Fate of
La Niña

A Novel

by

Debra Ann Ristau

*Miranda —
Keeping women
Beautiful!
Hugs —
Debra Ann Ristau*

The contents of this work, including, but not limited to, the accuracy of events, people, and places depicted; opinions expressed; permission to use previously published materials included; and any advice given or actions advocated are solely the responsibility of the author, who assumes all liability for said work and indemnifies the publisher against any claims stemming from publication of the work.

All Rights Reserved
Copyright © 2024 by Debra Ann Ristau

No part of this book may be reproduced or transmitted, downloaded, distributed, reverse engineered, or stored in or introduced into any information storage and retrieval system, in any form or by any means, including photocopying and recording, whether electronic or mechanical, now known or hereinafter invented without permission in writing from the publisher.

Dorrance Publishing Co
585 Alpha Drive
Pittsburgh, PA 15238
Visit our website at www.dorrancebookstore.com

ISBN: 979-8-89127-610-9
eISBN: 979-8-89127-108-1

Dedicated to
Every child with a dream.

ONE

Blanca

She sat on a scratched and faded bench near the edge of the playground. Blanca had been perplexed all morning. A storm was coming, and she did not know how to stop it, or even if she could. "Be with me," the angel prayed.

I am.

The small country school occupied a three-acre lot donated by landowners eighty years earlier. The classrooms were split by a center office, now vacant as the only two teachers employed were also the principal and vice principal. Parents made up the schoolboard and ran most of the events and activities at Klau Mine Elementary. The school was divided on purpose to separate younger students in the first through fourth grades from those in grades five and six. There was no football field, track or tennis courts. A sagging basketball hoop with a torn net and the faded remains of a half-court crudely painted on chipped asphalt dominated one side of the playground. An ancient swing set with rusty chains and cracked leather seats would have long ago been replaced at most schools in California. Blanca studied the faded outline of a chalk-drawn hop-scotch game. Someone had also drawn the outline for a game of four-square. A wooden bin holding a few mismatched balls sat forlorn and quiet, waiting for children to spill out of the classrooms. Three picnic tables on one side and two on the other provided space for outdoor meals for the twenty-four students enrolled this year. The persistent drought over the last few years left everything dry and lifeless. Forecasters predicted heavy winter rains, but locals with wells drying up feared the worst was yet to come. The school had been closed since the start of the Pandemic in March of 2020, and reopened this week. There was no cafeteria. No food or drink machines. No free lunches. If a student had lunch, the food came from home. The entire property was enclosed by a chain-link fence with padlocks on the gates, courtesy of changing times where fear dominated even the most remote schools in the state.

It was Friday. Late August. The start of a new school year. No one was quite sure what to expect. Several students were returning after the whole Coronavirus debacle, lockdowns and school closures. Some parents would continue to homeschool their kids rather than risk illness or a random mass shooting. Concerns and fears of the pandemic, illegal firearms, and their children's sexual preferences were now topics discussed by parents. What had happened to the world in the last two years? The question was rhetorical and brushed across Blanca's mind like a soft breeze. She gave an involuntary shudder and recalled her own joyous youth. She'd been a happy child and blessed with loving parents, two big sisters and one older brother. As the baby of the family she was a little spoiled, but mostly, she'd been loved. A blessing denied to many.

She thought of the missions she'd had over her time as an angel. Women used to gather and share recipes, career stories, family photos, morning coffee, or an evening cocktail. Men, who lived in that area of California, used to talk about careers, farming, vineyards, hunting, farm equipment, or the weather. Times had definitely changed. Yet, most students in this rural part of the world were ready to return to school and see their friends. Some of the younger ones had not yet experienced school at all. They were eager to learn and get out of the house. This first week had gone well, and the teachers were excited to report they were off to a good start.

It was Alicea's first full week of the first grade. She was already speaking both English and Spanish, anxious to learn to read and write. She had an inquisitive mind, sky-blue eyes, and creamy white skin, with a crowning mop of curly raven hair. One glance and anyone could see this little cutie would someday be a woman of incredible beauty.

The classroom door on the left burst open as the nine-and-under crowd scrambled out to their playground. Alicea was fourth through the door. Laughing, she moved with the others toward the swings that had become her new favorite place at play time. Blanca smiled as she watched those dark brown curls bounce up and down, then sighed. "So much life and joy in your heart, little one. I promise to get you through the storm . . . if I can."

She felt that small itch between her wings and eyed her majestic sword. "I might have to get reinforcements."

The door to the other classroom opened and now all of the students were on the playground. Three of the older boys made their way to the empty bench where Blanca sat in the afternoon sun.

"Maybe we can hike over to the lake this weekend."

"I wish. I'll probably get stuck with a mountain of chores."

"And now homework, too. But at least we get to hang out at school."

The boys had no idea there was an angel in their midst. Right there on the bench next to them was one of the prettiest Guardian Angels in the God Squad. Blanca was also one of the youngest to become a Warrior and Protector. She'd been assigned to Alicea the very day her mother learned she was with child. That had been a scary experience. Blanca shuddered at the memory of Sergio's reaction to hearing the news from Patsy. He was angry, and it was nearly a miracle that he did not choke the life out of Alicea's mother. The angels called on every holy resource they could to protect mother and child from evil that day, and Blanca was assigned with the ongoing mission of protecting them both.

Blanca left the boys to their youthful conversation and hovered above the swing set, to keep a closer watch on Alicea.

"Ah-lee-sea-ah," Blanca murmured. "Such a pretty name."

The small, yellow bus pulled up to the rural driveway with a jerky halt as the driver turned on flashing red lights to warn cars in either direction to stop. Alicea recognized their mailbox and knew this was where she was supposed to get off the bus. Mama wasn't waiting for her as she had earlier in the week.

The driver called her name to be sure the first-grader knew this was her stop. This was her fifth day at school. She wasn't dumb. She rolled large blue eyes with dark lashes at the driver, waved goodbye to her new friends, and hopped off the bus. Her purple backpack with silver sparkles was comfortably in place. She stopped at the mailbox as Mama had asked her to get the mail before making the quarter-mile walk down the driveway to their home which was hidden from the road.

I'm a big girl now, she thought with a smile as she walked toward home. *I can do this by myself.*

Blanca was with her step for step. She saw the plain white envelope addressed to Patsy Garcia, with only the numeral 14, hand printed in block letters as the return address. There was no postmark, someone other than the United States Postal Service had left the letter in the box for Patsy. "It has begun," Blanca whispered as her fingers tightened around the grip of her sword. Her wings held that now familiar itch between her shoulder blades when she was nervous or demons were near.

"Stop it!" Blanca chided herself. "You can do this."

I am with you.

Alicea skipped down the driveway, completely oblivious to the protective Guardian Angel at her side, the drama being played out around her, or the dire message she was about to give her mama. Their lives would soon change forever. Again.

TWO

Chuck

Detective Chuck Reynolds strode down the hall of the Monterey County sheriff's office toward his desk among the other detectives. His distinctive cowboy boots, black Resistol cowboy hat, and black leather jacket had long ago been accepted by his fellow officers. After thirty years on the force, he'd taken more criminals off the streets of Salinas than any other cop still alive or currently on the force. He'd worked just about every aspect of local law enforcement, including the city police force, K-9 unit, undercover, the sheriff's department, and homicide. He had a nose for trouble and an instinct about criminals. Chuck knew Salinas and Monterey County as well as anyone. He knew the criminals, gangs, addicts, and the good people, too. Farmers, ranchers, doctors, business owners, and families like his own. You could find generation after generation of those who settled the area more than a hundred years earlier. He also made it a point to get to know the fresh faces in town. His eyes were always open. His head on swivel.

Trouble was coming. He could smell it. He could feel it. Things had been too quiet. The criminal element in town was lying low. Even the drunks and drug addicts were not causing trouble. His informants weren't talking. He checked the visitor logs at the county jail. Nothing unusual. "What is it?" he wondered. "What is bugging me about this?"

"Hey, Joe," he called to a trusted fellow detective. "Do things seem awfully quiet to you?"

"Ah, dammit, Chuck. You know that you just saying that will jinx it. But yes. It's been nice to catch up on paperwork and even think about taking some vacation time. But you probably just blew it. Karma, buddy. Every time it slows down, we'll get a full moon or you just saying it out loud and wham! The proverbial poop hits the fan. Saddle up, pal. This won't last." Joe Medeiros was Chuck's best friend in the department. They could banter back and forth in complete confidence knowing each had the other's back.

Chuck grinned, tossed his jacket over the back of a chair, removed his cowboy hat, and ran his free hand through glossy black hair, a habit he'd had since high school. He locked his department issued Glock .45 in a desk drawer and pulled out a small stack of files. It wasn't like he didn't have a few open cases, but leads were cold. He ran down the list of follow-up calls to make and boxes to check.

In each file he looked again for loose ends. Were there any statements he hadn't followed up? Was anything missing? Was there a detail that seemed insignificant earlier, but might be key to solving a case? *Clues fall through the cracks when everyone is busy and we're all pushed beyond our limits*, he thought.

"You know, Joe, *La Familia* is up to something. I can feel it. Maybe it's time to pay Sergio Sanchez another visit. In person. I need to see his face. His eyes. Get a read on him." Chuck didn't expect an answer. He was musing more to himself than Joe. But Joe glanced up from his computer screen, a thoughtful look on his face.

"I hear you."

Chuck made a quick list of phone calls and visits to make. He had to be in court to testify in a homicide trial later next week, but today was wide open, unless a call came in. From the unsettled feeling that crawled under his skin, he knew that was a distinct possibility. *Soon*, he thought.

First things first. He picked up his list and punched in a number he had not called for several years.

"Hello?" she answered, her voice tentative. Questioning.

"Hey, Patsy. Detective Reynolds here. Just checking on you. All still okay? No problems?"

"Oh. Hi. No. Uh, no problems. All is okay here," she replied.

"Nothing from Sergio? No cause for any alarms? You haven't heard anything?"

"What? No. No. Nothing like that. Should I? Do you know something?"

"No. I'm just checking on you," he repeated, concerned now that his call had opened an old wound.

"Okay." Relaxing now, and feeling herself wanting to talk to one of the few people in the world she could trust, Patsy opened up. "I like my job, and it's quiet way out here in the country. Peaceful, you know? I've gotten used to it. You know my Alicea is six already? Can you believe it? She just had a birthday and started school. She's in the first grade already. I'm so proud of her! We're doing good. She is learning both Spanish and English and she's just cute as a button and smart as a whip, as my mother used to say."

"You enrolled her in school?" Reynolds asked quietly, his mind racing ahead to public records. It would make it easier to find them if someone was still looking. Someone like Sergio Sanchez.

"Yes. She was excited to go, and I really can't take her to work with me anymore. Do you think it's a problem? It's been so long, and I guess I feel safe here. I'm sure Sergio has forgotten all about us by now." But there was a new edge in her voice.

"I hope that's true, Patsy. But you keep an eye out for anything out of the ordinary and the same for Alicea. I don't have to tell you to make sure she understands never to accept a ride with strangers and all that."

"Of course! She's loving school. She's at Klau Mine Elementary, and there are only a few students. School has only been in session for a week. No COVID cases either. She rides the bus. I do wish I could have eyes on her twenty-four seven, but that's just not possible. I have to work at the main house, cleaning and all, but our little house is perfect for the two of us. I feel safe here, Chuck. No one can come down the driveway without me seeing them. I can never thank you enough for finding this home for us," she added.

"Hey, kid, you are welcome. You know I'm here if you need me. Just call. Anytime. You have the number."

"Okay," she said.

"By the way, how is your mom? Is she still in Greenfield?" he asked, remembering Melanie Montgomery as the young girl he'd known from his high school days.

"Oh, I'm sorry. I guess I didn't let you know. Mom died of COVID back in 2020. It was awful because we weren't allowed to be with her at all. I thought

I'd have a memorial service later, but by then it seemed a waste of time and money. Besides, I'm supposed to keep hiding because of Sergio. Right? He doesn't know where we are, and I don't want him to find out. I'm gonna ask you again, do you think he's a danger to us?"

Reynolds weighed her response about Melanie and her question about Sergio. He needed to answer with respect, but he wanted to yell, "What the hell?"

He said, "Patsy, I'm very sorry for the loss of your mother. Do you have anyone else? Any relatives or close friends you can lean on if needed?"

"Wait." Her voice went up an octave. "Does that mean that I do need to worry about Sergio and the Norteños?"

"Not saying that." Chuck spoke with caution. "Sergio has moved up the chain in the organization over the past six years. We have nothing to put him away. He's free to do as he pleases. But you are a loose end from back in the day. You know that. You need to be on guard. Watch your back. Now I'm going to ask again, do you have anywhere to go? I'm not saying anything might happen to you, because it's been a long time, but I'd like to know you have a backup plan. Or if I can do anything to help you make one."

"You're scaring me now. I don't want to hear this."

"I'm sorry, Patsy. I've been a cop too long to assume anything. I'd just be more comfortable knowing you have an escape route planned."

Her tone turned cool. "Okay, Officer Chuck. I gotta go. I'm okay. Alicea is okay. I don't want to take her out of school. Please do not stir these old memories. Let sleeping dogs lie."

"Sure," he said. "You have my number," he repeated. "Please call if you need anything."

"Goodbye," she said and disconnected the line.

"Damn!" he said aloud when the line went dead.

"You okay?" Joe asked.

"Yeah. I just hate it when smart people make dumb mistakes. This time I'm not sure if she made the mistake, or if I did by calling her."

"That's our world, Chuck." Joe shook his head and went back to his paperwork.

Feeling antsy, Chuck stood and unlocked his desk drawer again, holstered his pistol, secured it with the leather strap, grabbed his jacket and hat, and headed for the door. "Call me if anything comes in. I'm going over to East Salinas and take a look around."

"You going alone?" asked Joe. "I can go with you."

"Naw. It's no big deal. I just need to drive around and get eyes on the ground. If I see anything out of place, I'll call it in before going in. I'll be back in about an hour." With that, Detective Chuck Reynolds was out the door.

Joe Medeiros watched Chuck's back and felt something between admiration and jealousy. Chuck Reynolds was both confident and driven. Sometimes reckless, but always working for good. He cared a little too much about everyone. *That can eat you up in a job like ours*, Joe thought.

Driving down East Market, Chuck cruised the streets of East Salinas. Searching. For what? He didn't know. Something was out there. His mind drifted as his eyes traveled from side to side, front and back. He drove past an older couple on the chipped sidewalk. Each carried a full shopping bag in one hand. He carried a baseball bat in the other. She had a cane. Both could be used if a weapon was needed. Street smart. But sad to witness. He watched them for a bit, determined they weren't in any immediate danger, took the next left turn, and continued through residential streets. All was quiet. A knot of young men gathered on the front porch of a tired home on Toro Avenue. He slowed but didn't stop. They eyed the slow-moving patrol car but made no overt moves to scatter. Chuck recognized two of the men. They'd been in and out of the system for years. Nothing unusual going on there. Another turn. He made his way back to Williams Road and pulled into a fast-food parking lot. A young man crossed in front of Chuck. *XIV* prominently tattooed across his neck. He smiled at Chuck and gave a mock two-finger salute before reaching a tricked-out Honda Civic, with tinted windows and glass packs. Another normal day in Salinas. Chuck turned back onto the street and wondered what he was hoping to find. The police radio remained quiet.

And there he was. Chuck slowed for a red light and a black Cadillac Escalade pulled up next to him. Latino music pumped through speakers loud enough for Chuck to feel the resonance vibrate his patrol car. He slowly turned to face Sergio, who was driving the Escalade, with one passenger in the vehicle. Chuck and Sergio faced each other, and both smiled, an acknowledgement of each knowing the other with grudging respect. Chuck and Sergio. Not friends. Not enemies. Two men on opposite sides of law and order. One a career criminal and known felon. The other had earned the title of most decorated law enforcement officer in Monterey County. It was a matter of time. One or the other.

Sergio nodded, turned down the music, and lowered his window as he motioned for Reynolds to do the same. Polite.

"Officer Chuck. I got a question for you. Pull over next block?"

It was Chuck's turn to nod. He said nothing in response. The light turned green. Sergio eased ahead and Chuck pulled into the lane behind him. Following. Cautious. All senses on high alert. Sergio put his right turn signal on and pulled onto Monte Bella Drive, where he stopped near the basketball court. Chuck settled his sedan next to Sergio's Escalade, turned off the motor, and keyed his radio and let the dispatcher know his location and who he was meeting. Routine. A conversation, not a bust. Sergio remained in his vehicle. Hands on the wheel. He knew the drill. Although this meeting was his call, Sergio didn't quite trust Reynolds, either. They were like two prize fighters circling and sizing each other up before the dance would begin.

Chuck broke the ice and exited his vehicle. Sergio's windows were down.

"All right, Sergio. You want to talk out here? Or what? What's up? You aren't afraid of your boys seeing you talk to me?"

Sergio Sanchez opened the door of the SUV. The passenger sat quietly; Chuck recognized Diego as the owner of a local garage and one of Sergio's boys. Diego had his cell phone out. Chuck knew he would record the meeting. Chuck and Sergio met near the front of the vehicles.

"Wassup, Officer Chuck? Long time. I thought you'd be retired by now."

"No, Sergio. I'm still here keeping an eye on you and your homies. I should be asking you what's up. It's been pretty quiet around town."

"Nothing going on here, Officer. We been like altar boys. Just keeping our heads down and living the life. You know? We been clean and not letting those other fools mess things up for us. Life is good."

"What other fools?" Chuck asked.

Sergio laughed. "I honestly don't know. I just know business is down, and I'm thinking someone new is in town. But I want to talk to you about something else."

"Something else?" Chuck asked.

"Yeah. My girl from back in the day. You remember her? Patsy? Didn't you know her and her mother? I'm pretty sure you did."

Chuck eyed Sergio. "I did. Why?

"Well, you see, Officer, I think you might know where she is now. I'm trying to find her. The guys don't know it. They wanted me to kill her. Did you know that? I didn't. But I lied and told 'em she was gone and they didn't need to worry about her anymore. That was the end of it. I never saw her again, either. She just disappeared. Poof." He motioned with both hands as if throwing dust in the air and continued. "I think she had some help with her little disappearance act. I kept tabs on her mom until she died, but there was never a sign of Patsy or the kid. I don't even know if she had the kid, but I think she did. I'm thinking I'm a dad, and that's been getting to me. I want to see her again. And my gut tells me that I do have a kid, and he or she should know about me, too. I'm feeling this deep need to know they're okay. You feel me? Do you know where she is?" Sergio had kept his voice low and looked at Chuck with sincerity in his dark eyes. Chuck wanted to believe Sergio really did care about his ex-girlfriend and child, but years of experience told him otherwise. He didn't trust the gang member standing next to him.

Chuck didn't think Diego could hear the conversation. Sergio must have asked him to stay in the vehicle. He was only recording the visual meeting, but Chuck kept his own voice low to match Sergio's.

"I don't know where she is," he lied.

"Hey, Officer Chuck, Cowboy Cop, bro, you and me go way back. I remember when you first busted me. That petty possession rap. That was so wrong. But I did my sixty days at county, and I've kept clean. La Familia and the Norteños are legitimate now, too."

"Yeah. Sure you are, Sergio. Of course the Norteños are legitimate. Who would think otherwise?" he said facetiously. "Just keep it off my streets and stay away from the kids."

Sergio gave him a mock look of being offended. "Hey! A deal is a deal. I honor mine. So, you really don't know anything about Patsy? Or if I have a kid? I need to know."

"Here's what I can tell you, Sergio. Melanie died of COVID, but you already knew that. I don't know about Patsy or a kid, but last I heard she was moving to Vegas. You know I can't take on every woman with a sob story. Don't you have a new woman now?" Chuck hoped Sergio believed his partial lie.

"Dolores? Naw. That bitch is old news. But I do have a girl named Anna. Dolores left town. Hey, maybe she went to Vegas too. Or died of the Coronavirus. I never liked Mama Melanie. She was always sticking her nose in our business. She was evil. And this is coming from me. I just never liked that woman."

"Listen, thanks for the info, I've got to go. You're right, I don't want to be seen talking to Cowboy Cop. Could be hazardous to my health. Or yours. You put too many of mí amigos away. But I ain't snitching. You know that. Had Diego here record this just in case you tried something, and I needed to prove I didn't provoke you."

"Just a minute. What's really going on, Sergio?" asked Chuck. "You pulled me over for a reason and I'm not buying that it's about your old girlfriend. It's been awfully quiet around town, don't you think?"

"Nothing's going on. Business is down. Ain't nobody doing nothing. It's hot out. And man, it's never hot in this town. Everyone is just chillin', I guess." Sergio turned his head toward Diego in the Escalade and slid his eyes back to the detective. "Watch your back, Cowboy. It might not be safe for you here. You've made enemies, too."

Sergio didn't offer to shake hands. He turned away and gave his left hand a swipe across his neck to tell Diego to stop recording.

Chuck's voice cut the air as Sergio moved to get back in the Cadillac.

"Wait. Take my card," Chuck offered. "The day might come when you're the one who needs help."

Sergio took the card, gave it a look, and was about to toss it when he thought better about littering in front of Cowboy Cop. "Later."

He climbed into the Escalade, flicked the card to Diego, laughed, and said, "Yeah, right."

THREE

Patsy

Patsy was interrupted as she mopped the Meyers' hardwood floor by the insistent ringing of the telephone. A glance at the caller identification informed her that it was her employer calling.

"Meyer residence. May I help you?" she answered the phone as Mrs. Meyer had instructed, regardless of who was calling.

"Hello, Patsy dear. I was just calling to see how you are doing and if all is going well." Sarah Meyer always sounded so very sincere.

"Of course. Mrs. Meyer. I was just finishing up the floors. The house is ready as always for whenever you return. Do you plan to be back soon?" Patsy knew full well that Mrs. Meyer was calling to see if she was at the house—or taking the day off. She'd listen to hear if Patsy was playing music or for Alicea's voice in the background. Mrs. Meyer was checking up on her employee. Otherwise, Mrs. Meyer would have called her cell phone. Patsy smiled to herself. After all these years, Mrs. Meyer still didn't trust her. She wondered why the woman was so wary and distrustful. Patsy had never missed work. *Oh well,* she thought, *it's her nature and not my worry.*

"We might return next week. A little earlier than we previously planned. I'll let you know so you can get some grocery shopping done and have the refrigerator restocked for us."

"That sounds good. Just let me know," said Patsy.

"I will call again. Oh, and Patsy, please be sure to empty the cat's litter box daily. The last time we returned I could smell it," she added.

"Yes, ma'am. Is there anything else?" Pasty asked, not daring to defend herself because she knew full well that she emptied that litter box daily without fail.

"Yes. I have a question for you. Has your daughter been in school all week?"

It was the first time Mrs. Meyer had asked about Alicea since "the incident" seventeen days earlier.

"Yes, ma'am. She started Monday, and it's going well. Thank you again for not firing me. I really appreciate that you let me leave early enough to be home with her after school. I can't thank you enough, ma'am."

"You are quite welcome. But the child is growing up and you do realize that we simply can't have her at the house all day while you are working. You understand that. Right?"

"Yes, ma'am."

"Good. I'm glad you understand," she said.

"Yes, ma'am," Patsy repeated. "Is there anything else?" Patsy asked again.

"No. That's all. I will call later about the groceries. Goodbye, dear."

"Goodbye, Mrs. Meyer," Patsy said, and put the receiver back on the cradle.

She'd been employed by Norman and Sarah Meyer for nearly six years now. The childless couple lived in Los Angeles, where he was a partner in a law firm and she was a lady of privilege who took pride in the charity events she hosted both in Los Angeles and at their country estate where Patsy worked. She also devoted a great deal of time elevating her reputation as a patron of the arts.

Norman Meyer purchased the property near Paso Robles with a desire to raise quality beef cattle and plant a vineyard. He loved spending time at their beautiful ranch, but Sarah had never liked life in the country. She was more suited to lunch with the ladies and shopping on Rodeo Drive. Sarah, however, did love her husband and while she often thought about simply staying in Los Angeles when he came to visit the ranch, she was not about to let him travel without her by his side. She'd seen too many wealthy older men dump their aging wives for good-looking, younger women. She liked her lifestyle much too much to let that happen.

wave of frustration and negativity destroyed the peace of mind she was trying in vain to attain.

As she lay there, quite still, eyes closed, another scent assailed her sense of well-being. She could smell that distinctively unpleasant aroma of child body odor after playing outdoors in the heat. And something else? Another odor.

What is that? she asked herself as she lay there, not moving.

Then the aging Sarah Meyer slowly opened her eyes to see the face of her cat Mr. Buttons, mere inches from her own, and the sweaty body of little Alicea holding him. Both cat and kid were less than six inches from her face. "Are you okay, Mrs. Meyer?" Alicea asked. "Mr. Buttons can make you feel better."

"Patsyyyy!" Mrs. Meyer screamed.

With her hand on the brush cleaning one of the six toilet bowls in the house, Patsy heard her name called by a shrill and obviously distressed Mrs. Meyer. She dropped the brush and ran downstairs to the great room.

Trying desperately to take in the scene before her, Patsy's eyes scanned the room. Mrs. Meyer was in her usual position on the sofa. A few feet away stood Alicea, with a two-arm death grip on the Meyer's fat yellow tomcat.

Patsy's eyes darted from Mrs. Meyer to her daughter and back. The dull, disinterested expression usually worn by her employer was replaced with a wide-eyed, baleful glare between Alicea and herself. *This is not good*, Patsy thought.

"Get that kid and that cat out of here!" Mrs. Meyer shouted. "Now!"

Gone was the façade of the gentile lady of the house.

"We will discuss this later," she seethed. Her eyes shot undisguised arrows of hate towards Alicea and Patsy.

"Yes, ma'am. I'm sorry, ma'am."

Alicea was too frightened to run or let go of the cat. She kept inching backwards, away from Mrs. Meyer.

Patsy went to Alicea, placed both hands on her small shoulders, and turned her in the opposite direction and led her and the cat back through the kitchen to the outdoor patio and away from Mrs. Meyer. It was hot outside. The mercury said it was one hundred and two degrees in the shade.

The coastal fog that kept Salinas cool in summer rarely reached this eastern side of California's narrow Santa Lucia Range. The peaks climb up from the Pacific near the quaint village of Carmel-by-the-Sea and follow the coastline south for nearly a hundred and fifty miles.

"Mija, have some water. I know it's hot. We need to stay hydrated. That means you need to drink more water when it's hot out."

"Mama? I'm sorry. I thought Mr. Buttons would make her happy. She looked so sad."

"I know, mija. I know. But let's stay away from La Patrona today. She is upset. You know upset?"

"Yes, ma'am. When I spill something or don't pick up my things, you get upset. Not good, is it?"

"No, mija. Not good. *No bueno.*"

Patsy had taken to calling Alicea by the endearing Hispanic term of *mija*. It literally translates to "my daughter," but is used as an endearing term like *darling* or *honey*.

Patsy went on. "You and Mr. Buttons stay outside. Here is your water. Do not go near Mrs. Meyer again today. I am almost finished, and we will go home. How about pizza tonight?"

A radiant smile came from Alicea, as Mr. Buttons finally escaped her grip and jumped to the ground.

Before heading back to finish the bathrooms, Patsy stopped to check on her employer.

"I am so sorry, Mrs. Meyer. I don't know what happened. But Alicea and the cat are outside and won't disturb you again. I'm almost finished upstairs. Dinner is prepared and ready to put in the oven thirty-five minutes before you want to eat. Instructions are on the counter. Is there anything else I can do before I finish up and go?"

"Yes, Patsy. Come here, please."

"*Shit*," thought Patsy. *Shit. Shit. Shit. Shit.*

Standing in front of her employer, "Yes, ma'am?" she asked with a meek smile.

"Patsy, I've been very tolerant of Alicea for the past five years or so. But the time has come. I don't want her here at the house any longer. She is a darling girl. Don't get me wrong. But I need you focused on your work here. And she is a distraction. Not only to you, but her familiarity and lack of respect for me has become a problem. Do you understand what I'm saying, my dear girl?"

"I think so. You don't want Alicea here at the house. Not even if she stays outside?"

Mrs. Meyer cast her eyes to the ground before going on. "No. She won't stay outside. She comes and goes as she pleases. I've tried asking her to please stay outdoors, but then I'm not the mother, am I? She's been in our room. I'm certain of it. When we were back in Los Angeles. It's little things I've noticed. There was a red crayon in my lipstick drawer." Her eyes went back to Patsy. "You didn't put it there. Pray tell, who did?"

Patsy remained silent. She knew better than to get defensive or speak before Mrs. Meyer was done.

"This incident with the cat in my face was more than I could take. If I have to spend half of my life in this God-forsaken place because of my husband's love of beef and good wine, both of which he insists on producing here, the least I can do is savor the peace and quiet. Or is that too much to ask?"

"No, ma'am. I understand. Is there anything else?"

"No. Please leave. Go. I'll see you in the morning."

At least she still had a job and her house. For now.

"I'll just finish the bathrooms and be done in a few minutes."

Ten minutes later, Patsy retrieved Alicea from the patio where she was playing with her dolls. Mr. Buttons was curled on his bed nearby. He seemed to think it was his job to keep watch over Alicea.

"Come on, mija. It's time to go."

Turning to the cat, she added, "Mr. Buttons, you mind yourself now. No upsetting your mama. Understood?"

The big yellow cat yawned, stretched, and rolled onto his back. One eye stayed open and trained on Alicea. Within a few seconds both eyes were closed again, and he gave a soft and steady purr as Alicea gave him a little pat to say goodbye, little knowing it was the last time she'd ever see Mr. Buttons.

Mother and daughter left the courtyard and headed toward the hidden path through the woods that would take them home. The shadow of trees provided at least a ten-degree temperature drop. The cool shade was a welcome respite from the hot California sun.

While the air-conditioned big house was quite comfortable temperature-wise, Patsy's cottage without an A/C unit often got very warm inside during the summer. She would miss taking this walk with Alicea. She had a lot to think about. She needed this job. This home. This safe haven. She didn't make a lot of money, but she had her home, and the utilities were paid by the Meyers. She had security. As she walked up the hill, she pondered her situation yet again. *Just do your job and be polite*, she thought. They paid her. She was not a slave. Or was she? Would she feel different if she were Black? They didn't pay her minimum wage. The house and utilities were considered part of her wages. She had not had a raise in three years.

Sometimes Mrs. Meyer kept her for ten to twelve hours a day. Sometimes she was only there for four or five hours. Her schedule depended on the situation and the whims of her employer. They entertained a lot. Those were the hard days. The long days. Mrs. Meyer usually hired a fancy catering company from Paso Robles or one of the local wineries to help on those occasions, but the house still needed to be clean and beautiful. There were also many wonderful days when they stayed in Los Angeles. Work was easier then. Without daily interruptions Patsy could clean refrigerators and freezers, ovens, and the two outdoor grills. She also used that time to pay extra attention to baseboards and plantation shutters. The house was always ready when they arrived. More often than not, unannounced.

The Meyers had two men who worked full time and lived in another cottage on the far side of the ranch. They took care of the cattle and horses, barns and the pool at the big house, and most of the other outdoor chores, including the vineyard. Patsy would see them on occasion but kept her distance.

As she walked toward home that day with Alicea on the day of "the incident," she calculated the days until school would begin. Twelve. The worst of the Coronavirus pandemic was over. She could not keep Alicea hidden forever. She'd put her on the school bus in the mornings and she'd return in the afternoon. Patsy thought she could convince Mrs. Meyer to adjust her hours. Alicea could be trusted alone, if not for too long before or after school. Couldn't she? She'd pray Mrs. Meyer would agree to the new hours. She had no other solution at the moment.

Alicea had been very quiet as they walked home that day. "Mama? Am I in trouble?"

"No, honey."

"I thought *La Patrona* looked sad. I thought Mr. Buttons would help her be happy."

"I know, Alicea. You told me already. The truth is la patrona isn't very happy with anyone. Do not worry. School starts soon and you will ride the yellow bus and be a big girl very soon!" She reached down and picked Alicea up and swung her in a tight circle on the narrow path.

"I'm already a big girl, Mama! Please! Please! Can I really go to school? A real school?"

The next day Patsy left Alicea home alone. She'd made her lunch and organized her play time with lesson time. They'd always had lessons. Simple, but easy. She set the alarm clock to signal each phase of Alicea's life and schedule for the next few hours. She'd be back to check on her in four hours. Too long to leave a child alone. She wondered briefly if it was considered against the law. But there was no one to ask for help. She prayed this would work. Eleven more days.

"Mrs. Meyer?" Patsy asked the next morning.

"Yes, dear. What it is?" There was only a slight bit of exasperation in the elder woman's voice.

"I have to ask a favor." Patsy kept going, afraid if she stopped, Mrs. Meyer would interrupt, and she'd never get her request out in the open.

"Since Alicea is now to stay at home, and I cannot find proper care for her way out here, and you know my car is old and not very reliable, and school starts in less than two weeks, can I please only work four hours daily, two in the morning and two in the afternoon, but just until school starts? And once she starts going to school, if I can work only during the school hours?"

She blurted it all out in a rush, took a short breath, and continued, "I know you want me to work longer hours, but I have to ask. Please. I don't know what else to do. She's only five. She will be six next week, right before school starts. Please, Mrs. Meyer. I could also clean at night when she is sleeping if that will help. But I really hate leaving her alone. Even with the baby monitor for security, I worry."

Mrs. Meyer smiled at Patsy. But the smile did not reach her cosmetically enhanced eyes, with lavender contact lenses. At sixty-two, with vanity directing most every move, Sarah Meyer privately hated looking at her younger, more beautiful housekeeper and cook. The maid. She secretly wondered if her husband was diddling the wench. She didn't really think so, but the thought had crossed her mind more than once. *What is a pretty single woman like her doing living way out here with no social life whatsoever?* she wondered.

"Well, dear, normally I'd be inclined to just say no. But we've decided to head back to Los Angeles early. We're leaving tomorrow. We'll be back in six weeks. Possibly earlier. The boys will look after the livestock and pool. Please have the house ready for our return. Now, in light of our decision and my aversion to finding someone to replace you, the answer is yes. You may reduce your hours while we are away. Once your little one starts school, I imagine we can work something out. If not…" Her voice trailed off with a hint of a threat. "Well, dear, we'll cross that bridge when we get there."

She studied Patsy's face. "Please bring up our empty travel cases and leave them in our dressing rooms. Then you can go for the day. Mr. Meyer and I are dining with friends tonight. Goodbye, dear. I'll see you in five or six weeks."

Oh my God! Oh my God! Patsy's heart was pounding as she pulled out the luggage. She still had a job and a place to live. She did not have her wages cut. She had six weeks or so before the next confrontation. Six weeks to enjoy life with her daughter.

Patsy never thought about a social life or a man. She still loved Sergio. She knew in her heart he was dangerous. She had never tried to get in touch with him. Nor he with her, but maybe it was time to face him. She ached for him. She wanted Alicea to know her father.

She took the travel bags upstairs, tidied up the house, checked that fresh towels were laid out, the trash was removed, the litter box emptied, and the kitchen was clean. Then she called goodbye to Mrs. Meyer and let herself out. Though she knew Mr. Meyer was probably in his office or down at the barn, she rarely saw him, and he rarely spoke to her. *These are odd people*, she thought. But she was used to their formal ways and reluctant interactions with her. The help. Mostly, she was happy they left her alone, and she felt safe living there.

Alicea had been in school for five days. An entire week. Patsy was proud of her. She did not cry or whine or refuse to go to school, as some children did. In fact, she did not even want Patsy to walk her to the bus stop.

"I'm a big girl now, Mommy!" she'd insisted.

"I know, *mija*, but Mommy needs this! I need to see you off safely and make sure the bus driver stops and knows where you live. Remember, this is a new stop on their route." That was Monday. Patsy smiled as she remembered the conversation.

"Okay, Mama. Will you let me walk home alone?"

"Alone, mija?" She stared at Alicea. "Let me walk with you this week. I will come and make sure the bus stops. We will get the mail at our mailbox and walk home together. How does that sound?"

She saw the protest start to flare in her daughter's eyes and held up a finger. "And, if all goes well, we will talk again about being a big girl on Friday. Deal?"

"Deal! Thank you, Mama!"

Now it was Friday. As promised, Patsy had let Alicia walk home alone from the bus stop to the house.

Blanca watched over mother and daughter. Sword at her side. She scratched at that spot between her wings. *These are a nuisance*, she thought absently.

"I don't need wings. Or do I? How am I to protect these two? Lord, be with me. Help me. I'm not sure what to do. I pray for guidance."

I am here, my child.

FOUR

Alicea

Patsy watched the driveway for Alicea to emerge around the last corner. She'd let her walk home alone today, but that didn't mean she wasn't keeping one eye on the clock and the other on the bend in the driveway, waiting expectantly for her daughter to round the curve and come into view. Safe at home.

And right on time, she did. Alicea saw her mom open the front door and step outside, wiping her hands on that worn-out, old apron she'd had as long as Alicea could remember. She broke into a run and threw her arms open for a hug. "Mama! Thank you! I told you I'm a big girl now! See? I got home all by myself!"

"Yes, you did, my sweet girl! Shall we celebrate?"

"How?"

"Oh, I don't know. Hmm. Let me think. You, Miss Alicea, had your sixth birthday last week, and now you've finished your first week of school, and today you walked home alone for the first time. That's a lot of special stuff, isn't it?" Alicea nodded.

Then Patsy asked, "Are you tired at all?"

Alicea giggled. *Mama is silly sometimes.* "I'm a big girl! I'm not tired at all!" She stifled a yawn as she said it. In truth, the long days and new routine of learning in the first grade can be difficult for a child used to daily naps.

"How about some popcorn and your favorite movie?"

"*Anastasia!*"

"It won't spoil your dinner?"

"What are we having?"

"Liver and onions."

"What? Gross! Mom!" Her face scrunched up and she stuck out her tongue.

Laughing, Patsy admitted to teasing and confessed, "In your honor, Princess Alicea, on your first week of school and walking home alone, drum roll, please..." She began tapping the table with her fingers. "We've got basghetti in the crockpot and garlic bread the way you like it."

"Mama, it's called spaghetti. I can say it now. I thought I smelled that! Thank you!" She threw her arms around her mother, giving her a tight hug. Her face buried in Patsy's apron, where she inhaled the kitchen smells of fresh garlic, oregano, and hand soap on Mama's apron.

"Oh, mija, you'll get tomato sauce on your face! Come on, let's make popcorn and put the movie on. Did you get the mail?"

"Yes. I put it in my pack so I wouldn't drop it." Alicea leapt up to grab the purple backpack she'd dropped near the front door.

Blanca watched in silence. Knowing the color would soon drain from Patsy's face as fear gripped her heart and the drama would begin. Alicea unzipped the pack and put the white envelope on the table as Patsy took out a large bowl and put the folded bag of popcorn in the microwave oven and set it to start. When Patsy turned to look for the mail, she saw the envelope and her eyes registered the block *14* in the upper left corner. One. Four. Fourteen. N. The fourteenth letter of the alphabet. N for Norteño. Sergio? Or one of the others? There was no return address. No stamp. No postal mark. It had been left in the mailbox by someone. Who?

Alicea was already turning on the television and DVD player. The Meyers had not installed Wi-Fi for their employees, and Patsy could not afford it. She was saving every extra dime. That conversation with Cowboy Cop had made her think. Did she need to worry about Sergio? The Norteños? La Nuestra Familia? She had threatened him. Them. She'd made a mistake. Girls were killed for less. What of Alicea? That was all so many years ago. More than six years had passed. It was the day she found out she was pregnant.

She didn't have much in the way of savings. The detective had asked her earlier today about a back-up plan. She didn't have one. Her mind raced with possibilities. She'd have to open the letter. Not yet.

"Mama?" The microwave dinged. The popcorn was ready. Alicea thought her mother looked funny. A minute ago, she'd been smiling and happy. Now she looked sad and maybe sick.

"Come on, Mama. I pushed all the right buttons. The movie is starting!"

"Yes, mija. I'll be there in a minute." Patsy went through the motions of putting the popcorn in a large bowl, adding salt and melted butter. She grabbed napkins and poured two glasses of water. She set the popcorn and water glasses on the portable table between them, along with a stack of napkins. Alicea curled up in her favorite spot and Patsy sat next to her. Her mind on the white envelope.

Dear God, what is inside? She knew she needed to open it. Fear made her wait. Her hands were shaking.

Her mind raced. *I can't do it. This might be the last happy moment with my baby. Please God. Help me know what to do*, she thought.

Alicea munched on popcorn and took a sip of water as the familiar narration and music filled the room. Her big blue eyes closed ever so slowly and soon the sound of her gentle rhythmic breathing was all Patsy could hear. She shut out the noise from the television and softly pushed a fallen curl off of Alicea's forehead. "Sleep little one. Rest."

FIVE

Patsy

The envelope sat like a puma ready to strike. Patsy skirted the table, locked the doors, and checked that all of the windows were locked, too. She set the alarm code and stared for a moment at the device on the wall. *What is the point? Sure, it'll sound an alarm if someone opens a door, but who will hear it besides me? And if someone breaks in? What then?* Her mind had not really connected the dots before. But as she thought about it, the alarm was not connected to any police monitor or other surveillance. Who would come to their rescue? No one. It had made her feel safe to have the alarm, but at this moment it felt pointless. Her eyes traveled to her bedroom door, and she thought of the nightstand next to her bed. The small handgun Deputy Detective Reynolds had given her was there, locked in a small gun safe. Maybe she should take it out and keep it handy.

She looked back lovingly, but with fear in her eyes at Alicea napping on the sofa. She'd have to wake her soon. It would be time for dinner and a bath before dark. Patsy smiled as she recalled how her daughter had negotiated a deal with her to stay up later on Friday and Saturday nights.

"Okay." Patsy had given in. "But if you start becoming Miss Cranky Pants you go back to early bedtime. Eight o'clock on school nights and eight thirty or maybe even nine on Fridays and Saturdays. Deal?"

"Deal!" Alicea had squealed and hugged her mother.

Was that really just a week ago? Patsy's mind was a jumble of memories and fear.

"Oh, mija. You are growing up too fast," she whispered.

She glanced at the clock. Four forty-five on Friday afternoon. Did she dare read the letter while Alicea napped? *What if it's something I need to know immediately? What if he's coming for us? For me? For her?* Fear was causing her to lose control. Panic was rising like bile in her throat.

"Stay calm and open the damn letter," she told herself. They had stayed alive all these years. She'd keep them alive now.

The Meyers were in Los Angeles. The ranch hands were the nearest neighbors, but it was Friday. They'd be heading to town soon, if they weren't already on their way. She could hide in the woods if they needed to, but for how long? And the bigger question she asked herself, *who were 'they?'* The crunch on the gravel path would give her away and it might be too dangerous in the brush. *Wait. If someone is coming to harm me and knows where I am living, why would they send me a warning?* Her mind was jumping all over the place. She stared at the envelope. He'd found her. She knew it. It had been a matter of time.

"This is ridiculous," Patsy told herself again. "You are letting fear and your stupid imagination get the best of you. You are not thinking rationally. And now you are talking to yourself." Patsy didn't want to alarm Alicea. She didn't want her daughter to know the fear of someone wanting to hurt her. Ever.

Who could she call? Where could she go? What was her back-up plan? Her only rational thought was to call Cowboy Cop. Should she? Why had he just called to check on her after all these years, and now this letter arrived? Was that a coincidence? Was Sergio out there now? Had Cowboy Cop somehow stirred up trouble and caused Sergio to go looking for her? So many questions played havoc in her head.

"Damn him," she whispered softly as anger began to overtake fear.

In truth, these were the same unanswered questions and fears she'd faced six years ago. Maybe she was afraid of ghosts. If anything happened to her, surely the Norteños would be blamed. Or would they? She was nobody. She had nobody. She stirred the homemade marinara sauce. She looked again at Alicea, curled up so tiny as her favorite movie played on the small television screen.

Taking a deep breath, Patsy wiped sweaty palms on her apron, picked up the envelope, and walked to her bedroom. There, she quietly closed the door and sat on the edge of the bed.

In the other room, Blanca caressed Alicea's cheek, kissed the top of her head, and whispered, "Sleep a little longer, sweet girl." Then she sat next to Patsy, ready for whatever came next.

SIX

Blanca

"It is so good to see all of you again!" Blanca had called an emergency meeting with the Guardian Angels who had helped her find her own calling and permanent position with Patsy and Alicea. This was Blanca's first solo run as a guardian. Unlike the almost famous Warrior Guardian Angel, Hannah, who had hundreds of souls under her watch and had trained many guardians, Blanca was relatively new at this.

"It's okay to ask for help," Hannah had told her. And so, she did. Roy and Jeff, two of the guardians she had worked with in the past, were there, too.

This assignment was pretty straightforward, but Blanca saw trouble coming and felt uncertain about the source. Where was it coming from and what was she to do about it? She had as many questions and speculations as Patsy. Blanca turned to Hannah.

"Help?"

"Was that a plea or a question?" Hannah asked, then went on.

"Dear one, you are an angel special to my heart. And His. Worry does not come from Him. You know this. You simply do your best. The outcome is not up to you. They have free will and make decisions which have consequences. Your Patsy knows this. Little Alicea is still an innocent babe. Do not worry. He will give you the information you need, and He will be there with you. He always is. And if you need us, He will make sure we are with you, too."

Hannah went on, as Blanca felt her reassuring voice soothe her own fears.

"Use your strength. Focus. I promise you that whatever happens is God's will. Not theirs. Not yours. God's. To borrow a silly colloquialism from one of my humans, 'Put your big girl wings on and do this.'"

"How can we help? Tell us, Blanca. What is going on and what can you tell us?" Jeff was a unique angel with unique gifts. Blanca knew he watched over Sergio. Maybe Jeff could shed some light on Blanca's dilemma.

"Blanca, we're here for moral support and to reassure you. You know if there is anything we can do to help, we're all in." Roy gave her a big grin. His fatherly tenderness reminded her of her own earthly father. He'd been one of her favorites from the time he first arrived.

Blanca began to tell Patsy's story.

"You all remember that the last time we were together we helped Patsy escape Sergio's anger. He had his hand around her throat and considered killing her. She had just told him she was pregnant. She'd been so happy. He crushed her heart and her spirit when he wanted her to get an abortion. Then she threatened him and the whole Nuestra Familia. The Norteños wanted a hit put on her. But we got her through it. Both of them, actually." Blanca went on.

"That was six and half years ago. With the help of her mother, Melanie Montgomery Garcia; Detective Chuck Reynolds; and a little help from us, she's been safely hidden and working as domestic help and living at a remote location in Central California. All has been well. Her mother Melanie got COVID and died at the height of the pandemic. Thank goodness she found her way to the Lord before her last breath. Patsy and her daughter Alicea have remained healthy and well. The little girl is now six years old, and Patsy recently enrolled her in a small, rural public school. And now it seems the gang has found her. I don't know what is about to happen, but I feel this angst, and I'm not sure how to protect her. And before you say anything, Hannah, I know I should not feel this angst. Can you help me know what to do? I'm thinking you would not be here if I didn't need you."

Blanca filled in the blanks that led to the moment of Patsy sitting on the bed with the unopened envelope.

"At this very moment she is about to open this letter from Sergio, and she is so scared of what he plans to do to her and Alicea. Kill them? Kidnap them? Sell them? Torture Patsy? All of these things are running through her mind."

Against his normal, outspoken behavior, Jeff had remained silent and listened respectfully as Blanca laid out the scenario. Roy was proud of the restraint shown by his protégé, if he had the temerity to call Jeff his protégé. But he did feel he'd somehow helped Jeff find his place in the world of angels. Of course, Hannah was the driving force behind all of them.

Jeff spoke up. "Sergio sent the letter? Are you sure?"

"Who else could it be from? There was no return address. Only the number 14. The symbol for the Norteños. The fourteenth letter of the alphabet is N. 14."

"What's in the letter?" Roy asked.

"I don't know. She hasn't opened it."

Jeff cut in again with authority. "Listen, I don't think it's from Sergio. I've been stuck to him for all this time. He still loves her. But I can tell you that he does want to see his child. I don't think he means harm to either of them. His heart is softening. Not to brag, but with my help, he's actually been praying for forgiveness. If the letter is from him, I think he wants forgiveness, not revenge. And he would not have put 14 on the envelope. Let me fill you in on his back story."

Jeff thought back over the years he'd been a guardian to Sergio and said, "He has moved up in the organization and really does seem to be walking a fine line between Nuestra Familia and the Norteños. Some say both groups are one and the same. But from my vantage point, the Familia members are generals and the Norteños are ground pounders. They have a saying that goes for all, though." Jeff was thoughtful for a moment.

"Blood in. Blood out." Jeff let out a small sigh.

"It's really sad. I had trouble when I was a human, but nothing like what they go through. Their rules are simple. You kill to get in the organization. You are killed to get out. Blood in. Blood out. They call each other carnal. Pronounced like *car-now*. Meaning *brother in blood*. The demon stronghold with them is intense. I do what I can to keep Sergio alive and out of eternal damnation type of trouble. So far, he still has a chance. I got a few others I'm helping, too. I sort of have my own little ES club for lost souls."

"ES?" asked Blanca.

Jeff smiled. "Eternal Salvation versus ED, Eternal Damnation."

Jeff went on. "I keep praying for these guys. I do reach them on some level. They even go to church once in a while. A few have told the priest they're hearing voices. Father Richard doesn't know what to make of it, but he's happy to have them coming in. There is hope. As long as they aren't bringing trouble to the church. So far, so good. And Father Richard can't tell anyone because of his vows."

"Let's look at this," Jeff continued. "If not Sergio, who? But yes, it might be Sergio. We don't know!" He suddenly turned to Blanca.

"Blanca! You've got to get back there and find out what is in the letter!"

"You're right, Jeff. I do. I was just all worried and felt I needed you to help. Sometimes I feel so alone out there."

"You are never alone, Blanca. He is always with you! Do not let fear creep into your heart… Figure of speech, my dear." Hannah smiled and gave Blanca a hug.

Roy remained quiet. He was thrilled to be assigned to his earth family in Ohio. None of them had any problems that came close to what Blanca and Jeff were dealing with in California. The thought of all the missions Hannah had carried out caused him to cringe and shudder. *Thank you, God, for my very plush assignment*, he thought.

You're welcome, Roy. You earned it.

"What should I do?" asked Blanca.

Hannah was always the voice of authority. "Go back. Read the letter. Act accordingly. Assume nothing. Protect them as best you can. Help Patsy make wise decisions. If she is truly being threatened, she needs to take Alicea and disappear. Again."

With the dawn of an idea she asked, "Do you remember the 'Sisters' case we worked on?"

"Remember it? They were my sisters! For real!" Jeff chimed in.

Hannah kept going. "Thank you for the reminder, Jeff. But listen, they might be able to help. Patsy's mother Melanie had forged a friendship with Lee many years ago. Although that friendship devolved, and Melanie has passed, there was a connection. Don't forget that. And Officer Chuck used to be a close friend to Liz. They've lost contact, but I think Liz and Lee could help if needed. Liz has contacts and resources around the globe. Officer Chuck has proven his righteousness on many occasions. I think he might be your key. Go do your job, Blanca," Hannah said softly, with a reassuring smile. "You've got this. My intuition says to get Patsy to reach out through whatever connections she has. These people are all connected, and someone might be able to help. I know it seems like we are working without a net, but He's always there."

Hannah would forever be the leader of this team. "We walk this line between influencing them and praying we make a difference. We do what we can. They make the decisions. Any power we have comes from God. His will be done."

Blanca stood tall. "Jeff, please stay with Sergio and bring out the best in him if you can. I'll stay with the girls and find out what is in that letter. Roy, you can go home. Thank you for being here to hold my hand through this. I needed you. Hannah, thank you for the vote of confidence."

Hannah smiled again. "Blanca, that itch in your wings means you might have to spread them over your girls to protect them."

Blanca's eyes widened. "How did you know about that?"

Hanna laughed and Roy chimed in, "Don't you know by now? Hannah knows everything."

"Not everything, Roy. But I do watch and listen. I also stay focused."

SEVEN

Patsy

Her fingers were shaking. The only sound came from the drone of *Anastasia* on the television. Alicea napped. Using the letter opener that had been a gift from her grandmother, Patsy took out the single-page letter with stylized Norteño calligraphy. Handwritten with a felt marker. Two short sentences glared at her from the center of the page.

You are both mine.

I will find you.

No signature. It's Sergio. It has to be. Who else? Was she trapped out here, in the middle of nowhere, with no one around to help if he came to the house? Worse. What if he brought others?

There was no postmark. It was hand delivered sometime today. *He knows where I am*, she thought. But it read, "I will find you." Not, "I found you."

Blanca watched and read over Patsy's shoulder. Her thoughts mirrored those of Patsy. It had to be Sergio. Didn't it? Jeff was wrong. This is a threat.

"Oh Lord. What am I to do?" Patsy whispered to herself. *If they delivered this, they must already know where I am.*

Darkness was still several hours away in early September. Patsy felt sick to her stomach. *What now? Oh God. What now?*

"Mommy? Where are you? You're missing the good part!" Alicea called from the other room. Patsy hurriedly hid the letter in the drawer next to the handgun case and thought, *Oh, sweet baby, what have I done?*

"I'm coming!" she called, believing now that she and Alicea had to get away from the house as soon as they could. Before dark. Before she couldn't see their way through the woods. He would come at night. *Keep calm.* But terror gripped her throat just as Sergio had done so many years before. *Breathe,*

Patsy. Just breathe. Do not panic, she silently told herself over and over. In her heart she knew she could not just sit and wait.

"I'm here," she told Alicea and sat next to her while her mind raced through a variety of scenarios, none of them with happy endings.

"Think. Think. Think." But she was not thinking rationally. She kept imagining the worst that could happen. She chided herself for not having that back-up plan Reynolds had suggested. She'd grown lazy. Complacent. Taking another deep breath, she let it out slowly and said, "Mommy needs to make a phone call. You watch this part and I'll be back in a few minutes."

She called Cowboy Chuck. Even if he could come to her rescue, it would take him at least an hour and a half to get there. "Please," she begged as the phone rang. "God, please let him answer and please let him help me again. I don't know what to do or where to turn."

"Reynolds here," he answered.

Chuck
Chuck answered his cell phone and noted the "no info available" about the number calling him. This was usually the case with burner phones or informants. Rarely was it a wrong number, although he did get the occasional spam call, too.

"Officer Chuck? It's Patsy Garcia. I think I need your help."

He heard the unspoken cry in her voice. She sounded like a woman on the verge of hysteria. He hated that tone and felt the tightness begin in his chest. Adrenaline kicked in. His senses went on high alert.

Six Years Earlier
Patsy Garcia had threatened to testify against Sergio and the Familia but disappeared. Her disappearance was, in part, thanks to Chuck and a few trustworthy friends. Patsy's statement was taken, but there was a lack of any real help in her testimony for the district attorney to prosecute. Her statement was a lot of conjecture, innuendo, and hearsay. Nothing she said would hold up in

court, but it was enough to give the DEA and undercover agents a sense of direction for their investigations.

In return, Patsy wasn't worth the witness protection program, but Chuck Reynolds, being the kind of man he was, made it his mission to hide and protect her and the baby she was carrying. Chuck knew the Norteños would not be forgiving. Even if her testimony would never put anyone behind bars. She would still be considered a threat. She would pay the price of being disloyal.

His own home was out in the country, west of Salinas. The house sat back from the two-lane road and was protected by a locked gate and a long driveway that wove through several acres of pastureland.

After taking her statement and getting a firm no from the district attorney about protection, Chuck felt sure this young woman and her baby were in grave danger. He knew the gangs only too well. They knew him, too. He'd earned his reputation as a ruthless cop taking down drug dealers and solving every homicide that crossed his desk. With his black cowboy boots, leather jacket, and black 10x beaver hat, he went against the grain and did what it took to keep Salinas clean. Chuck Reynolds was respected by his peers and hated by criminals. His low profile as a cop ensured that most Salinas residents knew nothing about him. He shunned the media and stayed out of the public spotlight.

Chuck remembered when the district attorney refused to help Patsy. What were his choices after that? Move on as ordered? Another case? Another victim? Surely, he'd be signing a death warrant for this young woman and her kid.

"Shit," he had said.

Patsy had already been at the women's shelter for several months. She'd had the baby. A girl. The longer she stayed in one place the less her chance of survival. People talk. Even those at the shelter were lured out. This case was more than just domestic abuse. She'd have the whole of the Norteño army looking for her if Chuck's instincts were on target. And they usually were.

"Shit," he said again and called his wife.

Maria Reynolds answered the call while standing in the canned goods aisle at Star Market on Main Street. From the caller identification on her cell phone, and the special ring tone, she knew it was Chuck, though he rarely called in the middle of a work shift.

"Hey, love, what's up?" she answered, pushing the cart slowly past the green peas. Her dark eyes scanned the aisle. No one was in sight, but still, she kept her voice low. Casual concern edged her tone.

"Where are you?" he asked. His voice tight.

"Just left school and stopped at the market."

"I have a code TLD." His code was only for her, and it meant trouble. Life-or-death kind of trouble. They had rehearsed this scenario several times but had only used it once before. It meant he needed her help but did not want to put her in danger. It meant she would say nothing in this conversation, just listen. He'd talk. If she understood, she'd answer, "Sure!" If she had questions or could not talk, she'd say she was busy and would return the call. That meant they'd then arrange to meet in person.

When Chuck made that call to Maria six years ago, she'd been a lay teacher at Sacred Heart Elementary School. She loved her job and loved the Catholic nuns she worked with. Unable to have children of her own, she long ago accepted the inevitable and felt that thirty-two kids in her fourth-grade classroom were children enough. She did her best to give them the great start in life that all children need.

"I'm listening," she had answered and waited.

"I need housing for a young woman and her baby. A newborn. Only until we can find her a safe house. I've got some leads. We can trust her. No drugs. It might be three days or three weeks. Are you okay with this?"

Maria didn't know the girl and was not familiar with the case as Chuck never discussed work with her, but she knew this girl was in trouble. Chuck would not ask if he had other options or could not fully trust her. The room she'd hoped would someday belong to their own child had housed a few other victims over her years as a cop's wife. It was against the rules. But Chuck often followed his own rules. His gut. She worried it would get him killed one day. Or put her own life in danger. But they were a team.

"Sure!" she answered without hesitation and with great enthusiasm.

"Thank you. Talk to you later. I love you."

Maria dropped the phone back in her purse and finished shopping. *Life with my sweet Chuck is anything but boring*, she thought.

"That woman is a saint." Chuck sighed and made plans to move Patsy and her baby out of the shelter until he could find a home for them.

It took almost two weeks. He learned that a couple from Los Angeles had purchased a large ranch west of Paso Robles and were looking for domestic help. The job came with a house. She was hired. Chuck helped her move. She was cautioned to keep her head down and stay out of Salinas. She had done that. She'd been living off the grid for nearly six years. He checked in on her periodically, but she never called him.

Present

Now? She was in trouble again. He wondered for a moment if his conversation with Sergio had sparked this incident. Or, more likely, it was the school registration and public records. They'd have been watching for the kid to start school. But Garcia was a pretty common name in California. So was Sanchez.

He listened as she told him about the letter she'd received earlier. Once she started talking, and Chuck grasped the possible severity of the situation, his mind raced for a solution. He was familiar with her location as he'd scouted the area when Patsy first moved there.

"I'll be there," he said. "It'll take me a few hours, though. Let's plan nine thirty. It'll be dark by then. I'll take the service road toward the bunk house. Get there as fast as you can and wait by that big oak tree near the road, but stay out of sight. Bring only what you can carry. Wear dark clothes. Leave your car at the house. Don't take any chances. Get out of there and stay hidden as long as you can. I don't want to scare you. It's probably nothing, but let's take this seriously. Can you do that?"

Reynolds spoke in a calm, but authoritative voice. Patsy felt her own strength returning. He had thrown her a life preserver. She was no longer drowning in fear. She was no longer alone. She had a lifeline and a child to protect. She could do this.

"I'll pack a few things and we can walk down there. It's a little far, but we can do it. I'm scared, and I'm sorry, but I didn't know who else to call." The whine was edging back into her voice.

"Just keep your head down. Stay calm. If they show up while you're still at the house, get out immediately. Hide. Stay quiet and still.

"Pray for me, Officer Chuck. I'm so sorry if this is my fault."

"Don't worry about that now. I'll get you to a safe house. And Patsy, contact no one. No calls. No texts. No notes left behind. Nothing. No 911. Take only what you can carry. Shut off all appliances and put food away. Do not let them think you just left. If they are watching, they will know anyway. I will wait as long as I can if you aren't at the tree by nine thirty. Leave the lights on at the house. Again, if they are watching, I don't want them to think you went to bed. They'll be waiting for that. I will not call you. Shut off your cell phone and take out the SIM card. They might be tracking you. Grab that extra burner phone and the Walther PPK. Make sure that little handgun is loaded, and the safety is on. Keep it where you can get to it. Can you do that?"

"Yes."

"Will you use it if you need to? Aim center mass?"

"Yes." He'd talked to her about this when he first got her out of the shelter. *A gun is useless*, he'd said, *if you can't bring yourself to use it. Just be certain when you use it that you know who and what you are aiming at, and that you are protecting yourself or your child from mortal danger.* He had her practice daily when she stayed with him and his wife at their ranch before she started working for the Meyers.

"Good," he said now. "In the very off chance they are listening on your phone and already know where we are meeting, you go to back-up plan Bravo. Do you remember when we discussed that?"

Patsy's mind frantically raced back in time. "Oh, God! Oh, God! What was it?!"

"Yes!" She remembered, plucking the memory from some hidden reserve.

"I'll do that if I can't find you."

When she first moved here from Salinas, he'd told her they needed a back-up plan in case she was ever in imminent grave danger. This was not a back-up plan for a new place to live, but to flee. Escape was always a better plan than trying to shoot an attacker.

She was to go to the north side of Nacimiento Shore Road and get to any house there. Knock on doors until someone, anyone, opened. Call 911 from there. Could she do it? That was several miles of walking, but they could stay hidden along the way. Could Alicea do it? She prayed she didn't have to.

"Hold on, kid. The cavalry is coming. It'll be all right," came Chuck's reassuring voice.

"Thank you. Oh, God. Thank you," she reiterated.

She said goodbye, turned off the phone, and removed the SIM card.

Chuck's thoughts returned to the present. He'd just ended the call with Patsy.

"Shit," he said again.

He called Maria.

When the COVID pandemic hit the world and schools were shut down in 2020, the Catholic diocese laid off several teachers who were non-clergy. When they began to bring back the staff last year, Maria Reynolds decided it was time to take a break and call it quits at Sacred Heart. She found spending time at home with the horses gave her the peace of mind that teaching no longer supplied.

Maria's phone was cradled in the back pocket of her jeans as she fed the horses and swept the alleyway in the barn. She'd had a good ride today. The horses needed to be exercised and Chuck had little time to do it all.

She was about to close the heavy barn door and make her way back to the house for a quick shower before starting dinner, when her butt buzzed, and the familiar ring signaled a call from Chuck.

"Hey! If you're calling to tell me you'll be late again tonight, you've got the wrong number." She laughed and so did Chuck.

"Hi, hon. You know me too well."

Then his voice took on a serious note. "Actually, this is a TLD call. Not definite yet. Where are you?"

"Just leaving the barn and about to jump in the shower and prep dinner. Talk to me. No one anywhere near."

"Thanks. I have to drive down to Paso Robles tonight. Out of our jurisdiction and off the books. But I can't trust anyone, and I can't trust the radio. Okayed by the boss, but not sure what we'll find. Joe's going with me. Our girl's in trouble. You know who I mean. If she's still alive I need to get her the hell out of California. I don't want you in danger if I have to bring them to the house for a few days. I hate to ask, but if we bring her up here, I need to bring a female from the department to stay with her. Probably Jess Flores. I trust her. We don't have another safe house and I still feel responsible. Can you pack a bag? Go to your mom's? Just don't be at the house tonight. As soon as you can. Please? My gut is going crazy. Something is going down. I'm so sorry, hon." He spoke in that rapid-fire manner of his when he was nervous and wanted to get all the information out without forgetting something important.

"Sure!" Maria said with enthusiasm that belied her own fear. Her heart was not sure at all. "Please, Lord," she prayed, "keep him safe. Keep all of them safe."

Maria entered the house and pulled the door closed behind her. "Chuck," she said aloud to the empty house. "Maybe you should retire, too."

She sat at the kitchen counter where they had shared countless meals.

"Oh, Lord. How could I ever ask him to give up something he loves so much? He's my quiet hero. Helping others. Always. Putting away bad guys and solving cases is what he lives for. I can't ask him to quit. God, it's up to you. Either you make him quit, or he will continue as long as there is life in him. I love you, my crazy, darling Chuck. I would never ask you to quit. I guess that is what makes me a good wife to a cop. Living with this danger is not easy. Oh, Lord. Be with us. Keep him safe. And keep Patsy safe and that sweet baby girl."

Her heart softened with love. She showered, packed an overnight bag, and called her mother who lived a few miles away up San Benancio Canyon. It was a fairly short drive to the family home where her mother still lived. It had remained Maria's second home. Mom never said no, but she was getting on in years, too. She was out of the house and on her way by six o'clock that night.

EIGHT

Patsy

Alicea was awake and watching the video, as if she hadn't napped for the last hour.

"Did you have a good nap?" Patsy asked.

"I didn't nap. I'm too big for naps."

"Oh, mija. My mistake. Are you hungry?"

"Not really, Mama. Maybe I ate too much popcorn," she added sheepishly.

"Here. Have some water," Patsy urged.

"I know. I know. Hydrate. Hydrate."

"You seem to know an awfully lot."

"Yes! I do! Don't you know? I'm six now!"

Giggling, Patsy answered, "Yes! I do know that!" And continued, "So, my dear, big six-year-old, how would you like to go on a big-girl adventure tonight?"

Alicea squinted her eyes and brought her face close to Patsy's. "What kind of a'venture?" she whispered. She loved playing games with Mama.

"The kind where you get to stay up past your bedtime," Patsy whispered back.

"Even past the Friday bedtime?" Alicea asked.

"Yep," answered her mother with a grin.

"Oh, Mama. This sounds fun." Her blues eyes were bright with anticipation.

Patsy ladled spaghetti from the crockpot into plastic containers to put in the freezer along with the garlic bread they had planned to have for dinner. She put the salad in the fridge and cleaned up all signs of the meal. She couldn't dissipate the wonderful aroma that filled their home, but she wasn't about to unlock doors or open windows to air it out.

"Hey, Miss Alicea. Mija." Patsy kept her voice light. This was a game she was going to play as long as possible.

"The first thing we need to do is—"

Alicea cut her off with a loud wail. "Wait, Mommy! Wait!"

"What?" Patsy stared at her daughter. Eyes wide.

"The rules! What are the rules of the game? What do we need to do?"

"Ah." Patsy breathed a sigh of relief. Her heart pounded and her nerves were a tangled mess. Alicea had startled her.

"Listen carefully to Mommy. I'm trying to tell you. Okay?"

"Okay."

"Rule number one: Mom is the boss. But if for any reason Mama is out of the game, or you can't find me, you are the boss. Got it?"

"Got it!" She nodded with enthusiasm. "Are we playing hide and seek?"

"Nope. But we might be hiding during the game."

Alicea turned this over in her young mind. During the first week of school, she'd learned all about rules. She was now certain that rules were important to being a big girl.

"Okay. What other rules?"

"We might go hiding in the woods. Do you think you can do that with me?"

Patsy watched closely as Alicea processed this information. She made a little face then seemed to have made some sort of internal decision.

"Yes. But Mama, it's scary out there when it's dark. You'll be with me, right?"

"Absolutely! But if something happens, you have to remember the first rule. And what was the first rule?"

"Um, you're the boss?" Alicea said with a bit of doubt in her voice.

"Mama?" she asked.

"Yes, big girl?"

"I don't want to be the boss in the woods."

"Not to worry. I'll be the boss in the woods."

Patsy prayed again that all would go well. Maybe there really was nothing to fear.

"Rule number two," Pasty went on. "We are playing this game in silence. No talking out loud. Only the quietest of whispers directly into our ears and only if we absolutely must say something."

Patsy leaned down and whispered in Alicea's ear. "Like this," she whispered.

Alicea, quick to prove she understood, put her lips against her mother's ear and whispered back, "I can do that, too!"

"Good girl!"

"Next," said Patsy, "we have to think like explorers. I've got a black spy bag for you. We must take only the most important things for our spy mission!"

"Oh, Mama! We're going on a spy mission?" Her eyes were alive with anticipation.

"Yes!"

"Okay!" Alicea said in her normal loud voice. "But I don't want to be the leader in the woods."

"Oh no!" whispered Patsy. We must start whispering now. We need to practice our whisper voices so we won't forget later."

"Okay, Mama," Alicea whispered. "Sorry."

Patsy checked the time. After six. The sun would not set until nearly eight. Full dark might be about eight thirty. She didn't know about the moon. Would it be out tonight? How long would it take to get to the oak tree? She estimated the distance at about a mile and a quarter to a mile and a half. Navigating the woods and pasture with Alicea while staying out of sight would not be fast and easy. They'd need to rest. She wanted to leave before dark. She felt sure Sergio would not come before dark. She glanced again at the clock, then looked outside. The sun was getting low in the sky. She made a mental note to leave by seven. That would give them plenty of time to walk, and stop and rest. She hoped her timing was right. *I guess this is one reason to learn math in school,* she thought. Fifty minutes and they'd be out the door.

"Please, Lord, let us be safe," she prayed.

Patsy helped Alicea into a pair of black jeans and black socks and a dark long-sleeve sweatshirt.

"But Mama," Alicea whispered, "it's hot outside."

"I know, mija, but we don't want the trees to scratch us, and we need to keep our arms and legs covered. It will get cooler when the sun goes down."

Alicea was skeptical, but let Mama dress her. Patsy went to the kitchen and grabbed her emergency pack of six protein bars, four water bottles, two packs of trail mix, and an emergency blanket. She headed back to the bedroom, changed into her own black jeans, black hiking boots, and a long-sleeve black hoodie. She helped Alicea get her boots on, then went back for the pistol and burner phone. The Walther was loaded, and she had extra rounds in her pocket. She packed some underwear, a few toiletries, and a change of clothes for each of them.

As she glanced around the small house that had been home for six years, she wondered if she'd ever return. Could they get her things? Alicea's? Where would they go? What was going to happen to them?

"Is there anything special you want to take along?"

Holding the small, grey elephant that was her bedtime favorite, she asked, "Can I take Ellie?"

Patsy knelt down beside her daughter as the clock ticked forward and the sun cast longer shadows.

"If you can carry Ellie and your backpack, the answer is yes. Do you want to hold Ellie? Or can we attach her to your pack to make it easier to take her along?"

Alicea looked confused. This game was getting complicated. She was hot and wanted to take off the sweatshirt. The backpack was already heavy. Maybe she didn't want to play this game at all. Her eyes filled with tears that didn't fall as she looked at her mother, and her lower lip protruded and began to quiver.

Patsy wrapped her arms around Alicea and held her.

"It's okay, baby. Mama's here."

"I'm not a baby. I'm not!" she insisted. "I'm not scared. I just don't want to go anymore. Can we watch *Anastasia* again instead?"

Patsy didn't need this. It had been going so well. They were almost ready to go. *Just a few more minutes*, she thought.

"You know what? I think you're winning this game already," Patsy whispered. "But I have the best surprise for you coming up right now."

Patsy pulled out a packet of black-and-green camouflage make-up she'd kept after a Halloween party years ago. "You ready?" she asked. "Or should I go first?"

Alicea's eyes lit up once more. "Really? Yes!"

Patsy applied the mix of dark colors to their faces, but not as artfully as more time would have allowed. *This will have to do*, she thought, glancing again at the clock.

"One last thing before we go on our adventure. We both need a quick trip to go potty."

"I don't have to go." Alicea furrowed her brow. Her pink lips pouted and her blue eyes with bright whites were in stark contrast to her camo-painted face.

Patsy held up the mirror for her to see and said, "That's an order, soldier! We must never pass up an opportunity to drain our bladders!" she whispered, but with the voice of a drill sergeant, trying to be funny at the same time. It worked.

Alicea giggled. "You're funny. Can I call you Sergeant Mama? What's a bladder?"

They finished getting ready, and Patsy surveyed the room. Backpacks in place. Alicea was right. It was still warm out. It had been over eighty earlier. It would cool to the sixties tonight, but not until late. She left the lights on and kept the shades down. She restarted the video as if they were there, watching a movie.

Blanca was with them every step of the way. She was proud of Patsy. She'd faced her demons and defied them. She'd called for help. She'd prayed. She'd prayed for an escape and God gave her one. At least there was a plan. At best, Sergio was not there and he only meant to scare her. At worst… well, it might be a long night.

NINE

Chuck and Joe

"Hey, Joe," Chuck called across the desk.

"I got a problem that I might need help with tonight. Off the books, but I cleared it with Foster, just in case. I hate to ask, but are you up for a drive to Paso Robles? Might be back by eleven thirty. Might be longer." Joe stared at his friend. Thinking. Chuck went on. "Like I said, off book, but I cleared it with Foster."

Joe thought about going home tonight. His wife, Corinne, had been a holy terror lately.

"Why didn't he make more money? Why couldn't she get a new car? Do you think these pants make me look fat?"

It didn't matter how he answered any of the nagging questions she threw at him. He couldn't win. It would be the wrong answer and the tirade would begin. Just once he wanted to answer, "Yes, those pants make you look fat, because you are fat." But never would he say those words. Not ever. He loved her.

"I'm in," Joe said. "What's going on?"

How many times had Chuck had his back? Too many to count. Joe considered himself to be Joe Average in the department. He played by the rules and never tried to stick his neck out. Besides Corinne, he had two sons to think about. His life insurance wasn't enough to make Corinne happy, but it would help. Problem was, he really didn't want to die. Not yet, anyway. Chuck seemed to come way too close, way too often. He thought of the lyrics to that old song by the Hollies, "He ain't heavy, he's my brother."

It was usually Chuck who did the carrying. But tonight? Joe thought something was different about the way Chuck asked. His angst over the last few weeks, and the fact that this solitary lone wolf of a cowboy rarely asked for help, had Joe both willing to jump in, and scared he'd just grabbed the trapeze bar and might be swinging without a net.

"Thanks, Joe. I'm checking out now. Meet me at my car in twenty?"

"No patrol car?"

"No. Off book. No uniforms. I got a blue light and siren if we need it. Bring your service weapon and badge. And a vest."

"Ah shit, Chuck. What am I getting into with you?"

"Saving lives, bro. Saving lives. Protect and serve. It's what we swore to do. Defund the police or not, we got to protect and serve." Chuck grinned. "Thanks, Joe. It'll probably be a nothing night, but I want to be prepared."

Chuck's undercover car was a souped-up trans-am engine in a ten-year-old, dull black body. Not memorable, but dependable and fast, with extra steel-plate body armor throughout. Chuck had bulletproof glass installed, too. It was also equipped with a police scanner and radio. His personal car was the envy of most of the macho guys in the department.

Joe opened the passenger door and climbed in next to Chuck.

"Chuck, you know I love you, brother."

"Oh, for God's sake, don't get sappy on me." Chuck started the engine, buckled in, and pulled out of the gated police lot, turning left onto West Alisal Street. It was six forty-five. He didn't want to be late.

Making a right turn onto Salinas Street, it looked to be a typical Friday night in Salinas. A few classic cars belched Latino music. Others played country western tunes. The dinner crowd was heading out to local restaurants, and those with jobs were trying to get home after a long day at work. He followed the one-way street around to the left where the name changed to John Street. They crossed South Main with the green light and passed Norma's Family Restaurant. Chuck remembered when it used to be Sambo's. But that name had changed years ago, when it was no longer politically correct to make any reference to the classic tale of *Little Black Sambo*. It was considered prejudicial and demeaning to people of color. The illustrations and names were called racial slurs. While Salinas was home to a vast majority of Hispanics, the Black population remained relatively small by comparison.

Chuck sighed, as he did every time he passed the restaurant. Perhaps it was because he was a white male just trying to live an honest life, but he had always considered the character of Sambo as a Black hero. The book had been written and published in 1899 by a Scottish woman, Helen Bannerman. History was Chuck's secret hobby. He dug deep to uncover facts behind every case and every question. He'd seen his share of racists over the years, but in his mind, the fight was between good guys and bad guys, not the color of anyone's skin.

They passed Swenson and Silacci Flowers, a Salinas landmark business, now closed for the day. A few hotels remained on John Street. Their names and owners changed over the years and reflected the changes in town. His town. Joe's town. Yes, thought Chuck, they were here to protect and serve. Patsy might live in another county now, but she was Salinas. Born and bred. Chuck felt it was his duty to protect her, too. He thought briefly about her mother, Melanie. She'd been a good kid. He should have stayed in touch. He grew up in this town, but like many others, he lost touch with old friends. They'd grown apart. They were different now. *It is a sad truth, but there are only so many hours in a day*, he thought.

Crossing Abbot Street, Chuck slowed at the on ramp to Highway 101 South, then accelerated as they merged onto the highway. It was nearly a hundred miles to Klau Mine Road, where he hoped to find Patsy and Alicea, alive and unharmed. Threats made by the NF were serious. He'd seen too much tragedy to ignore this one.

Chuck filled Joe in on the facts as they drove. He brought him up to speed with the back story of Patsy and Sergio and finished with Patsy's call earlier that night.

"*I will find you?*" Joe asked. "Is he shooting in the dark? Maybe he left that same letter in several mailboxes because they had some sort of intel that she was in that area? Maybe the kid in school?" Joe thought aloud.

"Maybe," Chuck said.

The miles drifted by as the men let their minds go over the clues. Occasionally one or the other would bring up a thought. What if this? What if that? What was coming? Would they find her? They talked it out. As they traveled the last thirty minutes on back roads that would lead them to Patsy, they sat in silence. Each lost in his own thoughts, knowing they might be headed for a war neither wanted. Or they might be heading to a crime scene. *Please, God. Not tonight*, Chuck silently prayed.

Chuck wasn't much for church or prayers, but he believed in God. He'd come too close to death on too many occasions not to believe that he had some sort of divine protection. But he also gave the occasional thought to the fact that someday that luck might run out. How many times could he tempt fate?

TEN

Alicea

Alicea watched in the mirror as her mother applied the camouflage makeup. She thought about the game. *I'm glad she wants to play this game but I'm hot.*

"I think you're winning the game already!" Mama whispered in my ear.

We looked so different after Mama put the paint on our faces. She told me to keep my hands away from my face or I'd mess it up. But I really wanted to touch it. It felt strange and had a funny smell.

Then mama said we were ready to start the game for real. She unlocked the back door, and I started to go around her to be the first one outside, but she grabbed me and made me stop. Then she turned and locked the door behind us. It wasn't quite dark, but she didn't turn on the porch light for later like she usually did at night. Then Mama leaned down and whispered in my ear.

"The game begins now. Be as quiet as a mouse on the gravel. Stay right behind me. Hold my hand and don't let go unless I tell you to. I also have a piece of rope tied to my waist. Hold the rope, too. It might be easier than holding hands when we go through the woods. Are you ready, soldier?"

I nodded. I was a little scared. It would be dark in the woods. We've never gone in the woods before. Not even in the daytime. This game is scary, but I like it. I think.

ELEVEN

Blanca

Patsy and Alicea made their way down the path toward the big house. Their steps were slow and deliberate, but each footfall on the gravel seemed unnaturally loud. Blanca listened for other sounds, too. Sounds only she might hear.

Sergio. A car. Conversation. Demons. There could be any one of a hundred possibilities for trouble before this night was over. "Please Lord," she prayed. "Get them through this. They are good girls. I ask your protection for them tonight and always."

Then she heard the sound of a car engine on the road above. The sun was setting, but it wasn't dark yet. Blanca listened as the motor continued down the road.

Patsy stopped and stood like a statue when she heard the motor. Alicea stopped behind her and listened, too. They remained completely still. Blanca wondered if Patsy was holding her breath.

The narrow path through the trees was clear cut, but the canopy of foliage overhead cast eerie shadows in the fading light. It would be another two months before the leaves in this part of California would start to fall.

Crunch. Crunch. Patsy made a quick decision and moved like a cat. With Alicea right behind, she took several steps down the path before she veered off to the right. Blanca followed. She spread her wings slightly, to shield them from anything or anyone else behind them on the path.

Patsy and Alicea ducked into the woods and were completely out of sight. Blanca knew they needed to go down the hill through the woods to reach the pasture beyond. There, they needed to cross the open field, before reaching the oak tree near the service road.

Blanca looked at the darkening sky. "Please, Lord, let them make it," she prayed.

If that was Sergio up on the road, he'd have to go all the way to the back patio at the big house to see them as they crossed the pasture. He could not see them in the woods unless he had night-vision goggles. The horses and cattle in the pasture would not harm them. A greater threat would be that Patsy and Alicea might scare the livestock. Was there no end to the dangerous possibilities against them tonight? Blanca said another prayer and thanked the Father in Heaven for preparing her for any scenario.

Patsy stopped again. Listening. Her eyes had adjusted to the darkness of the woods as night fell in California. Alicea stopped and stayed close to her mother. All three strained to hear. As the sun set, there was the faintest hint of Fall in the air. The temperature had dropped a few degrees. After the past few weeks of record-breaking heat, it was almost pleasant to be outside. There would be a beautiful sunset on the coast at San Simeon and Hearst Castle. But Patsy had no such thoughts about the beauty that surrounded her or a sunset on the beach. She was running on nerves. All from a piece of paper. She had seen no other sign, threat, or person. Was this all her imagination? She wondered. No! She knew in her heart with certainty that the letter was a threat. She had to take Alicea and escape. When you know a snake is about to attack, you don't sit around and wait for it.

Blanca could feel Patsy's heart pounding in genuine terror. Little Alicea was still in the game. Patsy's mind was on fast forward. *What if Officer Chuck isn't there? What if Sergio finds us instead? Can I really protect Alicea? God? I'm so scared. Please help me. Please help me, Lord,* she prayed silently and continued to make a path through the woods and dense foliage. Her footing was unsure, and branches scraped at her hoodie. She kept Alicea close behind her.

Little did Patsy realize that the Lord heard every prayer she'd ever prayed. He'd sent Blanca. Not to intervene, but to pray for her. Guide her. But all decisions made were Patsy's. She was running toward safety. Whether the threat was real or imagined, she wasn't taking chances. She'd protect Alicea with her life.

Blanca heard her prayer. She heard another sound, too. Laughter? It was behind her. Close. Slowly. Softly they moved. The thick brush and growing darkness made it difficult. They tried to be quiet, but anyone or anything nearby could hear them as they made their way down the hill.

Blanca let them get a few yards ahead, then turned around, spread her wings, and pulled her sword.

Humans would not see her. Nor would she be able to stop humans. But they weren't being followed by humans. It was Chax. A demon. The Grand Duke of Hell. She'd faced him before, but that didn't make him less intimidating. He was a powerful demon, and it was not good that he had arrived.

"Why are you here?" Blanca asked. "This isn't your territory."

"Oh, it's sweet little Blanca. Do you think you can save those two? They are fearful, full of Satan's angst. Not the little one. But she will be. I'll see to that. Doesn't that woman trust your God? I mean really, running away in the night?" His voice dripped with derision.

"Dearest Blanca, your God should have sent a real warrior if He truly wanted to protect them. Seems like your God is not really serious about helping them at all."

"He did send a warrior, Chax. I'm here. And you will not harm them. Your Satan is no match for my God. No matter what you think." Blanca was shaking but felt stronger as she faced this demon from Hell.

"I love it!" Chax toyed with her. "A little pissing match with a pissant little angel. Sadly, I don't have orders to hurt you. Yet." And he was gone.

Blanca sheathed her sword and followed mother and daughter, who were practically swallowed up in the night. Darkness was nearly complete.

They heard another car approach. Patsy stopped again. It had been slow going since they left the house. She motioned for Alicea to get down and sit next to her. They were in a deep thicket, but only about thirty yards off the gravel path.

"Keep very still now," Patsy whispered in Alicea's ear and squeezed her hand at the same time. Alicea squeezed back and didn't make a sound.

Patsy stared up the hill toward her house and the big house. She could make out the few lights she'd left on and a few of the automatic yard lights from the big house. It was quiet. Then she heard the motor again. This time, she saw headlights turn slowly down her driveway. Fear gripped her heart. She let out a shaky breath.

Chuck would not come to her house. She never had visitors. It had to be Sergio. What to do? God? Run or stay still? This is the best place to hide. They were in the deepest part of the woods. They would make noise if they tried to run. Would Sergio have dogs? Probably not. Dogs were too much trouble. Night-vision goggles? She prayed he didn't have a dog or some other way to track them. She had to stop thinking about the ways they might be caught and focus on escape.

She asked God for strength and whispered in Alicea's ear. "We're going to pretend those are the bad guys. Bad like Rasputin. Bad like the Devil. We have to stay hiding."

Alicea squeezed her mother's hand so hard that Patsy winced and continued to whisper in her daughter's ear, "Alicea, you stay close to me. Got it? Hold my hand or the rope. If anything happens to me, you run all the way down the hill to the field with the cows and horses. Then you go to that big oak tree by the road down there. You know where I mean? Squeeze my hand again if you do."

She squeezed.

Patsy tried to see her daughter's face in the darkness. With the camo makeup on, all she could see were the whites of her eyes. They were no longer the eyes of a little girl playing a game with her mama. She looked like a frightened little girl who no longer wanted to play this scary game. Patsy wanted to hold her and cry and tell her everything would be all right. But would it be all right? she wondered. She put her arms around Alicea. "I'm here, sweetie. You are so brave and I'm so very proud of you," he whispered.

Alicea turned her head and put her lips to Patsy's ear, "I'm scared, Mama. I don't want to play this game anymore."

"I know." She watched the headlights blink off when the car reached the front door of her house. "I don't either, Alicea. But now we have to stay hidden and very quiet. It's very important. Do you understand?"

"Yes. But Mama? This isn't really a game, is it?" Her little body was shaking.

"No, sweet daughter, it's not. There are some very bad people at our house right now. But you're a big girl, and we can do this together. There is a nice man who is going to meet us at that big tree down there and help us get away. He'll be wearing a black cowboy hat. He's a good guy. He's a cop. We just need to stay quiet and hidden until that car at our house goes away."

Blanca felt sad for mother and daughter. She knew their legs were cramped in their small huddle. She knew that one of the Norteños had arrived at Patsy's house. She knew he was led by Chax. She thought Chax had been banished back to Hell, along with Mara and Abaddon, but he was a powerful demon. She guessed he'd figured out a way to get back to prowl the earth. Was there no end to the evil that comes this way? she wondered.

All was quiet. Whoever was at the house, was moving with stealth. No one was heading down the path, and there was no sound or movement at the big house. They sat and waited. When Alicea moved, trying to get comfortable, Patsy wiggled over to lean against the trunk of a large pine tree. She maneuvered Alicea to rest against her body. They were still hidden, but more comfortable. She guessed they'd been there for almost an hour. If that car didn't leave soon, she might miss her connection with Chuck and have to go all the way to Nacimiento Lake Road.

What was he doing in there? She still believed it was Sergio looking for her. Had he realized she wasn't there? Was he waiting for her? Searching her house? For what? She had no incriminating evidence against Sergio or La Familia. All she had was her baby. Her little Alicea. Her joy and love. Her world. Now sleeping beside her in this thicket. The night bugs had emerged with the setting sun. The buzz of the insects was maddening. At least their clothing and bug spray protected them from bites.

Blanca waited too. Ready. Alert.

Guessing it to be about eight forty-five, Patsy knew the time was coming to make that decision. Stay or go? Now or later? Could she make it the rest of the way? She heard the back door open. The sound was surprisingly loud in the night air. Alicea stirred slightly.

No voices. Then, the unmistakable sound of a man urinating off her back porch brought her up short. Disgusting. Still there. Only one? Only Sergio? Should she call out to him? Get this settled once and for all.

Blanca silently screamed, "No! Oh Father, do not let her call out!"

Then they heard him. "Patricia, Patricia, *salga, salga de dondequiera que ustedes.*"

"Patsy, Patsy, come out, come out, wherever you are," he repeated in English, singing like he was playing a game, too. But the voice! The voice was not Sergio's!

Her mind raced. Not Sergio? But who? This was bad, thought Patsy. He'd sent someone to kill her. Or worse. Yes. There are worse things than death. He was still there. She could not see him, but she had not heard the familiar squeak of the unoiled hinge on her screen door.

Then it opened and she heard him clearly. The sing-song voice of a moment ago had changed. "Fucking *puta!*" he yelled.

Then, muttered, but still clear and angry, he added, "*Esto es una puta perdido de tiempo.*"

"Fuck. Fuck. Fuck, Sergio! *¡Me voy de aqui!*"

Patsy silently made the sign of the cross and thanked God. She had no idea who was in her house, but he'd said this was a waste of his time, called her a whore and said he was leaving. Was he on the phone? Talking to himself? Was someone with him who might stay behind? She waited as her thoughts continued to race. Silence. She waited.

Ten minutes later, she heard the engine and watched with her limited view as the driver turned around and drove back up the road. She listened as he picked up speed on Klau Mine, heading back toward Adelaide Road and the highway. He was gone.

She sat for a few minutes longer, to be certain all remained quiet at both houses and no one drove down the service road. Alicea woke when the man yelled but had closed her eyes again. Patsy gently nudged her daughter and asked if she was ready to go.

"Home?" Alicea asked as she rubbed her eyes.

"No, big girl. We're going to reach that big tree tonight. You can do that with me. Right?"

Alicea stretched and reached out to touch her mother. They hugged.

"Mommy, I'm scared. I just want to go home."

"I know you do. But we can't. You were very brave tonight. But I need you to be brave for a little longer. We need to get to the police officer I told you about. We are still in danger, and we still have to be quiet. Can you do that?"

With enthusiasm returning and her confidence boosted, Alicea whispered, "Yes! Let's go, Mama."

Blanca went ahead this time. Unknown to mother or daughter, she smoothed the path through the brush and led the way, making it easier for them to navigate the wooded terrain.

This is going better than I thought, Patsy told herself. But they traveled slow and purposeful, one step at a time. When they reached the fence between the edge of the woods and the pasture beyond, Patsy said, "Let's rest a minute." She listened. Nothing. She adjusted her escape pack and asked Alicea if she wanted some water.

"No thank you, Mama."

They began to walk again, and Patsy pointed out the dark shadow of the giant oak tree near the road. It was still almost a half-mile away, but the worst was behind them.

"You see that tree over there? That's where we have to go to meet our friend. And then we win the game! Can you keep walking with me? And run if you can?"

Alicea was tired but trying to keep up. "Yes, Mama. I think so." Her voice was tired, too.

Blanca moved back in behind them once they were in the open field. She kept her wings out to shield them from whatever might be out there.

Patsy was pretty sure the car had driven away, but if whoever had been up there had gone down to the Meyers' house, he might see them. They'd be difficult to spot in their dark outfits, but once the moon came out, there'd be no more hiding.

Taking Alicea's hand again, Patsy started across the field at a jog. Alicea managed for only a few yards. "Mom, I can't!" Her voice was not quiet this time.

Patsy grabbed her and they both went to the ground. She tucked Alicea into the curve of her stomach and shielded her from the direction of the houses.

"Hush, baby. Let's just rest here for a minute." She waited. No sound. No lights. One. Two. Three minutes. Four. Five. All remained quiet.

Blanca was right with them and wishing she could do more to help. She watched as Patsy sheltered Alicea against any perceived threat and thought of the love a mother has for her child. Blanca had lived as a human but died at twelve years old and never had the joy of being a mother. *I'd have been a good mother*, she thought.

Patsy knew they had to keep going. They had to get to the cover of that tree. But she did think the worst was over. She thought if they were going to scout the area to find her, they'd have done so by now. She estimated they had about four hundred yards to go. Four football fields. "I have an idea," she told Alicea.

She shrugged out of her backpack, put it on Alicea, and adjusted the straps. Then she turned around and squatted, so Alicea could climb onto her back. She wrapped her legs around Patsy's waist while Patsy hooked her arms under those legs. Lacing her fingers together in front.

Blanca watched in amazement. Patsy had her forty-five-pound daughter on her back plus another twenty pounds in the backpack and the ten pounds of Alicea's own pack. She was carrying at least seventy-five pounds on her back. Four hundred yards to go. Could she do it?

She began to walk and picked up the pace. Alicea leaned to one side and Patsy nearly went down. "Uh oh. Try not to move back there, Alicea. When you shift your body from side to side, I could lose my balance. Please try to stay right in the middle for me?"

"Sorry, Mama."

"Okay. We're going faster now. If you move, I might lose my balance and drop you. We don't want that, do we?"

"No, Mama," she whispered. "I love you."

"I love you, too. We got this. We're gonna make it."

Patsy kicked it up to a slow jog and kept going. One. Two. Three. Four. Five. Six. Seven. Eight. She silently counted each step. Every twenty-four steps she slowed to a walk for the next twelve steps. Twenty-four. Twelve. Twenty-four. Twelve. The tree loomed closer. She dared not look back. She heard nothing except the sounds of the night and her own heavy breathing. One. Two. Three…

Headlights cut through the dark to her left from the direction of Klau Mine Road. Fear nearly paralyzed her to the spot. She had to get her emotions and fear in check. Was it Officer Cowboy? Or Sergio? Or whoever had peed on her porch? "Please, God. Please save us."

The lights went out. Patsy stopped and dropped to her knees and cautioned Alicea to stay quiet as she gently set her on the ground. She took the pack off of Alicea and lay prone on the ground, one arm around her daughter. Side by side they lay very still. Blanca waited. Alicea remained quiet.

For the first time, Patsy quietly unzipped the pack and slipped out the Walther P22 Chuck had given her six years earlier. She made sure the safety was on. Check.

"Please, Lord, don't let her have to use that thing," Blanca prayed.

They listened as the car moved slowly along the dark road without lights. It was not the same motor as the one at her home earlier tonight. Of that she was sure. She still couldn't see the car. She followed the sound of the engine. It was a heavy engine. Not some little compact.

She could make out the tree in the darkness and the car was nearly there. Her rendezvous point. She and Alicea were about sixty yards short. If it wasn't Officer Chuck, they'd be sitting ducks if they were seen. There was no cover. Not even a sleeping cow to hide behind. Although that was a dumb thought anyway.

The car turned around. She heard the shift in gears from forward to reverse and back again. The lights came on for just a few seconds. Twice. The engine purred near the tree. Patsy tried desperately to see in the dark. She caught a glimpse of the car when the brake lights came on and when the driver flicked the headlights twice more. She breathed a huge sigh of relief. She'd ridden in that car once before. It was Officer Chuck.

"Mama, did we win?"

"I think so, Alicea. I think so. Let's go. Slow. I'll get our packs."

She put the Walther back in the pack. Hand in hand, they walked toward the car. Then she heard his voice. He called softly, "Patsy? You okay? Alicea?"

"Who is there?" she whispered back. She needed to be sure.

"It's me. Officer Reynolds. Come on. It's safe."

Blanca smiled over them. "Thank you, Lord."

TWELVE

Chuck

He put the backpacks in the trunk and helped Patsy and Alicea into the back seat.

"This is Detective Joe Medeiros. We're gonna get you out of here tonight. What do you say, Alicea? Are your ready for an adventure?"

From the back seat came a small, tired voice.

"Maybe tonight was all the a'venture I need for a while."

They all shared a nervous laugh. The tension Patsy had felt since seeing the envelope was slowly beginning to dissipate. They were safe. At least for now.

"Did you have any trouble?" Chuck asked.

Patsy told him about the intruder. She could not see him but heard his voice.

"Chuck, it wasn't Sergio. I'm sure of it."

In the front seat Chuck and Joe exchanged glances.

"You're sure? You haven't talked to him in a long time."

"I'm sure. That was not Sergio's voice."

Chuck let it go. All was quiet on the drive back toward Salinas. Alicea had fallen asleep, and Pasty dozed as well. Blanca sat quietly with them. Chuck and Joe remained silent. There was always the possibility one of the females was awake. No use giving either cause for alarm.

Chuck pulled into the station. "Jess should be ready to go," Chuck said as Joe got out of the car. "Thanks, Joe. I owe you big time."

"Naw, Reynolds. You don't. I'm the one who owes you. We may not be even, but at least I'm trying to pay back what I can for all the times you've been there for me."

"Joe. Stop. You're embarrassing me. Man up and stop getting sappy on me. What's up with you, anyway? You're the closest thing I have to a brother, but I'm not comfortable chattin' about it. Okay? We're good. We take care of each other. We take care of the department. Right? EOD. End of discussion.

"Now, please send Jess Flores out. I'm having her stay with these girls tonight. I need to figure out the rest of this plan. Maria is staying at her mother's up the canyon. Glad all stayed quiet for a Friday night here in town. Go home. Get some sleep. Hug your wife. I'll see you in the morning."

Chuck was uncomfortable when anyone other than his wife Maria showed signs of affection or admiration for him.

It was nearly eleven thirty when Joe Medeiros closed the car door and went inside the station. Chuck sat in the quiet car waiting for Officer Jessica Flores. She'd been with the department a few years now. In Chuck's eyes, she was still a kid. But she was good police. She did her job and didn't make waves. She was always squared away, never grumbled or complained, and most important, he trusted her to protect Patsy and Alicea, so he could get some sleep.

Chuck didn't trust Sergio or the Norteños. His gut still told him trouble was brewing, but what? There'd be a full moon in another week or two. That's usually when all hell breaks loose. Chuck watched as Jessica Flores came through the door and headed for his car. She carried a decent-sized duffel bag. He popped open the trunk. She dropped the bag next to Patsy's backpack, closed the trunk, and got in the passenger seat next to Reynolds.

"Hey," was all she said, with a glance to the back seat at mother and daughter, both with eyes still closed.

"Thanks for doing this," Chuck said quietly.

"It's my job. I can't believe you got this approved. They asleep?" She kept her voice low, too.

"I think so. Let's limit talk. They've had a rough night."

"No problem." She adjusted her seat belt as Reynolds pulled out of the lot for the second time that night. He left by the same route, but turned right on South Main and followed it out of town toward his home.

Thirty minutes later Patsy and Alicea were safe in the guest room. Jessica put on a pot of coffee and took a seat in Chuck's recliner in the adjacent living room. No television or radio on, just her own police radio set low, but readily available if there was anything she needed to know. All was quiet.

"I'll be leaving again about three." Chuck told her as he walked down the hall to his own room. He was determined to get a few hours of sleep before heading back to the office. He planned to drive his pick-up back to town and leave the Trans Am for Jess.

The alarm woke him at two forty-five. He showered, dressed, grabbed his service weapon, and left the bedroom. Except for Patsy's story about the intruder at her home, it had been a quiet night.

Jess was properly on duty. She was wide-awake and still in the recliner, reading a John Grissom novel.

"Want a cup of coffee for the road?" she asked, getting up to pour it for him.

"I just made a fresh pot."

"Sit. My house. I know where everything is. Thanks again, Jess. Any news? Any noise?"

"Other than the fact that you snore? No. Quiet as a graveyard out here. I don't know how you stand this quiet. I'm so used to all the street noise from town. Traffic. Sirens. Parties. Neighbors fighting. It's just always loud in my apartment. But this quiet is nice, too." She gave him a smile and added, "The ladies are still asleep. I look in on them every so often. All is well."

"Thanks. I need to get going. I have a lot to do," he said.

"You ever going to tell me what this is all about?" she asked.

"Need-to-know, Jess. Need-to-know. And what you need to know is to keep your eyes and ears open. Someone showed up at their place tonight. Uninvited. To kill, hurt, or kidnap, or have a cup of coffee, we don't know. But not likely for anything good. I don't think anyone could possibly know they're here, but eyes and ears, kid. Keep them open. Call me for back up if you suspect anything. If there's going to be a problem, it'll be before daylight." Chuck already had his hand on the doorknob.

"Shouldn't you stay here, too?" she asked.

"Probably. But I've got to check on some things that I can't do from here. I truly believe you're all safe or I wouldn't go. Okay? Keys to the Trans Am are on the counter. The dogs are with my wife Maria."

"Got it. So, go already! I got this."

Blanca kept watch and prayed.

Chuck had just taken off his jacket at the station when the watch commander sent an urgent BOLO and called for units in the area and others to an address he recognized. His address.

"Officer pinned down. Shots fired. Situation unknown. Injuries unknown. No suspects or other information. Three potential victims. One officer and two female civilians. No other information. Repeat. All available units please respond."

"Ah shit! No!" Chuck cried as he ran to the patrol car.

THIRTEEN

Blanca

Blanca felt the demons approach. She was in the bedroom with Patsy and Alicea who slept peacefully. Blanca was full of love for them, and she had prayed they'd be safe here.

Chax was first, the one she'd met earlier on the trail. Then Mara came in, and Blanca could feel the heat of evil from her. Finally, Abaddon entered the room, too. Blanca could feel the fires of Hell coming off this evil trio.

"They are ours!" Abaddon shouted at Blanca. "We will turn her heart back to us. We are stronger now, little Miss Blanca. The three of us against this pitiful little angel? This is not even a contest, girlie. Why don't you go crying back to Hannah? You aren't winning tonight. Wait until you see what we've got coming this way."

Blanca drew her sword and spread her wings wide. She stood between the demons and the sleeping mother and daughter who were oblivious to the battle raging for their souls.

"Oh, dear. Look who has got her feathers ruffled." Chax laughed.

Mara joined in the laughter. "You're a riot, Blanca."

"Let's go see how our boys are doing outside," Abaddon said. And they were gone.

Blanca felt stronger than ever. She had to warn Jessica. They needed to be ready. There wasn't much time.

Jess had just poured herself another cup of coffee and was about to return to her seat and book when there was a tremor in her hand, and she spilled the coffee.

"Hot!" she said aloud with an involuntary catch in her throat.

How did I manage that? she thought.

She went back to the kitchen sink, and that's when she saw them. She hadn't heard a thing. There were two cars parked down the driveway and dark shadows were moving toward the house.

"What the hell?" Jess set the cup on the counter and doused the kitchen light as she moved toward the guest room. Her service weapon already drawn.

"Wake up! Wake up! Both of you. Come with me. Now." Her voice was urgent, but now loud as she shook Patsy and Alicea. Both were startled awake. "Come with me."

The house wasn't large, and Chuck had never built a safe room. He didn't have a basement. Her best bet was the inside closet in the primary bedroom. All doors and windows to the outside were locked and double reinforced. That would help, she thought.

Jess scooped up Alicea in one arm and helped Patsy with the other. Both were still fully dressed except for shoes and hoodies.

"Let's go." She had just hustled them into the closet when the house lights went out. Whoever was out there had cut the electricity. Her cellphone was in her pocket.

She pulled it out and was able to call Headquarters and give a brief sitrep and call for backup when shots rang out. Blanca spread her wings wide over and around all three, shielding them from bullets that pierced the walls of the closet. As Patsy, Alicea, and Jess huddled together, Blanca wrapped her wings tighter. She prayed with them. *Please, Lord, be with us. Protect us. Put your wall of protection around these beautiful ladies.*

"Officer pinned down with two civilian females," Jess repeated. "Shots fired. Shots fired."

As she spoke, the sound of automatic gunfire blasted around them. She dropped the phone. All expected to be hit at any second. The noise seemed to last forever, but the gunfire only went on for about thirty seconds. Then it stopped. They heard glass falling from windowpanes. Pipes had burst. Water was running. "Is anyone hurt?" Jess whispered. "Patsy? Alicea?"

"I'm okay," came Alicea's soft whisper back.

"Thank God," said Patsy. "I'm not hurt either. What now?"

"Hush. We don't move. We wait." Jess knew they'd never have a chance if they went out now. Their only hope was that whoever had just shot up Reynolds' house would assume no one had survived and they'd leave. Or law enforcement would arrive in time.

Jessica was processing information. How many guns? From what direction were the shots coming? She knew that whoever was out there would most likely come into the house any second. They'd use caution. At first. But if they had a police scanner? They'd know she was inside, too. Was it worth going to prison for killing a cop? Would it be a badge of honor? Or would they get the hell out of there before back-up arrived? She waited. They all waited. Alicea started to cry.

"Hush, mija. We must stay very quiet."

The three had no idea that it was Blanca who protected them or that she was in the closet and shielding them with her powerful wings. The Lord was with them. Blanca followed orders.

They heard a crash as a door was kicked open. Jess figured it was the front door from the direction of the sound. She strained to listen. Footsteps. Hurried. Then the back door crashed open. Furniture was knocked aside. Inside doors were kicked open. Cabinet doors were pulled out. Dishes not already broken crashed to the floor. Someone entered the bedroom. They were close. Any minute now. Jess gripped her weapon and aimed it at the closet door.

Then, a siren in the distance. A voice came from the other room. "*Vamonos*! Let's go! Now! Now! Now! Out! Out! Out!"

Feet hurried in retreat. Car doors opened and slammed shut. Engines roared to life. They heard the sounds of tires spinning on the driveway as they headed back toward the county road. She heard them turn south. Law enforcement would be coming from the north. The perps would get away.

The sirens grew louder. But Jess held her position. They were safe. She was sure. But she would not move until she got an all clear from a fellow officer.

"Thank you, Lord." Blanca continued to pray, her wings still wrapped around her charges. Officer Reynolds' house was a mess. She heard Chax then.

"We'll be back, Little Blanca."

You'll be ready, Blanca. I am with you.

FOURTEEN

Chuck

It was four forty-five in the morning when Chuck turned on the lights and siren and sped toward home. He called in. On his way. He did not claim it was his home. Too many bad guys had police scanners. He'd be a target forever. But then, if they shot up his house, it wasn't random. Maybe this wasn't about Patsy after all. Maybe this was about him.

He pulled out his cellphone and started to call Jess. Then thought better of that move. She had not called him, which meant she didn't have her phone, or it was too dangerous. Calling her could put them in worse danger. He had to get there. He had put them there and left. Damn! He accelerated as he crossed Blanco Road and left the lights of the city behind.

He called the watch commander instead. "This is Detective Chuck Reynolds. That's my address. Officer Jessica Flores and two female civilians are there. My wife is not there. I repeat, my wife, Maria Reynolds, is not at the house. I'm en route. ETA is twelve minutes."

The watch commander practically yelled into the phone. "Chuck?! What the fuck did you get Flores into? Ah shit, this is gonna come down on my head."

Chuck replied, "Maybe. But it was my house that got shot up. No reports of injuries yet. Let's see what happens next. Any word? Anyone there yet? Any more shots or trouble? Have you heard from Jess?"

"No. Keep your radio on. And get out there!"

Too late to set up a roadblock. They'll be long gone. Maybe. Let's hope they are gone, and the girls are safe. Chuck's mind raced with possibilities. Not all were good.

"Please, Lord. You know I don't pray too often. But I seem to be making a habit of it lately. Let them be okay."

Chuck made the left turn onto the narrow country road. A few more miles. His siren screamed in the night. He decided against calling Maria until he knew she'd be up. No sense disturbing her sleep, too. Nothing she could do anyway.

His cell buzzed. Caller identification said it was Jess Flores. "Hey! You okay? What happened?"

"Chuck Reynolds?" A man's voice.

"Yes. Who is this. Where's Jess?"

"This is Officer Williams. We're first on the scene."

Chuck interrupted. "Are the girls okay? Is Jess okay? Can I talk to her? I'm almost there. That's my house!" Chuck was getting uncharacteristically loud as adrenaline fueled anxiety. His right foot pressed harder on the accelerator.

"Hold on. We have procedures and protocol. But I can tell you this, miraculously, yes, they are physically unhurt."

Chuck eased off the gas pedal and dropped his speed back to sixty-five miles per hour. He was still driving too fast on this narrow road. His heart continued to pound in his chest but there was a thread of tension easing back, letting him breathe again.

Officer Williams went on. "But for the life of me, us, we don't know how they weren't hit. We'll have questions for you, too. As will the crime scene investigators. Something's off here. I'm not going to let you inside until Forensics finishes and they aren't even here yet. That's all I can say. Sorry, pal. See you in a few."

The adrenaline returned. "But it's my house!" Chuck yelled.

"And you of all people should know. Calm down, Officer.

"Calm down? Calm down?" How many times had he said that to someone else? Countless. But this Williams was beginning to seriously piss him off.

"Do you know who I am?"

"Please, Reynolds. Everyone in the department knows who you are. This is all for your own good. You know that. The three females seem unhurt. We've got two buses coming to get them checked out. We're sending them to Salinas Memorial."

"Are you kidding me?" Chuck was going ballistic again. "That is the first place the NF will look for them."

Chuck clicked off the phone, not trusting himself to speak rationally. The last thing he needed was a reprimand, but he knew that might be the case anyway.

Five minutes later he pulled into the driveway, the place was ablaze with red and blue flashing lights.

FIFTEEN

Patsy

More noise. More footsteps. Several people walking around. Then someone very close to the closet door. Quiet. Another set of footsteps. Two of them. Being very quiet. The bad guys back? Or officers to help? They'd heard the sirens, but Officer Jess took no chances and told them to stay still and quiet. They did.

Then the closet door was pulled open. Flashlights blinded them. Jess held her fire. The two officers had guns drawn, as did Jess. What a sigh of relief all breathed when the suspense ended.

"Thanks, guys. They're gone? All clear? Truly?" she asked with a slight shake in her voice.

Patsy stood on wobbly legs and propped Alicea on her hip and held her close with her right arm. Patsy kept Alicea's head and eyes hidden under a shirt she'd pulled off the hanger in the closet, not knowing the extent of carnage beyond. It was pitch black without electricity. Flashlights carried by officers offered fractured glimpses of splintered wood and a home destroyed by gunfire, but she didn't see any blood or bodies. It had all happened so fast and been so loud. She threw her free arm around Jess and pulled her in.

"Thank you. Thank you," Patsy gushed.

Jess was clearly uncomfortable being hugged and pulled back immediately, her eyes scanning the darkness.

"Where is Chuck?" Patsy asked. "He was here when we went to bed."

"He went back to work. But he'll probably be back soon," Jess offered.

Patsy had been too afraid to talk to Officer Flores in the closet but had wondered if Chuck was out there trying to protect them.

Automatic gunfire had ripped through the house, destroying windows, walls, cabinets, and furniture. She stared as one officer examined the wall behind the closet. It was riddled with holes. How was it that none of them were hit?

"Can we go get our shoes and stuff from the other room?" she asked of no one in particular.

"Just as soon as we take a few photos in there, ma'am. We'll bring them out to you. Where are they?"

"Our shoes are by the bed. Sweatshirts on the chair. Our backpacks are in there, too." She thought of the Walther and burner phone in her pack. Would Chuck get in trouble because of her? She hoped not. She stepped on something. It hurt.

"Ouch. I need my shoes," she said again and stopped moving.

"Just a minute," Williams called to someone. "Get photos in that first bedroom and bring their shoes out here. The ones by the bed. Nothing else."

As he spoke, and her mind tried to sort out what had just happened, she realized she could no longer concentrate. She couldn't think. She was holding Alicea, who kept her head buried under the shirt. It was dark with a kaleidoscope of flashlights bouncing off ruined walls. She saw broken windows, splintered wood, a broken coffee pot, a lamp shade that looked like a fishing net. Her mind was beginning to shut down with trauma. Then she suddenly opened her eyes wide at the officer.

"I'm sorry. What? What did you say?" Patsy asked.

"Let's get you outside. We've got blankets. Are you sure you weren't hit?"

They were escorted out through the open doorway, but Patsy turned back to look for Officer Flores who was still inside. The door lay partly attached to the broken frame. Jess was arguing with Officer Williams about taking her cellphone.

"I need to call Chuck," Patsy heard her say.

"Why are you taking my phone?" She was getting angry.

"I mean it," Jess said in an unnaturally loud voice. "You can't take my phone."

"I'm sorry, Jess. This is a crime scene, and we need everything for evidence."

At least that is what Patsy thought he said. She wasn't sure because her ears were still ringing. But the next voice she heard was louder and unmistakable. Officer Jess yelled at the one called Williams.

"What?! You fucking moron! You think I did this? Or Chuck? You have got to be kidding me!"

Williams shook his head. "I'm not. If we can link the Norteños to this, we might finally have some serious pull with the district attorney against them. But if things aren't done by the book, their lawyers will scream evidence tampering."

Patsy thought Jess was about to grab her phone anyway. The officer outside was asking her to move away from the house, but she stood rooted to the spot just outside the door that was no longer there.

"Flores, that means we bag and tag everything."

"But we aren't dead! It's not a homicide," she argued.

"Actually, it is. And I need your weapon, too." He held out his hand. "I should have taken it the moment we opened that closet door."

"What? What are you talking about?" Jess was confused. "We're all here. Who is dead?"

Patsy heard the catch in her voice. "No! Not Chuck?"

Then the outside officer insisted that Patsy bring Alicea and escorted her to the backseat of one of the cruisers, to wait for the ambulance. More sirens were heading toward them.

Officer Jessica Flores

"My weapon? A homicide? What are you not telling me? Am I a suspect of something?"

Williams stared hard at his fellow officer. "There's a body outside. Reynolds is on his way. He's not hurt. He won't be allowed in either. I'm not going to let you talk to him. I told him you were all on your way to Salinas Valley Memorial, but you're not. We're sending you to Monterey Community. Unless you think you don't need medical…"

She cut him off. "I don't need any medical attention. And neither do they. Other than trauma, they aren't hurt.

"There might be injuries you can't see. I'm not Forensics, but there's no way some of those bullets didn't penetrate that closet."

"Then have the EMTs do a quick assessment and release us. Those guys meant business tonight. You don't have a clue who they are, but we can guess. Chuck's made a lot of enemies, and that lady and her kid were a target. They are a target. You know Sergio Sanchez is probably behind this. Why don't you start there?" She was close to being insubordinate, but Williams wasn't her boss. She couldn't stop herself. Chuck had not told her what was going on, but she could guess. She'd read old case files, too.

"They're out there. Free. Armed and absolutely dangerous. They'll be checking hospitals."

Jess wanted to talk with Chuck. He'd know what to do. She paused to take a breath, and it was Williams' turn to cut her off.

"You don't know. Do you?"

She stared at Williams. "I don't know what?"

Her mind slowed to register what she'd heard him say a moment earlier. "And what do you mean, there's a body outside?" Her voice rising again, her mind not accepting. "I didn't shoot anybody, and that lady and that kid never left that bedroom until I hauled them into the closet. We are the only ones here. The only one who was ever outside was…" Her voice trailed off. *Think, Jess. Think. And shut up.*

Now her mind sped into dangerous territory. Chuck said he needed to take care of some business. She heard him leave. But no one had come or gone until the two cars pulled up. She was sure. Or was she?

More vehicles were pulling up to the house. Sirens were turning off.

"This is jacked up," she said. "The whole damn county is probably awake by now."

"I need you to go outside. Now." Officer Williams took her by the arm this time. His grip was firm. His fingers pressed into her solid bicep as he escorted her out of the house.

Chuck

He parked the cruiser at a haphazard angle along with the other law enforcement vehicles on the scene. He was careful not to block an exit and turned off the motor. Chuck was born in this house. It was built by his grandfather and became a wedding gift to his parents. On their fortieth wedding anniversary, they built a larger home at the back of the ranch and gave this one to Chuck and Maria.

"She's a good woman," they'd told him.

Yes. She is.

The dynamic of families living together on a family ranch in homes built to last for generations is no longer the norm, but it worked for the Reynoldses. His parents had passed long before the Coronavirus Pandemic of 2020. His older sister and her family now lived in the newer home, but Chuck and Maria had always loved this old house built by his grandpa. He was thankful his sister was on vacation. They had a locked gate about another half mile up the road. Chuck's own gate stood wide open when he pulled in. He'd personally closed and locked it behind him when he'd left earlier. As his headlights grazed over the gate, he could see that someone had cut the lock.

All was quiet. The house was dark. He could see flashlights from the officers inside. No more sirens blared but red and blue lights still flickered. He counted five cars on site. He figured he was ahead of the buses. Forensics probably not here yet either. If they came at all tonight. Thank God no one was hurt. He needed to find Jess, Patsy, and the kid. It was his job to keep them safe. *God*, he thought, *how did this happen?*

He'd been so sure they'd be safe here. Sergio surely wasn't dumb enough to shoot up a cop's house? Was he? Why? Chuck still had more questions than answers. He wondered if they'd been followed. Tracked? *Was it her cellphone? I told her to leave it.* The school enrollment haunted him, too. Was that it? His mind went over every possibility and scenario. But he kept coming back to the main question. Who knew they were here? Joe? No. Maybe they weren't the target at all. Maybe whoever had done this had come gunning for him. A coincidence that Patsy was here? He didn't believe in coincidences. What if Maria had been home?

He chastised himself for letting anger and emotion cause his mind to bounce from one impossible scenario to another without any kind of evidence. He knew better. *Take a breath and handle this like any other case*, he told himself.

He searched again for the obvious question. Who knew they were at Chuck's house? He rejected the idea that Joe had anything to do with it as soon as it entered his head. His boss? Jess? He realized a little late that he had let this information slip to too many people. "You idiot," he chided himself.

Chuck wanted to check on the women, but knew they'd keep them away from him for a while yet. He'd assess the damage to the house and figure out his next move. Maybe he couldn't help Patsy after all. But he was determined to try. It was always the kids that pulled his heartstrings.

"Shit." He got out and started to walk to the door.

"Officer Reynolds." Williams nodded in acknowledgement as he spoke. "I can't let you in. We need Forensics in here first."

"What is the problem? Where are the women?" Chuck felt agitation rising in his throat against this officer. He knew Williams was just doing his job, but he seemed to be being an ass about it.

"Mother and daughter are in one of the patrol cars until the ambulance gets here to have a look at them. Jess, too. Separate cars."

Chuck reconsidered as Williams gave him the information. *Okay, maybe he wasn't being a complete ass*, thought Chuck. *I'd probably be a dick, too, if I were in his shoes and this was his house*. But he wasn't in Williams' shoes. This was his house and he wanted answers.

"And Chuck, we're going to need you back at the station to answer a few questions."

Chuck set his jaw. "I take it back. You are an ass." Then turned a walked away, leaving Williams to wonder what he meant.

He saw Jess first, but his eyes missed nothing. He wondered about several officers gathered near the back of the house. Something was going on over there. He started toward the car where Jess was waiting. He'd worked with her on and off for a few years. She was a good cop in Chuck's book. Whatever went down out here, he didn't think she had anything to do with it. He'd take his cue from her. If they were bringing Internal Affairs into this, he needed to know what she knew. He needed to know what had happened out here. He'd been on the other side for his entire career. The good side. He was a good cop. He didn't like bending rules. But like he told Joe earlier tonight, protect and serve, that's what we do. *What the heck*, he thought. *I'm still on the right side. The good side. I'm not going to be railroaded into thinking I did something wrong.* He turned back to the house and Williams. His stride long.

Being a cop was risky business these days. He thought back over his career. *We're no longer trusted. We are no longer respected members of the community. Protect and serve, put your ass on the line, and get it handed back to you for trying to do your job. Maybe it is time to retire*, he thought. *I'm close.*

Chuck called back to Officer Williams, "Hey, Williams, I'm not coming in, but come talk to me for a minute."

Williams stepped into the early morning air. The night was no longer so dark. Dawn was coming. "What do you want, Reynolds?"

"Hey, I'm not going anywhere until you tell me what's going on here. Last time I checked, I still outranked you."

"I have my orders," Williams told Chuck.

"Orders from who?"

"The sheriff himself called me once he knew this was your house." Williams put his hands on his hips. "Don't make me cuff you, Reynolds. I need your badge and weapon. Weapons, too."

Anger rose at the absurdity of the situation. Chuck raised his voice again. "This is bullshit! I was just at Headquarters. That's my house. You're standing on my property. I'm glad the women are safe. But you are seriously pissing me off." Chuck could actually feel his blood pressure rising as he spoke.

"Yes. That's convenient. Isn't it?"

Chuck stared at Williams, trying to comprehend and calm down. He knew that getting angry would not help.

"Okay, Williams. Here you go." He handed over his badge, started to clear his service weapon, but Williams stopped him. "As is," he said.

Chuck held it by two fingers and let Williams take it.

"All of them." Williams seemed to be enjoying this.

Chuck reached beneath his jacket. "Slowly," said Williams.

Chuck pulled out the Sig Sauer P938 and held it up for Williams.

"Sweet," said Williams. "Next?"

Chuck reached down and pulled up the left leg of his thirty-six-inch, long Wrangler jeans over the top of his Tony Lama cowboy boot and pulled out the Baretta .32 ACP Tomcat. Once again, he started to clear it, then stopped.

"Habit," he said and handed the loaded weapon to Williams.

"Is that all?"

Oh, yeah, Williams was enjoying this way too much, Chuck thought.

"What did I ever do to you, Williams? What is your problem? None of these have been fired since I went to the range last time. I've cleaned them all since then, too." Chuck wasn't used to being treated like a criminal. Protocol was one thing, but the smirk on Williams' face in the dim predawn light told Chuck that Williams was enjoying taking his fellow officer down a peg. *That's just not cool*, thought Chuck, knowing full well he'd be cleared of any charges, because the only thing he'd done wrong was to try and protect a woman and her kid when he had good intel that they were in danger and had no one else to help. He'd used his own car and was off the clock.

"This is crazy. You know that?" Chuck went on even though Williams hadn't answered.

Chuck watched as Williams bagged and sealed each weapon.

"Come on, Williams. What is really going on here? And what is going on over behind the house?"

Just then he caught the sound of more sirens. The ambulance. Maybe two.

Another car pulled up. It was Sheriff Mike Foster. Chuck had been focused on Williams, Jess, and the house. But his ever-roving eyes took in all of his surroundings. His house had been shot up. That was clear. Chuck assumed this was all about Patsy and the kid, but something more was going on here. There were too many cops huddled at the back of the house. He could see the flashing lights of photos being taken. Foster had parked his car and was headed across the lawn toward the other officers.

Being a bit sarcastic, but knowing he needed to tread carefully and follow the rules, he asked, "Officer Williams, may I please go speak with Sheriff Foster?"

"Sure. Though I'm not sure he wants to talk with you, Officer Reynolds."

Chuck turned his back on Williams and intercepted Foster.

"Reynolds." Sheriff Mike Foster was the top cop in Monterey County. "Are you okay?"

"I am, sir. But what's going on? Williams here won't talk to me or let me talk with Flores. You know I talked with you about bringing the Garcia girl and her daughter here for a few days. Flores came and stayed with them. I grabbed a few hours of sleep then went back into the office. Maria's at her mother's. Joe Medeiros went down to Paso with me, but we got back before midnight. He should be home now. I'm telling you all this now because I don't like secrets, and something is up that nobody will talk to me about. I know my house got shot up and Jess and the girls were not hurt, but there must be something else going on. I have no problem with Internal Affairs. I know I've done nothing wrong. Foster, can you tell me what's going on? Please." Chuck was begging for answers.

"Good to know, Chuck. Good to know. There'll be an investigation and I'm sure you can clear everything up with IA. You're one of my best. But I'm afraid there's a target on your back. And it just got bigger," Foster said.

"Will you please tell me what is going on. Williams took my badge and weapons. He says that was on your orders. Why? I'm assuming you'll want to clear out my gun safe, too? It's in the house. Or it was when I left at three this morning. It was locked when I left. And I'll tell you straight up, none of the three weapons I just turned over have been fired since I cleaned them the other night. I am not going to be set up for anything, either."

"Whoa. Slow down, Chuck." Sheriff Foster didn't like games, either. He'd always trusted Reynolds but knew that everyone was capable of murder under the right set of circumstances. He thought about it for a moment, stopped walking, and turned to Chuck.

"Okay. You deserve to know because it seems you really don't know. That, or you are a really good actor."

"Oh, for Pete's sake, Mike, you know me or not? What else happened here?"

"Sergio happened, Chuck. He's dead. Here. On your property. Any explanation?" Foster paused. Chuck stared at him.

"Because Officer Reynolds, the media is going to have a field day when this news gets out. And you know it will."

Chuck was dumbfounded. His mind raced over the last few hours. Days. Weeks. He thought of his recent visit with Sergio. He stared at his boss. Sheriff Mike Foster. This was going to be a media disaster. The Norteños would go ballistic. The public would be upset.

"Do you see why I needed to take your badge and guns? Standard procedure. But this is first blush, Chuck. We need to go by the book with Forensics on this."

The sky had turned a soft shade of pinkish gray. Chuck could not wrap his head around what he'd just heard. Sergio is dead? Here? Why? Who? How? Again, who did this and why? His mind raced with questions he didn't dare ask aloud.

Chuck stopped the sheriff with a hand on his arm. "I thought Sergio was responsible for the threat to Patsy, but if that's true, who killed him?"

"Exactly," said Foster. "And then they will ask if you took matters into your own hands and moved in and killed him before he could get to Patsy."

"What? I would never do that, and you know it."

"I don't know anything, Chuck. You have a reputation. The media could spin this in a way that really points a finger at you. I know you'll see it if you take a minute and open your eyes. And then what? You're going to have the entire NF after you. It won't be safe for you or anyone close to you. They might even try to get revenge with an all-out war against law enforcement."

"I can almost read the headlines now. 'Rogue cop brings woman and child to remote location to bait NF leader and kill him. Norteños retaliate with shootout. Fortunately, no other victims. The NF denies any responsibility but claim they'll get revenge against the sheriff's department and Officer Reynolds to avenge the death of Sergio Sanchez.'"

"Holy shit," Chuck said.

"Exactly," Foster answered.

"Boss, all I did was try to save that girl and her kid. I swear. We need to find out who did this."

This is not the time or place for this conversation, thought Foster. He didn't like it, but he might have to arrest one of his best officers. And if he did, he didn't want to let Chuck keep talking without an attorney or having been Mirandized. He wanted to believe Reynolds, but there was another piece of incriminating evidence against him. He took a deep breath and said it.

"Chuck, Jess says you left just before three this morning. You clocked into Headquarters at four twenty-five. Where were you for that missing hour and a half? Given drive times, you're missing a little over an hour. Please give me a solid alibi."

Chuck stared at Sheriff Foster. He registered two things at once. First, Foster was questioning him without having Mirandized him. He was asking for an alibi. Next, Chuck's shoulders relaxed. He had not realized how tight he'd been gripped by tension.

"You know, boss, I've wanted Sergio for a long time. I watched him go up the ranks. But I didn't kill him. I haven't got my report filed. But I went to extract the Garcia mom and her kid because she called asking for help and I figured he was going to find them, and nothing good would come of that. She had gotten a letter from the Norteños. I thought Sergio was behind it. But now? Now I don't know. I think something else is going on. Maybe a takeover in the organization? Maybe they thought they could kill all of us tonight and blame Sergio's death on me, too. I don't know. I haven't really had time to think through it all or see any evidence. But I'll tell you this, boss." He paused and grinned as he looked intently into the eyes of the sheriff.

Chuck's smile lit up his face. "I've never been so glad that I was hungry and stopped for breakfast before heading to check in. I've got my receipt, and I'm sure the cameras and the ladies on the late shift at Denny's on Blanco Road can corroborate that I walked in the door at three ten and left about an hour later."

SIXTEEN

Chuck

By Tuesday, pieces of the puzzle were beginning to fall into place.

Sheriff Foster pushed open the door to Homicide. "Chuck. Jessica. You've been cleared by Internal Affairs. By some miracle we've kept the media out of this mess. But I don't see how that can last. We need to find out who killed Sergio and who wants that girl dead." Adding, "Or who wants you dead, Chuck. But I've already decided that list is probably way too long."

"I can now tell you what you probably already know. Sergio died from a double tap to the head. An execution. All shots into his body at the scene were postmortem. Coroner puts the time of death between four and eight p.m. on Friday. Your weapons have been cleared and you can pick them up. We matched the murder weapon to two unsolved gang killings. Keep your heads down and find out what's going on in my town. My county. I don't like this at all."

Chuck stared back at Foster. "I know you're just doing your job, but you really didn't think Jess or I had anything to do with this, did you?"

"No. But someone had it in for Sergio, and you're on the same list. Listen, Chuck, you've built up a ton of vacation time. I don't want to lose you. You're one of the best on the force. But it would be worse to lose you permanently and let them brag about taking you out. You aren't far from retirement. I'm only saying this because I want you to think about your future. And Maria's. I want you to have a future. This hit was a wake-up call for all of us. We need to be on high alert. As I said before, there is a target on your back and it's bigger than ever. We want cases solved, but more than that, I don't want my officers to die in the line of duty. You think about it and do what's best for you. Okay?"

Chuck mulled over Foster's comments and read between the lines.

"Whoa. You think I should quit? I appreciate what you're saying, but why do I feel like I'm being punished?" he asked, then quickly added, "No. I take that back 'cause I've seriously been thinking the same thing. I might take you up on that time off suggestion. I've got Patsy and her daughter living in a rental house over in Modesto. It's temporary. I put her on a bus Saturday. The house belongs to a friend of a friend, who met her at the bus stop and helped her get settled. They're safe for now. I hope. I don't want to go around you or work on this on department time, but I owe it to that woman to help get her out of the country."

"Look, Reynolds. What you do on your off time is your business. But while you're on my clock, you solve cases, and you're too close to this one. I want nothing compromised. Medeiros is lead on this investigation. Keep your head down and think about that vacation time you're due."

"I will," Chuck promised. "I've got a court appearance Thursday to testify in the Johnson case, but other than that, I've got nothing on the books but a few cold cases."

Foster paused, looked thoughtful, then snapped his fingers. "One more thing, Chuck. A package came for you today. It's with the watch commander. Amazon box, but with a handwritten label and no return address. I only know about it because the mail room people said it looked suspicious. They had the dogs clear it. No drugs, bombs, or poison. Let me know if it's anything to do with any of your cases. Will you?"

"Of course." Chuck wondered briefly who sent a package to the station for him without a return address. That in itself was suspicious to him, too. Foster turned and walked out the door, leaving his detectives to figure out their next moves.

Jess and Chuck stared at each other. Joe Medeiros heard it all.

"What are we going to do now?" asked Joe.

"We?" Chuck looked at Medeiros with a puzzled frown.

"Yeah, we." Medeiros went on. "Until today, I couldn't talk to you about any of this. I got my ass handed to me for going with you to bring them back here. I know you're off the case, but I know you. Foster knows you, too. You won't rest until this is solved, whether you're on department time or your own. I'd rather you work with me than against me."

"You heard Foster. Do we jeopardize our careers? You're right, Joe, I'm not going to rest until we know what happened. I'm going to find out who did this and why my house was shot up, if I have to retire to do it. Maybe I should just take some time away. I've got a ton of vacation and personal time still on the books."

"Maybe that's the best idea you've had yet," Joe said.

Both men turned to look at Officer Flores.

"Jess?" Chuck asked. "What's your call on this?"

"My call?" she asked with eyes wide as she stared pointedly from one officer to the other.

Jess Flores could get worked up over an injustice, but she did her job efficiently, without much emotional baggage. She was single, and while no one talked about it, most of the guys on the force believed she was gay. She never went on dates or talked about men. She didn't hang out at any of the local cop taverns, and she never talked about her personal life. Which was fine by most of those she worked with. She was straightforward and a good cop.

"Listen, guys, that was by far the scariest night of my life on the force. I don't know or understand how none of us in that closet were hit. Nor have I begun to fathom how the first on the scene were able to get there before the shooters found us in the closet. They were right on us when they all pulled up and left. Why? How is any of that possible? How many miracles can happen in one night? If the shooters knew we were in that house, why didn't they finish us off? That's what's going through my mind. Look, I'm not a homicide detective. I'd like to go back to doing what I do and stay out of this whole thing."

She went on. "Chuck, I respect you. You too, Joe. But I'm not part of this investigation other than as a witness. And frankly, I agree with Foster that you are too close to this. With all due respect, Reynolds, I think you should take time off and keep your head down. Don't do anything stupid. I do think someone out there is out to get you. But as far as I'm concerned, I know nothing about anything you two are doing with regards to this investigation."

Jess left her chair and headed for the door. She turned her head back over her shoulder. "I'm out of here and staying clear of you both. Got it?"

Chuck stared at the back of the door that closed behind her. Smiling, he turned to Joe. "She's got a point." His mind was already back on the events of the last few days.

"I need to find out if Forensics is done at the house and do some research of my own. Then I need to try and get repairs done. If I don't, the weather and wild animals will destroy anything that might be salvageable. The more I think about it, the more I like your idea. But you have to promise to keep me in the loop on anything you discover. Deal?"

"Of course," Joe replied. "You do the same."

Chuck gave Joe a knowing look and a slight nod. "Agreed."

With Sheriff Foster's blessing, and an audible sigh of relief, Chuck was granted a month off.

"But you are not working this case!" Foster thundered as Chuck walked out of his office. Mike Foster stared at the open doorway and watched his best officer walk away, knowing full well that Reynolds wasn't about to let this case go.

"Be careful, my friend," he whispered to the empty room.

Chuck stopped to sign for the package. It was a cardboard box about the size of a large carry-on bag. With the events of the last few days crowding his thoughts, he'd forgotten that he'd ordered a new shoulder holster a few weeks ago. Holding the box, he remembered the order and wondered if this was it. *Feels too heavy*, he thought. *Oh well. I'll find out soon enough.* He popped the trunk and tossed the box inside. It landed with a dull thud. He took a long look back at the station door and then got behind the wheel and headed for Highway 68.

Now he'd have time to solve Sergio's murder and find out who it was that shot up his house, who was after Patsy, and finally get her and the kid out of the country. It would also give him time to get the repairs done to the house and see what he thought of actually retiring. He'd put in enough years. But could he stand not being there? Not solving cases? It was his life. He needed to talk with Maria about it. They'd decide as a team.

Chuck thought about their life together as he drove. She was a good woman and a good mate. They were friends, too. Now that she was retired, she did more around the ranch, but they'd always shared most of the household and ranch life duties.

No, he thought. *That's not true. She's always done more around the house than I ever did. Thank you, God, for giving me such a good woman. Not sure what I did to deserve her. But I do thank you for making her my wife.* Chuck didn't pray too much in the usual sense, but he often talked to God like a friend when he was alone and uninterrupted by work. Chuck had given Maria a brief report the morning after the shooting and told her to stay at her mother's. He'd fill her in later.

The fact that Chuck had asked his wife to stay with her mother and not at the house was a concern for the team at Internal Affairs. They thought it odd. Had he been expecting the danger and warned his wife to get away? The simple truth was that it wasn't the first time he'd sent Maria to stay with her mother. His sixth sense about danger followed him everywhere. He wasn't sure what they'd find when they reached the rendezvous point with Patsy, and he didn't want to take chances. It seemed a normal precaution to him.

Unable to stay at home until the investigation was complete at the scene, and not wanting to call attention to his mother-in-law's home where Maria was staying, Chuck booked a room at one of the nicer hotels in Monterey. He'd stay there until the house was patched up and it was safe to return. He and Maria needed a date night and time together. Four days apart and he already missed her more than ever. He never considered staying in Salinas. The danger of being seen was too great. The city too small. His role in this latest gang-related activity was too large. Monterey was only a thirty-minute drive and eighteen miles away, but it was a world apart from Salinas. More importantly, Officer Chuck Reynolds, with his distinctive cowboy attire, was not known there.

He knew Maria would never suggest he retire from the force, but he believed it would be her choice if she were to make one. They needed to talk about it. Time and good luck tend to run out for a lot of peace officers. *Peace. Wouldn't it be nice?* he thought.

SEVENTEEN

Blanca

"I did not realize our wings were so powerful!" Blanca shared the news with Sergio's Guardian, Jeff, who stepped in to help her after Sergio was killed.

"Yep. I remember the first time I took a bullet for Serg. Stings a bit, but I think that's just the surprise of it. Those guys thought he was invincible after that. Problem was, so did he. Sergio got too cocky. His heart was in the right place, but his ego was too strong. A bit like me, I think. Hardheaded and stubborn."

Jeff stared at Blanca for a moment. "Do you ever wonder what it might have been like if we had lived longer? I mean as humans? Like, if we had made it to old age like Roy, the farmer from Ohio? Or even Hannah."

Blanca pondered the question. "I don't. I was only twelve when I passed. But somehow, I've been granted the wisdom of a Guardian Angel after death. I love what I do. What we do. Whether I'd lived to be an old woman with children and grandchildren has no bearing on who or what I am now. I am energy. I am an Angel of God. I do what I'm assigned as best I can. These humans are willful and often thoughtless and stubborn. I'm rather glad I never had the chance to be like that. I do love being here with them, though."

"What do we do now?" Jeff asked. "What is the plan? The assignment?"

"We still have to protect Patsy and Alicea. Come with me to the safe house in Modesto where they are now. Officer Reynolds, the man who protected them before, is working on a plan to get them away from the Norteños. Sergio was their only protection. But the NF still sees them as a threat or loose ends. The house in Modesto is only temporary. It's not a permanent solution. They are going to need to change their names and start a new life far away. It won't be easy for Patsy, but it's our job to protect her and Alicea and help them start that new life. Are you ready?"

"As I'll ever be," said Jeff. Blanca drew her sword and planted the tip on the ground. Jeff placed his hand above hers on the grip. "Let's do this," he said.

The angels arrived at the small house near Modesto Community College where Patsy and her daughter were staying until Chuck could get them out of the country, or at least far away from California. Alicea sat at a small desk in her bedroom with an open coloring book and a box of crayons. Patsy was on a burner cellphone in the kitchen.

Patsy

"Listen to me, Officer Chuck. I am very thankful we weren't hurt at your house, but that honestly scared the shit out of me. We've been in this new place for three days now and I'm afraid to leave. Please tell me what is going on. Have you heard from Sergio? Is he the one who tried to kill us? Are we really safe here? Giving me a bus ticket, an address, and a key to this house doesn't exactly make me feel protected. But nobody is snooping around, either."

Blanca and Jeff listened as Patsy begged for answers. There were no officers on duty to protect her. She and Alicea were alone in this unfamiliar city.

"I know, kid. I'm sorry." Chuck truly did sound remorseful. "I want to be there in person to tell you this, but it's too dangerous for me to drive over there. I know you weren't followed, but they might try to tail me." He paused, giving her time to accept his explanation and get prepared to hear the worst.

"Sergio is dead. There is no easy way to say this. He was shot execution style and his body was left at my house the night you were there. I had nothing to do with it. It's possible we were followed from Paso. I didn't see another vehicle and I don't think we were followed, but I'm not ruling it out."

Reynolds continued on the other end of the phone. "Patsy, I'm going to find out who did this. We are not out of danger. Not you. Not me. Staying apart and using burner phones is our best bet. I'm going to get you out of there soon, but I need you to sit tight for another week or two. I have a friend of a friend there in Modesto with no discernable ties to me, the department, you, or the Norteños. He owns the house you're in. It's a furnished rental and was available. You will get food and groceries delivered. No names. I want you to please stay out of sight, and don't put Alicea in school. No walks around the neighborhood, dinners out, nothing. Okay?"

Patsy listened as Chuck kept talking, but her mind was hung up on the fact that Sergio was dead. She was dealing with this new information that Sergio was not her enemy. Or was he? Who else would want both of them dead? Who?

"I'm sorry. What?" she asked Chuck to repeat the part about groceries. "How long will we be here? What about Mrs. Meyer? My job? My things?"

"I'll take care of it. From what I see, you have two choices. You can go back to the ranch in Paso Robles and continue to work for the Meyers, which will probably put all of you in harm's way. Or you can change your name and get out of the country. I can help you do that."

Patsy thought about the money she'd inherited from her mother, Melanie. It wasn't much, but maybe enough to find a safe place to live.

Chuck

There was a timid knock on the door of his hotel room. He'd given Maria the room number to save her from a stop at the front desk. That didn't stop him from checking the peephole in the door and hoping someone on the other side was not about to put a bullet through his left eye. He turned the deadbolt, opened the door, and nearly melted on the spot.

"Wow! How did I get such a stunning wife?" He closed the door behind her and took her in his arms. The hint of perfume teased his nose and reminded him of her tantalizing femininity. She was his treasure. Working with the public, he'd seen countless women let themselves get soft around the middle or pack on pounds with a heavy rear or flabby arms and thighs. Not Maria. At fifty-seven, she was still petite, with strong muscles. She was probably a size or two larger than when they first married thirty-plus years ago, but she wore it well.

Maria giggled and balanced on her toes to reach her toned arms around his neck and pull him in for a kiss that was long and deep.

"I am so glad to hold you after the emotional drama of these last few days," she said. "But maybe I'm even more excited that you are taking me to the Sardine Factory for dinner," she teased. "Is this a celebration that we are both still alive or is there some other special reason we are splurging tonight?"

"Yes, and yes," he said with a sly grin as he shrugged into his leather jacket and pulled it over his shoulder holster.

"Are you going to replace that holster? It's looking a little warn."

"That reminds me," he said. "I think the new one came today. It's in the trunk. I'll take it out when we get back. Are you ready?"

"If we stay here any longer, I won't want to go at all," she said as her hand slid gently over his crotch.

"Oh, don't do that!" he laughed. "They won't hold our reservations, and I want to be able to walk in there without embarrassing myself." He winked and added, "My sly little wench. Let's go eat. We'll come back here for dessert."

At dinner, Chuck gave Maria details as he knew them about what had happened on Friday night. He rarely opened up to her about cases he worked. For one, they were often gruesome. Second, the less she knew about certain things the better for both of them. It was dangerous out there. He trusted her implicitly, but he was the law enforcement officer in the family. It was not her job to worry about these things.

But this time was different. Her home had been violated because of him. Was he the target? He didn't believe in coincidences and his gut told him that Patsy and Sergio were keys to this conundrum. He'd solve this riddle. He always did.

Chuck eyed her grilled wild abalone medallions. A house specialty, these tasty treats were not available everywhere like they used to be. His own plate of Parmesan-crusted calamari steak, scallops, and prawns was quickly disappearing. The half-bottle of Ramey Chardonnay from the Russian River Valley was just enough for the two of them. Neither was much of a drinker.

Prices at this exclusive restaurant were on the high side, but service was spectacular, and the food did not disappoint. They ate a lot of beef at home, since they butchered a grain-fed steer annually, and the freezer was always stocked with beef, lamb, and pork. Seafood in Monterey was usually the norm for date night. They had only been to the Sardine Factory once before. The night he proposed.

"So, my darling husband, talk to me. I know there is more going on in that beautiful mind of yours." She took another sip of wine. "Or do you want to wait until we get back to the room?"

Chuck took a deep breath and glanced around the room, noting their proximity to other diners and the chance of someone being able to eavesdrop on their conversation.

"I'm taking a month off to fix the house and get Patsy and the kid out of the country," he said.

Maria eyed him suspiciously. "And?" she asked, knowing there was more. He'd never taken a month off in the thirty-two years they'd been married.

"And," he said slowly, drawing out the word into several syllables. "And I think it's time to talk about me retiring. Maybe we move away. Someplace safe. Remote. Take your mom, too."

She stared at him, a bite of abalone halfway to her mouth. Frozen in mid-air.

"Don't tease me," she whispered without a trace of humor in her voice.

"I'm not."

"You've always said you didn't want to retire until they forced you out. Did something happen?"

"Yes. Our home got shot up."

"Besides that."

"Foster thinks it's time. The bad guys are coming for me. How long do I want to take these chances?"

"Can we leave tonight? After making love, that is." Her grin was back in place.

"Not tonight. Look, honey, I'm not sure about this at all, but I don't want you to be in danger and I'm smart enough to know when I might be on the losing end of a gun fight."

"What do you need me to do?"

"Stay with your mom. Take care of her. And you. If you feel like it, start scanning the internet and look for property that might be right for us. We've got money put away. I don't want to sell the family ranch, but we could lease it out. We need a home. One for your mom. A barn. Acreage. A long driveway with privacy. You figure out the rest of what you'd like and where you'd like to be and let's go home hunting. Pick several." He laughed. "We can narrow it down by visiting them." Pausing, his expression turned serious again. "Whatever happens, we are in this together and I don't want to lose you. My job is not worth losing you. So, whatever we do, let's do it together."

Maria's heart was doing cartwheels in her chest. "Is this really happening? Are you serious or telling me what you think I want to hear?"

Chuck looked lovingly into the eyes of his wife and took her hand across the table. "I honestly don't know where this is going, but something has changed in my heart since the other night. I won't call it fear. I'll call it reality. There comes a time when a man has to hang up his spurs. It feels to me like that time is coming for me. But I will also tell you honestly that I'm not sure. I do know that I want to solve this case and protect that woman and her kid, before I walk away."

"Understood, my love." She could not stop smiling. "Are you finished eating? I will honestly tell you that I'm very sure I'm ready to go back to the room."

"Yeah?"

"Yeah."

"Okay then. Let's go."

EIGHTEEN

Chuck

Several anomalies jumped out at Chuck as he poured over notes about the case. He needed to take them one by one and come away with answers. It was already after ten in the morning. Maria had gone back to Mother's after breakfast. She was excited to start her internet search for a potential new home.

"Maybe I'll get to grow old with you after all," she had said and kissed him goodbye that morning. "Stay safe, my love. We'll figure this out."

Alone again in the hotel room with a lukewarm cup of coffee, Chuck scratched his head and started a new list on the yellow legal pad in front of him.

How did the gang know where Patsy was living?

How did they know where he lived?

Did they know Patsy was at his house?

Who was the real target of the shootout?

What did Sergio have to do with this?

Why was Sergio killed?

How did Jess, Patsy, and the kid survive in the closet without getting hit?

These were the predominant questions on his mind, but not necessarily the predominant order.

He leaned back in the desk chair and studied the ceiling. How did they survive? How was it possible none of those bullets penetrated the closet? Not even one?

He jerked forward and grabbed his cellphone, punching in the number he knew all too well. "Joe. Is Forensics done at the ranch? Am I allowed to return?"

Joe Medeiros let him know that Forensics had indeed finished at the scene. They'd worked in record time. Their report was not yet available, but he did have copies of the crime scene photos.

"Thanks, partner. Foster probably told you, but I'm officially on vacation. I'll be at home for the rest of today. Doing a little target practice. Will you send the photos to my phone as soon as you can? Especially anything taken in the closet where Jess hid the girls. I'm staying in Monterey for now. Call me if there is anything I need to know. I will do the same for you. Thanks again, Joe. I'll talk to you later."

He hit the red disconnect button; pocketed the phone; donned his shoulder holster, boot gun, jacket and hat. Thirty-five minutes later, he pulled up to the bullet-riddled house that used to be his home.

Sheets of plywood had been nailed over broken windows and gaping doors. The team had secured his property when they finished going over the mess. "Thanks, guys. I appreciate this," he said aloud to no one.

He loved the peace and quiet of this place. Two horses trotted up to the fence by the barn and nickered softly.

"Okay, boys. I'm coming. I guess the grass is getting a little thin out there."

After throwing some hay out for the horses and checking on the other livestock, he made his way back to the house, noting that all the brass from the other night had been carefully cleaned up. He didn't go over to the spot where they had found Sergio's body, but he did glance that way. He already knew the cause of death and that it had not happen here. He pried the plywood off the back door and pulled out his flashlight.

The gun safe was standing where it had always stood. It was too heavy to steal and strong enough to withstand the shootout. He could see a few nicks where bullets had grazed the exterior, but none penetrated.

As a collector, Chuck kept a good arsenal of firearms, as well as several antique collectables, in his safe at home. He was surprised Forensics had already tested and returned them. Things don't normally move that fast. He'd given the crime scene investigators the combination to the safe and was amazed that it was done so quickly. He knew it was an homage to him that they finished as soon as possible.

He knew none had been fired since he last cleaned them, and the forensic experts knew it, too. There was not much point to waste the department's time and resources testing weapons they knew weren't connected to the case. They could attest that none of these weapons had been fired that night and that all were legitimately registered and owned by Chuck.

He unlocked the safe and took out four automatic assault rifles: a colt AR-15 A2, an M4 carbine, an UZI submachine gun, and a Soviet AK 47. *This should do it*, he thought.

He set the weapons aside and walked back to the bedroom. Using the flashlight, he examined the inside walls of his closet. The contents had been removed and his clothes were still strewn across the bed. "At least you boarded up the house," he said, as if they were standing near him.

He expected to see smooth walls. None of the women were hit, so he had assumed none of the bullets had penetrated the closet. But that was not the case. He had intended to do some shooting of his own to see why the bullets were stopped. Maybe he should check with forensics and see what they thought. Still standing in the closet, he opened his text messages, to see if Joe had sent any photographs. He had.

Chuck felt the small hairs at the back of his neck begin to rise.

How is this possible? he thought. *This can't be right.*

He turned the flashlight to examine the walls again. The holes were there. At least a dozen marked three of the four walls. The fourth wall, with the bathroom on the other side, had no marks on it. Three walls were severely pockmarked. "How did you not get hit?"

Chuck had to get out of the closet. He needed air. He grabbed his weapons on the way out and set everything down on the wooden barbecue table in the back yard. He sat on the bench and touched the screen of his phone once again.

"What the hell? How?" he asked himself.

The photographs taken by the forensic team showed the closet both before and after the clothes were removed. Bullets were scattered around the edges of the closet, as if they'd been swept aside to clear the center of the floor.

"Come on. This doesn't make sense. And now I'm talking out loud to myself. Maybe they moved them around when they were in the closet? But how is it not one of them had even a scratch?"

"Well, old house, you're in need of a facelift anyway. I don't think a few more bullets can cause much more damage." He picked up the AK and went to the other side of the house. Standing in front of where he knew the closet to be, he fired a short burst. Working methodically, he moved around the house, firing into the closet with each weapon.

Before going inside, he sat down again and reread the forensics report. They had determined that at least six different firearms were used to shoot up the house. The bullets retrieved from four of the weapons were already in the system from unsolved cases. Two homicides, three robberies, and six drive-by assaults. The weapons themselves had not been found, but all were believed to be tied to the Norteños and Sergio. None had come from Chuck's gun safe.

Chuck cleared all four weapons, policed his brass, cleaned his guns, and returned them to the safe. Since every hole in the closet was now marked by forensics, the fresh holes were obvious. He'd made his own specific shot patterns. After years of research, including a stint in the Army near the end of the Vietnam War, he knew instinctively which holes were made by each of his weapons. He'd used both regular and armor-piercing bullets.

Two and a half hours later, he finished his experiment. Chuck had fired a total of twelve rounds per weapon, per side of his house. In all, forty-eight bullets on each side. He put 192 new holes in the walls at various heights. He wanted to simulate the random shots fired by the perpetrators. He took a deep breath and went back inside.

The wall behind the bathroom that had been unharmed before, now bore forty-eight holes from where Chuck had fired directly into the opposite wall and the bullets crossed the closet and lodged into the unmarked wall. The other two walls each had ninety-six new holes. Because each of those two walls had forty-eight bullets go in on one side and out the other. His bullets crisscrossed the closet, where the bullets from the other night penetrated, but were stopped.

"How?" He pulled up the photo again. The bullets had obviously hit something solid and stopped. His walls were not bulletproof. Nor were his clothes that had been hanging on the closet rod. The walls were fairly thin and had not stopped any of his bullets. They'd kept going, except those that were stopped by the tile and plumbing in the bathroom. What stopped the bullets from hitting the three of them in that closet on Friday night? Why weren't they hurt?

He boarded up the house again and walked over to the spot where they'd found Sergio. He stood and looked at the ground where they had found his body.

"Talk to me, Serg. What happened? What did you do to piss them off? A takeover? Who? That punk Jorge? He'd be my first guess. Sergio, you were a pain in my ass for years, but I didn't wish you dead. In fact, I'll swear there was a good side to counter your tough, badass self."

Chuck turned back toward his car. "Godspeed, kid."

NINETEEN

Sergio – Friday afternoon, when Alicea was at school

He taped up the box and stashed it behind the sofa at his grandmother's house on Alma Avenue. She had wanted him to stay for dinner, but he had things to do. Important things. She'd made tamales all day and would sell some to the neighbors to augment the small Social Security check she got each month. He'd take a few with him to eat later.

"I gotta go, Abbi." The shortened name he'd always used for his grandmother. His *abuela*. His Abbi. "I left something behind the couch. Just leave it there and I'll pick it up tomorrow. Is that okay?"

"Of course, *míjo*. Don't be getting in trouble. I worry."

He gave her a kiss on the cheek and told her not to worry.

"I'm doing great. In another year I'll buy you a new *casa*. You'll see."

"I don't want a new casa. I want a grandchild. Whatever happened to that beautiful Patsy you used to bring around? I never see you with any new girls. You work too hard."

Sergio stared at his aging grandmother and wondered why, after all these years, she mentioned Patsy. How did she even remember her name?

"Abbi, Patsy is long gone. Someone said she moved to Las Vegas. I don't know. I have more important things to do than worry about *niñas* and *bambinos*. I'll see you tomorrow. I love you! *Besos!*" And he was out the door.

His abuela had become a United States citizen back in late 1962. She'd been very proud of that, but he didn't see the big deal. His parents were both born in Salinas, and it was the only home he knew.

"Sergio, mí niño, you take life in this country for granted because you have never known true oppression or real poverty," she once told him.

What did she know? he thought.

He was supposed to meet up with Jorge soon. His palms were sweating as he drove.

"Get it together," he told himself. "No one is going to find out. You were careful. You covered your tracks."

But his mind jumped and his heart beat fast as he thought of what might happen if anyone found out what he'd done. Jorge was a punk. He'd been acting all tough lately and Sergio had had to remind him of his place a couple times. Diego, too.

"Damn. Maybe the Cowboy Cop was right. Something is up."

They were waiting for him when he arrived at Diego's garage a little after five. He took a quick visual count and quickly realized these were not the most trusted members of his team. In fact, he'd had minor conflicts with several of these guys. Toughs. Hotheads. He thought some were using the product they were supposed to distribute. Jorge wanted to meet because he had some ideas to go over. He thought they needed to boost their presence against some new guys in town who were claiming to be Bloods, Sureños, and they'd been disrespecting the NF on their home turf.

Sergio hadn't heard a word about any Sureños being in Salinas, other than from Jorge. It didn't make sense. Why would the Southern gang want to infiltrate, make trouble, and bring trouble on themselves by coming to Salinas and agitating the Norteños? He looked around the room again. His eyes landed on Jorge. He sat in Sergio's usual seat, a smug grin on his face as he continued a muted conversation with two of the newer members.

"Wassup, Serg?" he called across the garage that smelled of oil, gas, grease, and body odor.

"You tell me. You called this meeting."

He heard chains being pulled to close the big metal doors behind him. He walked across the oil-stained concrete toward Jorge and, too late, he noticed the large sheet of heavy plastic on the floor. He was already on it when he sensed rather than heard the man behind him. He knew at once that the real threat was in front of him. His friend. He stopped and stared straight at Jorge.

"What's going on?" he asked, and felt the gun pressed to the back of his head. "What the fuck? Jorge?"

"Don't move, *mi amigo*. I have some questions for you. And you are going to answer them."

Sergio didn't move or say a word.

"Did you hear me, *pendejo*?" Jorge was louder. There was an edge in his voice.

"I heard you," Sergio said softly.

"Where is that *jaina* of yours? The one who was going to rat us all out a few years ago?"

"How the hell should I know? For all I know you snuffed her already."

"I'd have told you if I did. Weren't you supposed to do that? Didn't you have orders to do that? And didn't you tell them you did? She was gone. End of story, you said. They believed you, even though her body never turned up, but neither did she. You been all high and mighty ever since." He paused and pulled an invisible piece of lint off of his shirt. "But I've been watching you. You been up to something. Haven't you?"

Sergio's mind was grasping for anything to help. *Where is that little voice when I need it?* he thought.

"I'm right here," said his Guardian Angel, Jeff. "But we're in a tight spot and the best you can do is keep quiet, my friend."

Sergio had a sense to keep quiet, though he never actually heard Jeff speak to him.

"You never thought our bosses would actually talk to me about that. Did you? Big surprise, old pal? And how do you think they found out you didn't kill her? No answer? Nada? Well, I'll tell you, because you seem to be the only one who doesn't know. Because La Familia is organized. We make sure loose ends are always tied up. So, what do you think we discovered?"

Sergio stood very still. He could feel the barrel of the pistol at the back of his skull. And sweat beading on his forehead and underarms. He didn't say a word.

"Still not talking? Well, mí amigo, it seems a kid was registered at a little school down by Paso Robles and guess what her name is? Alicea Garcia. Mother, Patricia Garcia. Father, Unknown. Seriously? She registered the kid in school? As I said, it's a small school. A small area. We found her. At least we think we did. But you know what? She disappeared again. Poof! Just like that. You know, like someone warned her. You?" He waited for an answer that didn't come.

"Yeah, I think it was you. I'm thinking you've known where she was all this time. So now what do we do about that?" He paused for only a moment, not expecting an answer. "Which brings me to the next part of our little chat." Jorge stared at Sergio. "Get on your knees, pendejo!"

Sergio still didn't move. "I said, get on your knees." His voice was seething. Three men grabbed Sergio and forced him to his knees. Then they grabbed his arms and zip-tied his wrists together behind him. Sergio started to pray. But not out loud. Without making a sound he said, "Oh Father in Heaven, if you are real, help me please. I've made some really bad choices in life. Please forgive me of my sins and let me forgive these men, as you forgive me. Our Father, who art in Heaven, hallowed by thy name. Thy kingdom come, thy will be done, on earth as it is in Heaven. Give us this day our daily bread and forgive us our trespasses as we forgive those who trespass against us. Lead us not into temptation, but deliver us from evil. Amen."

Sergio knew his time on earth might be coming to a quick end. *Live by the sword, die by the sword*, he thought. *Blood in. Blood out.* And suddenly he clearly heard the voice.

"I'm with you, Sergio. Hang on, *mí hermano*, from another *madre*."

Sergio looked up at Jorge. "What did you say?" he asked.

"What do you mean, what did you say?' I said get on your knees! And now you are. Good. Because now we go to part two. And you better give me an answer this time." The two men stared at each other. Sergio was no longer afraid.

"Where is the money?"

"What money?" Sergio answered.

"You know what money."

"I don't know what you're talking about."

"Don't make this harder on yourself than it needs to be." Jorge was losing his machismo and remembering back to their childhood friendship. They had been good friends. They had even been altar boys together when they were kids. Life had been good, before they both decided to swear allegiance to the Norteños. The change was slow at first. As they got older the tasks became more difficult. The day Jorge told Sergio that Patsy had to go, their relationship changed forever.

Jeff was drawing on everything he had to fight the demons trying to control Jorge. He was losing the battle.

But Sergio did know about the money. He knew all about the money. It was in a box behind his grandmother's sofa on Alma Avenue. They knew where she lived. He would never tell. He'd be signing her death certificate. It was bad enough that they were going to kill him. They had probably already killed Patsy and Alicea. He would take this to the grave.

Then he began to pray aloud. "Our Father who art in Heaven, hallowed be thy name."

"Stop!" Jorge screamed and covered his ears. "Do it, Diego! I can't stand this. Kill him."

Two shots rang out. It was over. They wrapped him in the plastic sheet and made plans to dispose of the body.

Jeff cried in despair as he watched the scene unfold.

"Why, God? Why couldn't I save him? I'm so sorry, Sergio. I'm so sorry, God. Why do I always fail? Please, God, help me do something right."

Jeff

The Guardian Angel called Jeff opened his eyes to see that he was no longer in the garage in East Salinas, but back in the beauty of Heaven. His mentor, Mamie; Hannah; Blanca; and Roy were all there.

"Welcome home, Jeff." Mamie held him tight. "I'm here. So are these wonderful angels from your training team. Oh, my son, you did not fail. You saved his life."

"But I saw it. They shot him." Jeff wanted to be strong, but he felt weak and powerless to fight the emotional loss he felt.

"They did," said Hannah. "But you saved his soul. He's heading this way."

"He'll have another mentor. You aren't ready for that role. But you did save him from Eternal Damnation, as you call it. He turned his heart back to the Lord, and he was forgiven. The Father sees the truth in all of us. He rejoices when the lost lamb is returned."

"I guess even angels can go from the darkest of emotions to walking on air with good news. Wow. And Jorge? What will happen to him?" Jeff asked.

"He remains tormented by demons, but all hope is not lost. You will go back to Salinas after a short rest. Perhaps you and Sergio might even work together someday. But that isn't our call."

TWENTY

Blanca

Blanca filled them in on Patsy and Alicea. Mamie went back to her current assignment. While God keeps track of every human, every creature, every living thing on earth, these angels receive specific instructions and tasks. They are not all-knowing, all-seeing beings, as Hannah often reminds the newbies.

"They are safe for now. About a hundred miles away from the gang that is after them. Have we figured out who killed Sergio and why?" she asked the angels.

"I know who killed him and why," said Jeff. "I was there. I held him and comforted him. I prayed with him. He prayed with me." Jeff paused to collect himself while the others waited. There was no hurry. No rush. "It was his former best friend, Jorge, who ordered the execution." He paused as he recalled the scene. "I thought he was going to have Sergio tortured to get the answers he wanted, but Sergio stayed quiet. When he started to pray out loud, Jorge thought back to their time as altar boys. The demons couldn't force the torture they wanted him to carry out."

"What did Sergio do to warrant their anger?" Roy asked.

"He stole money from them. He stole a lot of money," Jeff answered. "It's in a box behind his grandmother's sofa."

"Is she in danger?" Blanca was concerned.

Jeff answered. "I don't think so. I haven't been called in. She has her own Guardian, and he's been on the job taking care of her for years. He'll find a way to protect her. Or maybe she's being called home, too. I'm not privy to that information."

Jeff seemed older and wiser to his teammates. He'd changed more than a little over the last six earth years. Although none of them looked any different to each other and all held positions of importance protecting humans, Jeff was the one who fit the old earthly adage of being the Guardian Angel who worked overtime. It had taken a toll, but he was wiser, more patient, more understanding, and a better Guardian because of the challenges he'd faced working with Sergio and others who bordered on the thin line between good and evil.

"Okay then," said Hannah. "Let's get back to work. Jeff, rest up. Blanca, you have some heavy challenges coming up. We'll be there if you need us. Do not let Chax intimidate you, because you are stronger than you know. Roy, I haven't heard a word about anyone in Arcanum, Ohio, having any problems or going astray. Keep up the good work. They say pride is sinful. Some say it is the greatest of sins because pride leads to all other sin, but I am proud of you. Not boastful pride. You, who you are, your accomplishments, and all that is part of your work as an angel, are all directed by God. Pride is the wrong word. Instead of proud, I will say that you have morphed into a beautiful Angel of God. He created you. He loves you. And He knows the role you will play for generations to come. All praise and glory to God." Hannah looked lovingly at the others. "Now don't let my compliments go to your head or you will be guilty of pride, my friends. Just keep doing what you do, pleasing the Lord."

Blanca left her friends and returned to Earth. She sat perched on the bed next to Patsy and watched her rhythmic breathing. She'd had a rough week, but Blanca knew plans were being made to keep her safe. Plans were also being made to find and kill her. Which plan would succeed? Could Blanca save her human life again? She'd already been close to death three times. Would there be a fourth attempt? A fifth? Would they never give up? *At least I know her soul is in a good place*, Blanca thought.

Chuck
"Hey, Joe. Anything new?" Chuck asked his partner over the phone on Thursday afternoon. He'd been at the courthouse to testify earlier. That was a fairly simple case, and he was asked only to corroborate his written statement taken from an early interview with the defendant. He called Joe on his way back to Monterey.

"Some chatter about Sergio stealing money from La Familia and Jorge being tasked to find it. But so far we've got nothing solid," Joe told him.

"We've also had eyes on that garage over on Market. Diego's. He's kept a low profile. He's clean, but there's been a lot of activity in and out of his garage. More than usual. We don't have anyone undercover to get good intel on that, but we're watching."

"If we can pick someone up on a lesser charge, maybe we can get them to roll over on this. Give us the bigger dog for letting them off. It's all we've got for now. What about you? What's going on?"

Chuck didn't hold back, but he wasn't going to mention anything about Patsy or his plans for her and the kid. The less anyone knew, the better her chances. Maria was still at her mother's. His house still boarded up.

"Look, I'm not sure what you got from CSI, but I did a little test of my own at the house. I added a few more holes to the sides of the house. Guess what? There is no way those three in the closet weren't hit. But they weren't. Look at the photos. There are bullets in that closet all around the edges, but none of them had even a scratch. That's impossible. I proved it the other day. Shot the shit out of things. Bullets went right through all walls except the bathroom. They should have all been hit and all be dead. Something is just not right. This is impossible. Either they weren't in that closet when the shooting went on or they were covered by some bulletproof blanket. And Williams swears they found them in the closet, and I believe Jess, too."

"What do you make of it, Chuck? How do we put this in a report? Evidence doesn't lie. People do. But who? Why?" Joe was as perplexed as Chuck on this. "Set that aside for now. You got anything else? Any of your intuitive theories about how they knew where Patsy was living or whether she was even the target?

"Part of me wonders if this whole plan was to take you out or get you blamed for Sergio's death," Joe said.

"I'm asking myself the same questions. The answers are out there. We'll find them."

"I hope so."

"Listen, I'm good. I'm working with a confidential informant to get mother and daughter out of the country. The less you know the better." Chuck gave Joe the number to another burner phone he carried.

"Call me at that number if you need me. I'll be out of touch until I get things settled. I'm good. No need for back-up. I'll call if I get into any trouble. But know this, I'm not looking for it. My hunch is that Jorge knows what went down. He and Diego got something going on. If Sergio took money from the Norteños, my guess is they ordered the hit, not Jorge."

Joe pondered the phone conversation with Chuck. Was he holding back? Did he really shoot up his own house again to prove what they all suspected? With a shrug, Joe knew it was true. One truth about Chuck, he was honest to a fault. He might hold back information, and push the envelope, but he'd never lie. Well, unless, of course, it was absolutely necessary to save a life or stop a criminal. He'd also protect those he thought were innocent or deserved another chance, and he'd do everything in his power to bring a criminal to justice. If he could prove who killed Sergio, who was after Patsy, and who shot up his house, he would do it and he would follow every lead until the job was done. On or off the force.

TWENTY-ONE

Chuck

He had a busy few days after verifying ballistics and the impossible scenario that everyone swore was true. He spent most of Thursday in court, where his testimony did little but verify the report he'd filed on an old investigation that was just now coming to trial. A wasted day, he thought.

After talking with Joe and learning nothing new since the other day, he coordinated with the contractor working on the house repairs. Then he called Maria. It was four thirty on Friday afternoon. It had been one week since their lives were turned upside down with the phone call from Patsy.

Patsy and her kid were still in an unsanctioned safe house in Modesto without police surveillance. If he was wrong, and they found her, whatever happened would be on him. Without backup from his boss or the district attorney, he couldn't think of another way to help. He believed she was better off with whatever help he could give, versus being out there on her own. It was hard enough when they all believed the threat came from Sergio, but now they were fighting a hidden enemy. An enemy with a score to settle. Patsy and the kid would be collateral damage. He questioned everything. Was she lying to him? Was she the bait for him to take and get himself in a vulnerable position? Did she plan this whole little scenario? He didn't believe it, but he did consider it.

A confidential informant he'd worked with several years back owed him a favor or two. He'd planned for this eventuality and had grabbed passport photos of mother and daughter before putting them on a bus to Modesto the day after the shooting. He'd also traded his black hat and boots for a "California Rodeo Salinas" logo ball cap and the all-black athletic shoes he wore at the gym, on a stakeout, or undercover. No sense throwing out his personal calling card to anyone who might recognize him.

After getting them on the bus, he paid a visit to his CI and left him with the photographs, personal details, and new names. It really was not as difficult as most people thought to create a new identity. It just needs to be done right. Chuck's guy was one of the best. Or he had someone who was one of the best make them for him. Chuck didn't ask too many questions.

"I need them early next Monday morning. Can you make them that fast?" Chuck had asked.

"A week? Sure. No problem. But you'll have to pick them up in Modesto. Otherwise, they'll be here on Tuesday. Either way. Let me know."

"Modesto? I can do that. Just get me an address."

His informant wrote out a name and address on a torn piece of paper.

"I'll tell him to expect you. Don't wear a uniform."

Chuck took the paper, memorized the address, and handed it back.

"I'll be there about seven in the morning."

Chuck didn't have a plan at the time but was working things out as he went. He didn't like coincidence. Modesto? He had a week to figure this all out.

The more difficult task was managing his own identification, if he were to accompany them on this journey. He might have to sit this out and find another escort. Someone not tied to anyone with any sort of remote connection to him, the case, the police, or the gangs. That might take some doing. But he'd get started with the new IDs and get things in place as best he could. And as fast as he could.

Chuck had also hired a contractor to start the repair work on the house and talked to his sister about watching the place. She and her family had been on vacation when everything went down. They returned Thursday night, and he got a phone call and an earful from his only sibling.

"Uh, Chuck? What the hell happened to your house? Do we need to be on watch?" she asked, and added, "You know we're always locked and loaded up here, but I'd like to know if anyone might be heading back to finish the job. Are you okay?" she asked, but didn't wait for an answer.

"No one called to tell me you were dead or in the hospital. Now I'm talking to you, so I'm guessing you're safe. You weren't home when it happened?"

He laughed into the phone. "I'm fine, sis. Again, it's a long story, and I don't have time right now. Keep the electric eye across your gate and keep the gate locked. Your dogs will let you know if anyone's coming past our house. I don't think you need to worry. Got a guy coming to make repairs. It'll probably take him less than a month to finish. Can you keep an eye on things? Maria's staying at her mother's house. I'm in Monterey. Again, long story. We're good. We're safe. You stay safe, too. Love you, sis."

"Love you too, bro. You ever going to retire?"

"Funny you should ask."

"What!?"

"Not yet. Just thinking about it. Listen. I need to go," Chuck confided to his sister.

"Next time, keep me in the loop, baby brother. Don't you ever make me call you like this again."

It wasn't the first time his family had come close to danger because of his job. He wondered if it would be the last.

One last favor to call in. At least he hoped it would be the last. The problem was that he wasn't sure who to call. He needed to talk this part over with Maria.

She answered on the third ring.

"What do you say to dinner tonight?" he asked when Maria answered his call.

"Sardine Factory, again?" she used her sexiest voice.

"Uh. Probably not. Maybe somewhere a little less expensive?" he pleaded.

She laughed. "You know I'm teasing you. Too many expensive dinners out and the guys at the department will think you're on the take."

"Oh God, Maria. Don't even joke about that. It's been the downfall of too many good cops who suffered for too many years with too little pay. But we can still have a nice dinner. Maybe on the wharf or one of those places on Cannery Row?"

"Sweetheart, you choose. I don't care if we grab fast food. I just miss you, and yes, I want to have dinner with you tonight. All quiet here. Mom is good. What time?"

"Whenever you can get there. I'll be there in a few minutes. We aren't doing fast food. It's four thirty. I'm gonna jump in the shower now. I'll see you in a bit. Love you."

"Love you more," she said and hung up.

He was pressed and dressed when she arrived an hour later.

"Damn, you are looking good, my sexy Cowboy Cop."

Chuck stared into the eyes of his wife, then swept her off her feet and twirled her around the room with strong arms around her waist. "Woo hoo! I think I like going on dates with you, big guy!"

"I guess we need to find the good in all this. Right?" he said.

"Absolutely! I've got news for you, too. But it can wait until we get to dinner. I'm hungry!"

"So, let's go already! Are you wearing walking shoes, or do you want to drive? It's only a few blocks," he asked.

They walked to the restaurant and were seated immediately. The view of Monterey Bay was spectacular from their table. "This never gets old," she said.

The waiter took their order and delivered drinks. Relaxed and feeling the pressure of the last week begin to melt, she asked, "Do you want to go first?"

"Probably. I need your brain, your charismatic personality, your excellent memory, and your intuitive instincts to make a very important decision." He said it with a glimmer in his eye and a smile on his lips, but she sensed this was also quite serious and important.

"What if I just said, 'Yes, do it'?" She paused and looked at him over the rim of her water glass. "That is, if you are going to ask about retirement." She smiled, but his eyes did not.

"Uh oh. Not it? Okay. I'll be serious. I'm your girl. Shoot."

He reached across the table and took her hand. "I've got Patsy in a safe house in Modesto until Monday. I've got new passports for both of them. I've got a plan and a contact to get them from Puerto Rico to London and then to their final destination. I've even got a job for her there. I don't need to tell you where that is. But it's amazing when you start calling in favors and realize the connections people have. What I don't have, though, is an escort to get them to Puerto Rico from Modesto. I don't trust sending them alone. I'd go, but they'll be watching for me. I want someone who has no ties to her, me, or the department. That's where they'll be watching. And it seems they have someone on the outside who monitors public communications, too. I don't know how they do it, but the Familia seems to be all over this case." Chuck was still holding Maria's hand. His right thumb slowly caressing the back of her hand as he spoke.

The waiter came by to tell them their food would be out soon. When he was out of ear shot, Chuck went on.

"I've also got a good idea about who was behind Sergio's execution."

"La Familia?" she whispered.

"I think so. And a good friend of his from the old neighborhood. They're rotting in prisons and pitting these young men against each other like it's some sort of cock fight. It makes me sick," Chuck said.

"How can I help?" she asked.

TWENTY-TWO

Patsy

She woke with a start early on her tenth day of living in Modesto. The burner phone was jarringly loud as it rang on the table next to the bed. Alicea stirred in the next room. Her small arms pushed up and out from the covers as she stretched and tried to stifle a yawn. Patsy groped for the phone and accidentally knocked it to the floor. Still ringing, she threw off the covers, rescued the phone, and answered with a breathless, "Hello."

"Are you okay?" It was the Cowboy Cop.

"Yeah. You woke me up. What time is it?"

"Six in the morning. Pack your stuff. I'll be there at seven fifteen."

"Do I need to be afraid?" she asked.

Chuck held the phone away from his ear and looked at it for a half second. Oh, how he wanted to say, "Hell, yes! But fear and worry won't help."

Instead, he answered in a calm and reassuring voice.

"Everything is fine. No cause for alarm, but I need to move you again. Today."

Blanca listened and worked to soothe Patsy's fear. The woman believed in God and prayed often, but she didn't know she had a legion of angels working to save her life as well as her soul.

Alicea was up now, too. "Mama, are you okay? Who called?"

This little one needs her Mama, Blanca thought. *I'll be the one working overtime to keep them alive. Lord, give me strength*, she prayed.

I'm with you always.

Chuck

He was halfway to Modesto. Heading northeast from Monterey, the blinding sun had now risen high enough that he didn't have to squint behind the mirror lenses of his sunglasses. Traffic was heavier in the opposite direction. It was still early, but the Bay Area commuters who lived in the Central Valley of California were already on their way to work. The GPS on his phone said that his estimated time of arrival at his destination was seven o'clock. Perfect, if no delays. He'd arranged to pick up the new passports before getting Patsy and her daughter.

He and Maria had talked long into the night after returning to his hotel room. She stayed with him and left when he did early this morning. They slept cuddled together. Spooned. Holding on to each other. Finding peace and comfort as their naked and vulnerable bodies found solace in each other. Together. They fit.

Chuck liked long drives. He didn't turn on the radio. There was no police radio to interrupt his thoughts. This is a good time to think. He used it well. He also prayed again.

"God. This is me, Chuck. I don't talk to you as much as I should. I get busy. I forget. I make excuses. But lately? Lately I've been calling on you a lot. But right now I want to thank you. I've had a good life. I believe in you. Thank you for my Maria. She's the best wife a man could ask for. Now I need to ask you something else. Is this a wake-up call? Am I supposed to retire? Is it time for me to do for myself and Maria and her mom the same thing I'm doing for Patsy and the kid? 'Cause that's what I keep coming back to."

An impatient driver sped past him on Pacheco Pass. The four-lane highway through the mountains was dangerous enough without reckless drivers making it worse. Not his call today. He needed to get those passports, get Patsy and her daughter, and start driving south. It was going to be a long day. He was glad to be driving the Trans Am.

"And hey, God, thank you for giving my Maria the wisdom to help me figure out what to do today. And please, one more thing. Please help us be successful. Help me get them safely out of the country and safely to this final destination. And one more thing. Thank you for my friends. It took a lot of people to make this happen. It takes a lot of people to make a successful life happen. It takes a lot of favors. We aren't out of the woods yet. But please protect us from our enemies. Please help me help others. And help me know if it's time to retire. And where we should go if we leave Salinas. Amen."

Chuck didn't think he was very good at praying. But God heard his prayer. Chuck turned his attention back to the road. He'd be passing through the small highway burg of Santa Nella, soon. He glanced at his watch, wondering if he had time to grab a cup of coffee.

This wasn't the nicest part of Modesto. But it wasn't the worst, either. He knocked on the door. The yellow porch light was still on. A curtain moved on a window with a view of the porch. The door opened a crack. He could see the chain of the extra lock still attached.

"Name?" asked the man on the other side of door. Chuck could only see part of his face. Pitted. Aged. He could see a dark eye with dark circles underneath. Dark hair with a scattering of gray. He was wearing a gray tee-shirt and gray sweatpants. He was barefoot. He was shorter than Chuck. He guessed him about five-nine. Overweight. Chuck noticed things like that.

"Chuck Reynolds." There was no point in lying.

"Money?"

"Here on the porch?" Chuck asked.

The door closed momentarily, and he heard the chain removed. The man opened the door. The odor inside was not pleasant, but Chuck had been exposed to worse. He stepped inside and stayed within two feet of the door, giving just enough room to close it behind him.

Chuck heard someone moving in the next room. He assumed that was the kitchen. He could make out the sounds of silverware and plates. He heard the sizzle and the smell of bacon frying, soon replaced the offensive odor he determined was urine.

"Money?" the man repeated.

Chuck pulled out five one-hundred-dollar bills.

"This was the agreement. Yes?" he said.

"Yes. Thank you. Here. Check them now."

Chuck opened the very official-looking US passports. There were the photos he'd taken of Patsy and Alicea. Date of issue: six months ago. Not too new. But new enough for the photographs to be correct. Especially Alicea's. Patsy's expiration date for ten years. The kid's for five. Good. No errors there.

"These look good. Thank you."

"Yes, they're good. I'm the best. And you got the bargain price, too. Only my best customers get that. You have the right friends. Now go. I don't like owing anything to you."

Chuck was out the door and back in his car in thirty seconds. He looked over the passports again. They looked legit. Would they get flagged? He had to hope they would not.

The computers were all linked these days. He had no idea if this would work. But again, he was doing what he felt best. To protect and serve.

He circled Patsy's block twice. Then rolled up to the door and parked the car. It was seven ten in the morning. He rang the doorbell. It was one of those doorbells that take a photo of whoever is outside. He noted cameras mounted to the eaves, too. The small red lights indicated they were working. He waited. What was taking her so long?

With each passing second his worry meter went up. She should be ready.

The door opened in a rush and there they were. Both safe. Packed. Dressed. Ready to go.

"Sorry. We were saying a prayer. We're ready." Patsy looked down at Alicea. "Ready? Another adventure?"

Alicea rolled her eyes. "Mama likes a'ventures. I like Mr. Buttons. I miss him."

"I think things are going to be better, Alicea. But we've got a long way to travel first. You need to be a big girl for this. Can you do it?" Chuck asked.

She looked up at Chuck and smiled. "I *am* a big girl. I can do it."

"With that kind of confidence, I'm sure you can." He opened the trunk to put their luggage inside and saw the box with the new holster he'd dropped in there the day he left the station. His own duffle with a change of clothes was still in the back seat where he'd thrown it that morning.

"Let's get your bags in here. We've got a long drive today."

He grabbed his duffle from the back seat and threw it in the trunk with their backpacks and the box. He'd forgotten they left with so little. There had been no time to return for more of their things. He thought briefly of his short conversation with Mrs. Meyer, to let her know that Patsy would not be returning. She seemed more concerned with finding an immediate replacement than for Patsy's welfare.

"And what am I to do with the things she's left in the house? You don't intend for me to pay someone to pack them up and ship them to her. Do you? Because I won't. She can come get them herself or I will send them to charity. Is that clear?"

"Crystal," he'd replied.

It was a problem he'd deal with later, if at all. Life is precious. These lives are in danger. *Protect and serve, Chuck. Protect and serve*, he told himself again.

All in and seat belts buckled, he headed for the freeway. Southbound Highway 99.

"Where are we going?" Alicea asked.

"Can it be a surprise?" Chuck asked in return.

"We like surprises. Don't we?" This from Patsy.

"Sometimes," said Alicea. "Sometimes not."

"I will tell you this," said Chuck. "We are going to drive for several hours. Did you have breakfast?" Eyes on the rearview mirror and at his front seat passenger confirmed the answer was no. "Well then, we will drive for about an hour, then stop for breakfast. I know a great place for that."

His voice took on the quality of a swashbuckling captain in a children's fantasy. "Then, my Princess, we will be back on the road for another few hours." He elongated the word hours, for effect. Alicea was grinning and rolling her eyes in the back seat, feigning distress with the back of her hand upon her forehead.

"And," he added with more drama than necessary, "we will then stop the car and spend a couple of days with friends, before we go to a remote and hidden airport where we will board a private jet, taking us to the first stop on the way to our final destination on this a'venture."

"Oh, Mama! Is this real? I'm 'cited!"

"I'm excited, too! Oh, Officer Reynolds," she said respectfully. "How can we ever thank you?"

"By staying alive," he answered quietly and repeated. "By staying alive."

"That's the plan," said Patsy. Her heart felt at peace for the first time in more than a week.

"Should I ask our final destination? Or what the rest of my life that you are creating will look like?"

"I will tell you. But not now. The less you know, the better, until we get there. Do you understand? We aren't out of the woods, yet. I've called in a lot of favors on this. Didn't realize how many truly great friends I have. I also didn't realize the benefit of knowing a few characters of dubious distinction, that are actually good guys at heart."

"Like Sergio?" she asked.

"You know what," he said in the quiet car. "Sergio and I were on opposite sides. But I learned something about him. He wasn't all bad. Was he?"

"No. I don't think so. Although he did try to kill me once." She glanced into the back seat. But as expected, Alicea had already plugged headphones into her ears and was tuned out completely to the conversation in the front seat.

"But there was a good side to him. I know it in my heart."

"Patsy, I need to ask you something very important. And I need you to be completely honest with me. Okay?"

"Okay."

"Did Sergio give you any money? Either before you left six years ago or recently?"

"What? I haven't had any contact with Sergio since he almost killed me that day."

Another glance to the back seat.

"You're sure?"

"What the fuck do you mean, are you sure?" She always lashed back and got defensive when angry. Chuck believed her. He didn't think she had any idea about whatever money Sergio might have stolen.

They drove in silence. Chuck pondered the situation. If Sergio didn't give the money to Patsy and didn't trust the Norteños with it, where was it? Not in a bank. *Think, Chuck. Think like Sergio. Where would he put it?*

The miles drifted by and so did the towns. Turlock, Merced, and now to Chowchilla and breakfast at Farnesi's. Best breakfast on Highway 99, he'd been told. Unassuming. Good food. Lots of it. Mostly locals. No gangs. This was a pretty safe bet for breakfast. It was eight thirty on Monday morning. They'd be on the road again by nine forty-five.

They were expected in Southern California by nightfall. Plans were still being arranged for the private jet to get them to Mexico, but it was confirmed to happen within a day or two. He needed to have them on location so has not to miss the connection when it came through. They were looking at a narrow window for transportation to Mexico. From there, they'd take a commercial flight to Puerto Rico, maybe. The plans were not yet definite. But he would not be going with them. He'd fill her in on the details later. But he trusted his instincts. Moreover, he trusted Maria's.

TWENTY-THREE

Blanca

The angel smiled as she watched the three of them eat the hearty breakfasts served at the roadside diner. The other patrons included a few local cowboys, two long-haul truckers, and a family of six with four boisterous boys who all quieted when their father returned their digital tablets. The table was now quiet. No laughter or shared stories. No pushing or shoving to change seats or argue over a box of crayons. The times had certainly changed since she was a child in the early 1960s. What new inventions were on the horizon? She was daydreaming and contemplating the future of humans when she felt a presence behind her. That itch between her wings returned.

Slowly, she turned toward the demon she knew was there.

"You don't belong here, Chax. Go away."

Suddenly, there were three of them. Abaddon and Mara were on either side of Chax now. She moved her hand to the grip of her sword and repeated her words with authority. "You don't belong here. Go away. All of you."

"Do we have to play this game again?" Mara asked. "I'm tired of this little twit of an angel. She's hardly worth the effort, but orders are orders, I suppose. What's the plan, Abaddon?"

Blanca stood her ground. Her massive wings twitched ever so slightly. Her grip was firm on the sword, though she kept it sheathed. She didn't say another word. She waited and watched. This was some sort of a showdown. Why? she wondered. It was like that case she worked on with Hannah and Roy and the sisters. Jeff had been on that one, too. Why were these same three demons returning to cause trouble now?

Without anger, Blanca pulled her sword and held it in front of her. "I have sworn to keep them safe, and that I will," she told the trio. "Why don't you find another playground? There are no souls to steal here."

"Oh, dear little Blanca. Aren't you just adorable trying to be all badass and grown up?" Abaddon was taking over now. "What fun would it be if we didn't have a challenge? Do you have any idea how easy it would be for us to simply swoop in and turn that cop against them? Or how much fun we'd have making her distrust the cop? Maybe we can get her to take his gun and shoot him with it?"

"Oh! Oh! Even better than that!" cried Mara. "We could convince one of the already damned to cause a road accident and really amp up their anger levels. They'll turn away from your God and come to our side. They often do. Even the really good ones can make bad choices with enough incentive and heartache."

"Blanca, face it. You are simply not strong enough against us to stop us from doing whatever we want with your girl there. We know it and you know it."

In an instant and with the strength of an army of angels, Blanca hefted her four-foot-long sword, pulled it across in an arc, and sliced through the middle of all three demons from right to left. They disappeared in a cloud of smoke, as Blanca once again sheathed her sword and sat at the table next to Alicea.

"These are really good pancakes," Alicea told her mother. "And I was really hungry."

"Where are we?" she asked the vacationing detective.

Chuck

"We're in a town called Chowchilla. A friend of mine used to live here. He was a guard at a prison that's not too far from here."

"Really? A prison? Isn't that where they put bad people?"

Too late, Chuck realized the slim possibility that a criminal from Salinas might be housed in one of the nearby prisons. If so, he supposed there was also a slim possibility that visitors might stop at this very restaurant. He glanced around the room. No, he thought. That slim margin of possibility would be the same for any restaurant in the country. Just the same, the thought gnawed at him. He was anxious to get back on the road. His breakfast was delicious.

Breakfast had arrived for the boys and their parents, too. The tablets were put away and the noise level rose again until it was replaced once more with silence as they ate. Chuck smiled to himself. Little girls are easier. Princesses, versus little hellions. But then, he was stereotyping. A practice he usually warned others not to do.

Blanca

After the incident with the demons, Blanca was back on high alert. Wherever they were seen, trouble was close at hand. She did not doubt her strength to banish them, but she knew they planted treacherous seeds of destruction wherever they went. She had to be aware of everything. This was not the time to sit and enjoy being with these humans she loved so much or let her guard down.

She needed to confer with Jeff. He might know the greater danger out there. She closed her eyes, prayed, and held a firm grip on the handle of her sword.

"Hey, Blanca. How can I help?" Jeff asked.

It was the same Jeff. The unlikely angel with the sassy attitude who had been Sergio's Guardian.

The angels' work is unseen by humans. They are energy and raw power. Not physical. Time does not exist as it does for humans. Blanca had laughed when she first heard the phrase, "Once a Marine, always a Marine." It was the same for angels. Literally. Eternally.

"Jeff, the same three demons we fought with Hannah, back when Patsy was pregnant with Alicea, were just here. I think my girls are in trouble. They are in the protective custody of this law enforcement officer, who is trustworthy. I know his mind and he is trying to get them to the safety of a new life. But there is trouble ahead. I know it the way we know these things. But I don't know what the trouble is. Do you have information that will help?" Blanca asked.

Jeff looked thoughtfully at Blanca.

"We are both still pretty new at this. Young by angel standards. We've been entrusted with this situation. I already have new humans again. Once Sergio passed, Hannah told me to rest, but I got another assignment right away," he said.

Jeff continued, "You can do this, Blanca. Listen to the Lord. Trust Him. He will give you the answers you need, when you need them. Always. He sent me here today."

Blanca sensed the change in Jeff. He seemed to have aged. Grown up. He'd become more respectful. But she could see no outward change in him at all. It was his demeanor and a sense of quiet strength growing in him. She'd noticed it earlier, too. The last time they were together.

"Listen," he said, "Sergio took money from the Norteños that he believed was due to him for all the bad things he was forced to do for them. Sergio knew if he gave it to his grandmother or spent it on her or himself, she'd be in danger, too. His theft, so cleverly executed over the years, would be discovered. He thought he'd covered his tracks. He did. But suspicion loomed and fell on him anyway. He put the money in an unmarked cardboard box, along with a note that it was for Patsy and her kid, sealed it up, and addressed it to Officer Reynolds at the sheriff's department. That is the only person on earth he actually trusted other than his grandmother, of course. Then he hid the box behind the sofa at her house. He planned to retrieve it and figure out what to do with it, but never got the chance. Jorge didn't really want to torture the information out of his former friend, nor his grandmother. Sergio knew his life was nearly over. He'd been in the game too long. It was getting too ruthless, and he'd lost his love of violence. When Jorge ordered his man to pull the trigger, it was quick. Sergio was praying. I was with him all the way. That was my first time."

Jeff had a faraway look in his eyes. Remembering. "It was awful at first. But Sergio crossed over into the light and then I was happy I'd helped him make it. His abuela, his grandmother, was a big help, too. She prayed every day for his soul. She's alone now, but she has her own Guardian, and one day they'll be together again."

Jeff brought his attention back to Blanca.

"Sergio put around a million dollars in unmarked bills in that box. After he passed over, his grandmother found the box and her Guardian asked me to help her decide what to do with it. I knew she had to get rid of it. There would be consequences if she didn't."

Jeff stared at Blanca and momentarily forgot what he was telling her. His mind randomly jumped to the idea of so many very different angels helping humans with all their trials and tribulations of life.

"We're all so different. Aren't we?" he said, losing his train of thought. Completely changing the subject.

"What?" Blanca was confused. "Jeff, are you telling me the box in Officer Reynold's car contains that money? The Norteños missing money?"

"Yeah, I am. Grandma found it after he was murdered. As I said, it was all sealed up and addressed already. She thought it might be something that would help solve his murder. Whatever was in the box, she did not want it in her home. She loved Sergio more than anything, but she was smart enough to know he led a life involved with sin. Drugs. Guns. She did not know and did not want to know the details. But she heard snippets of conversation here and there that led her to pray constantly for his soul to be redeemed. In a very real sense, she saved him. She took the box to the post office and mailed it. She did not want to be seen going into the police station. It's hard to be innocent and still live a life of fear because you live on the edge of a violent world."

"So how is it that Officer Reynolds doesn't know what's in the box?" she asked.

"That the bizarre part," said Jeff. "Chuck got the package but didn't open it. He made the very human error of assumption. He'd ordered a new holster for one of his weapons and assumed that was what had just been delivered. He threw it in his trunk and got too busy to bother to open it. Wrong. He's been packing a million dollars in cash around with him for more than a week."

Jeff went on. "Blanca, that money was meant for Patsy and Alicea. Money the Norteños will do anything to retrieve. But they don't know where it is. Their orders are to find it and get it back and punish whoever took it and whoever has it now. Right now, it's Patsy, Alicea, and Chuck Reynolds. But they don't know it, yet."

"Jeff, what am I supposed to do?"

"Trouble will follow the money. But if they try to give it back? They'll still be killed. The only safe thing for them to do, and live, to live the lives God created them to live, is to escape. That's your job, Blanca. You got this. Keep your eyes and ears open. The demons will return disguised as anything they want to get your people to turn and make mistakes. You know the devil thrives on turning good people toward anger and greed. They are being tested. The choices they make will affect the rest of their lives. Long or short. You remember that other old adage about *what would Jesus do?*" He didn't pause for an answer. "Well, that certainly applies here. What would He do? But also, what is the right choice? Is there a way to return the money anonymously? It's blood money. Money from the sale of illegal drugs and illegal guns and more that harms innocent people, even children. Should it be returned to be used for more evil? Or should it be used for good? How? How do you hide that much money? The box? It's unassuming. Not too large and not too small. But is that wise? To leave it there? Where to put the money? They can't put it in a bank. Not in the States. They can't just go around carrying that kind of cash. Someone will notice. So, you see the dilemmas they will soon face? Once Chuck discovers the truth about what is inside that box, his life will change forever. What is he going to do with it?"

Jeff went on as Blanca contemplated all he'd shared. "And what of the Nuestra Familia?" he asked. "What are they doing to find the money now that they killed Sergio? They won't stop looking until they believe it's gone and they can never get it back. Danger is near, Blanca. You smote those demons, but trouble is already here in this place. I'm here to warn you and help."

Jeff kept talking. "Reynolds is a good man, but he doesn't realize a tracking device was put on his car. They've been watching for him ever since the night they shot up his house and he wasn't there. Just before he left for Modesto, to pick up Patsy, they spotted him at a local gas station and attached the device under his car. They didn't trust him then and they don't trust him now. It was a matter of time before they caught up to him. Jorge called a contact of his who lives near here. Martha. He sent her here to check out Reynold's car and see who was with him at this restaurant. She's on her way now.

Jeff looked around the dining room. Chuck, Patsy, and Alicea were still at the table. Then Chuck's cellphone rang. He checked the number. It was Joe Medeiros.

"I'm going to take this call. I'll be out front." He laid a fifty-dollar bill on the table and walked toward the front door.

Blanca and Jeff watched. Powerless to do anything as Chuck took the phone call, left money on the table, and stepped outside, leaving the girls alone.

Jeff touched Blanca's arm. "It begins now. Keep them safe. I'm here. When she gets a chance, Jorge's woman will try to take out Patsy or kidnap the kid. She won't take on the cop, but she might try to break into the car. Probably not. Most likely she will inform Jorge. This is all about to happen soon. We will know what to do. The evil one is near."

Chuck

Outside, Chuck answered, "Chuck here. What's going on?"

"Hey, Chuck. There is a package here for you. It's from that place you told me about that makes good shoulder holsters. You expecting something?"

Chuck's mind went into overdrive. The box in his trunk. If it wasn't the holster, what was it? He felt nauseous and began to sweat. His mouth went dry.

"Hey, pal, could you open the box and tell me exactly what's in it?"

"Sure. Hold on a sec."

Chuck heard Joe set the phone down and put it on speaker. Then he sliced through the tape and Chuck could hear him lift the box flaps and the rustle of paper inside.

"It's a shoulder holster. Nice one, too. I take it you ordered this, yes?"

"I did. Thanks. Listen, I need to go. I'm fine. I'll check with you later tonight."

Back inside, the friendly waitress had brought his change and cleared the table.

"Alicea, let's use the bathroom before we go." Patsy stood up and dusted a few crumbs off the leg of her jeans.

"I don't have to go," said the girl who got a "look" from Patsy that said otherwise.

Mother and daughter moved toward the door marked "Cowgirls."

Chuck left a generous tip and used the "Cowboys" room, before heading outside once more. He briefly wondered how long it would be before this restaurant would be forced to change the names on the restroom doors. He didn't see Patsy inside, and they weren't out front waiting for him. He thought mother and daughter must still be in the restroom.

More than anything, he wanted to check that box in his trunk. But he held back. He'd need privacy for that. This parking lot on the side of the freeway with a possible contract out on his life or the woman's life, was not a smart idea. He stood by the front door and waited for them to finish and come outside.

Blanca

When Patsy and Alicia entered the restroom, Blanca went with them. Jeff waited in the hall as Chuck brushed past him and disappeared into the men's room. At that same moment, the woman named Martha came around the corner. Jeff saw her first. There were two demons with her. Jeff didn't know these demons personally but recognized the evil in them. Pulling his sword, he stopped them before they could influence Martha further. Inside the restroom, Blanca made sure that Patsy recognized the dangerous woman, and that she grabbed Alicea and ran out the moment the other woman closed the stall door behind her.

As Jeff held the demons back, Blanca helped Patsy and Alicea find hiding places. Patsy in the closet and Alicea behind the bar. The woman with the XIV tattoo came out with unseeing eyes and walked right through the energy of

Jeff holding back the demons. She shrugged her shoulders and went out through the back door she'd used to enter the restaurant.

Fuck. Nothing here. Jorge is nuts. Why do I ever listen to those guys. Nothing but trouble, Martha thought, but no words left her mouth. Back in her car, she pulled around the old Peterbilt truck and headed for home. Everyone working at the restaurant was busy. No one saw her come or go.

Blanca had her wings wrapped firmly around little Alicea behind the bar, and Jeff stayed in the janitor's closet with Patsy. The demons were gone. They stayed with Martha.

Chuck

"What is taking them so long?" Chuck wondered.

He went back inside and headed for the restroom. He knocked on the door marked "Cowgirls." No answer. He knocked again. "What the hell?"

He knocked a third time and asked, "Anyone in there?"

Hearing nothing, he opened the door. Empty.

"Shit," he said and ran back outside.

He scanned the parking lot. His car was still there. The trunk was closed. No one was in the car. She didn't have the keys anyway.

He went back into the diner and asked the waitress who had served them if she'd seen them and if there was a back door to the restaurant.

"I didn't see where they went, but we do have a back door. We got two. One through the kitchen there and one through the banquet room in the back. You go down the hall by the bathrooms," she said, pointing. "And through the saloon on the other side. Then you take that hallway on the left to the banquet room in the back and we got another exit. Are you thinking to have a party back there? We do all kinds of events."

Chuck stopped listening and ran toward the bar area that was closed until later in the day. Bar stools were stacked on tables and the room was dark. He found the next hallway and the large room at the back. He charged out the back door. She'd had a good five-minute head start, but why would she run? He was protecting her.

"Dammit." He examined the ground at the bottom of the stairs that led away from the building. Did he notice signs of a scuffle? Or was that his imagination? Was he sure they weren't still inside? It was a large building, with a lot of places to hide. But for the life of him, he couldn't figure out why she would be hiding. He was used to people running from him, but those were perps and people he'd arrested, not people he was trying to save.

His eyes took in the parking lot behind the restaurant. Employee cars. A battered pick-up truck. A couple of big rigs were there, too. He saw an older Peterbilt and a late model Freightliner. All empty. Nothing stirred out there on this quiet Monday morning. Chuck let out a deep breath. Should he get on the road? Where to look for them? She could be anywhere. There was a nearby motel. He stood there for another half-minute, watching. Thinking. Most likely, she was still inside. She had to be. But would he be wasting time looking for her if she'd been taken against her will? It seemed pointless to search out here. He went back inside.

"Dammit," he said again.

"Patsy," he called softly. "You here?"

Nothing.

He started back down the hall toward the bar. He stopped there in the darkened room. The only light came from the hall. There were no windows to let daylight into this adult side of the restaurant.

"Patsy," he called again. "If you're in here, come out. This is Reynolds. I don't know what happened, but if you're here, you're safe. Come out."

He was about to head for the main dining room when he heard a noise behind the bar and drew out his Sig Sauer. Could someone else be hiding back there?

Cautiously, he called again, "Patsy? Alicea? Are you there? Who's back there? Then he raised his voice slightly. "This is Detective Chuck Reynolds. Come out with your hands up."

He saw two little hands emerge above the top of the bar and heard a soft sniffle.

Needing to be sure she wasn't being held hostage, he moved slowly around to the open edge of the bar. Alicea was alone. Frightened and alone. He returned his weapon to the worn holster and knelt down to give her a hug.

"It's okay, honey. I'm here. What happened? Where is your mama?" he asked with urgency but tried to keep his voice soft and reassuring. "Is Mama all right? Where did she go?"

Alicea held on and buried her face on his shoulder that was now down at her height. Chuck realized how small and vulnerable she was as he comforted her. He knew this was not a good defensive position, but at the moment he was more concerned about the girl. He sensed that whatever danger had come this way was now gone.

Alicea sniffed again and wiped her eyes and nose with the back of her hand. "I want to go home," she said.

"I know, sweetie. But we need to get Mommy first. Where is she?"

"She went in the closet and told me to hide in here until you came."

"What closet?" he asked. "Show me."

"That one."

Chuck prided himself on his observation skills, yet he'd completely missed seeing the door that was made to look like part of the wall. He guessed it was to keep late-night guests from mistaking the janitorial closet for the water closet.

He held Alicea's hand and together they walked toward the closet. What would he find on the other side? Was she hurt? Was she still there? What or who had she seen to cause this reaction? She'd been pretty level-headed so far. This seemed completely out of character. Something caused this.

"Please, God," he prayed with barely a whisper. "Let her be all right. Let her be safe." He was focused on his objective, but the words of a song he'd heard by Jelly Roll also flashed through his mind, "I only talk to God when I need a favor, and God, I need a favor."

Whatever was behind that door, he didn't want Alicea to see until he knew there was no danger. He positioned the child on the other side of door, where she couldn't see inside, and told her not to move. He drew his Sig Sauer again and stood on the opposite side of the door. He knocked. Alicea's eyes went wide.

"Patsy? Are you in there?" They were out of sight and earshot from the main dining room, but he wasn't taking any chances. He kept his voice low. If someone was in there with her, the last thing anyone wanted was another shoot out.

"Chuck? Is that you?" came a quivering reply.

"It's me. It's safe. I'm opening the door now. Is it safe for me to do that?"

"Yes. I'm okay. Alicea? Is she okay?"

He opened the door to find Patsy cowering at the back of the closet behind several mops and holding toilet bowl plunger like she was going to use it as a weapon.

"Come on out. I'm here. Is someone here that caused you to hide?"

Just then, Alicea ran into the closet and knocked over an empty mop bucket with a loud crash.

"It's time to go. Now," Chuck said and hurried both of them out of the closet.

"We're going to walk out of here right now. I'm going to put my arm around you as if we're a couple. Okay?"

He knew she was getting herself together when she wrinkled her nose, curled her lip at him, and said, "Ew."

They left the building through the front door without seeing anyone or anything suspicious.

Patsy waited until they were outside and on their way to the car before answering.

"Yes. I saw someone in the bathroom. I don't think she knew me, but I was afraid. You were outside. She came in the bathroom just as we were finishing. I knew her from the old days. And she had the XIV tattoo on the back of her hand. When she went in the stall, I grabbed Alicea and told her to hide. I knew you would eventually find us. I just prayed she didn't recognize me and tell someone or try to find us. I panicked. Please don't leave me alone again."

Chuck felt her fear. "I never saw anyone come in through the front door. Maybe she works here? Or maybe she's familiar with this place and came in the back door to use the bathroom. That door was not locked. Wherever she came from, I think the danger is over."

Patsy kept her eyes roving from side to side as they crossed the parking lot. Chuck did the same. Nothing looked out of place. The car was parked exactly as they had left it. He opened the right-side doors for mother and daughter and walked to the back of the car. He popped the trunk open, noted that all bags, backpacks, and the now ominous box were still inside.

He closed the trunk and got behind the wheel.

"Everything okay back there?" Patsy asked with a questioning look.

"Yep. All good." Chuck examined every car and truck on the way out. They waited for traffic to pass and were back on the highway in less than three minutes.

Blanca

When Chuck had gotten them both safely back to the car, Jeff warned Blanca. "They will continue to track him. We are lucky Martha decided to leave. They might bide their time, but they will follow the cop. He is their only lead. Take care of them. Him, too. He wore out his last Guardian. If you didn't get the message already, I'm supposed to tell you he's now one of yours, too. At least until this phase of their life together is over. Which probably won't be long."

It was Blanca's turn to stare at Jeff.

"Don't look at me like that, Blanca. I'm just the messenger. Take care of them. All of them. I will come again if you need me. For now, the job is yours." He was gone as quickly as he'd appeared.

Chuck

"Do you remember her name? Her associates?" Chuck asked Patsy in the car.

"Who?"

"The woman in the bathroom. Who else would I be talking about?" *Why am I being snippy with her?* he thought. *I'm on edge now, too.*

"Oh. I'm sorry. I guess I'm still shaking inside." She glanced into the back seat. Alicea was once again plugged into her headphones and playing a game on her tablet.

"I was so scared." She looked out the window, turning her face away from Chuck as the car sped down the highway.

"Her name is Martha. She's about my age. She used to date a guy named Diego, but I think they broke up. He owned a garage in Salinas. Worked on cars, that sort of thing. They were friends of Sergio's. Sometimes she'd hang out with me when the guys were off doing guy things. That was before I got pregnant." Another glance to the back seat.

"She didn't have that tattoo before."

Patsy didn't say anything more. Chuck let the silence between them stretch as there wasn't much else to say. He glanced at his watch and the GPS. They were still on target to reach their destination on time, despite the delay in Chowchilla.

Chuck wondered if he was making a big mistake. Was he going overboard trying to cover her tracks? He reassured himself, as they drove in silence, that he was not. It was not just her. The kid. His Maria. Her mom. Joe. Jess. He felt like they were all in some sort of danger. He couldn't take out the entire organization. He couldn't even take out the leaders. And now? Now he was about to involve innocent bystanders. *Please, Lord,* he prayed, *no collateral damage. Especially not to these good people I got involved in all this.*

They drove through Bakersfield and merged with Interstate 5. When they passed over the Grapevine, Alicea announced that she had to use the bathroom again.

"We probably all need a break," he said and turned off the highway at Valencia Boulevard.

Without incident, they were back in the car twenty minutes later with a full tank of gas and nearly three hours to get to their destination.

"Are you driving us to Mexico?" Patsy asked.

"No. We're meeting up with some good people I trust. They will go with you to Mexico. But you will not be in one place too long, and you won't be in Mexico for more than a week or so.

She turned to stare at him. "What?"

"I might be extra cautious, but I think it's for the best. I've been thinking about it throughout our drive. Mapping out the final details in my head. Wondering about the consequences of your encounter with that woman in Chowchilla. I don't believe in coincidence and that was too close for comfort. Although I can't figure out how she got past me either coming or going. And why they haven't shown their hand by now if they are really after you. And if they are after you, why?"

He didn't tell her about the money. He'd asked her once. That was enough. He'd find out soon enough what was in the box in his trunk and if it was connected to the case.

"I think that is the most you've talked to me on this whole trip. Thank you."

She looked out the window. He had stayed on the Parkway, heading east, and she wondered why he didn't get back on the freeway.

"Where are we going now?"

"Los Angeles traffic will be horrendous this afternoon. This route is longer without traffic, but it'll save us at least an hour at this time of the day," Chuck explained.

"But can you tell me where we are going? Like where we'll be living? What kind of a job will I have? And the thing that really concerns me, who is paying for all this? You, personally? I don't get it. Why are you doing this for me? You are the one who told me to get a back-up plan and I didn't. You have come to my rescue too many times. I'm grateful. I really am. But why? How can I repay you? I don't know how I can ever do that." She turned and looked out the window again. She was lost in a sea of what-ifs and worry about a life she could not control. Maybe she'd lost control when she first met Sergio.

As they rode in silence again, he thought about the team he'd put together for this mission. None of them were being paid. All were just good people who offered to help when he had asked. He hadn't seen or talked to some of these people in years.

The friend who owned the rental in Modesto, served in the Army with him. The couple he was meeting tonight at the VFW Post in Fallbrook, California, were both former US Marines. She was the daughter of a friend from high school. The daughter had served with 7th Engineers at Camp Pendleton. Her husband had a particular skill set that would come in handy if they ran into trouble. After six combat tours in the Middle East, he'd finally reunited with the love of his life, and they settled in Fallbrook.

When Maria suggested that he call his old friend Liz Davidson, because she'd met her at a class reunion and remembered that her daughter was a Marine and that she owned time share units in Mexico and traveled a lot.

"Maybe Liz has connections, so they aren't flying out of airports here in the States. They probably won't be looking for her in Mexico, and especially not if you can get them new identities," Maria had said.

"You're a genius," he had told Maria when she'd suggested it to him the other night.

She had immediately smiled and came back with, "That's why you pay me the big bucks."

They laughed and kissed. He began making calls and asking for favors. At first, he was surprised that so many people and virtual strangers were willing to help. But as he closed his eyes that night and sleep overtook his tired mind, he remembered how many really good people there are in this world. A lot them were his friends.

"Thank you, God," he had whispered into the night.

Liz Davidson Miller was the biggest super trooper of all. He'd had a small crush on her in high school and even took her to the Harvest Ball one year. But their friendship was never destined to be more than that. He'd seen her once or twice when he first got out of the Army and went into law enforcement, but she had her own life, and he had his. They drifted apart on the river of life. They married different people and moved on. At the class reunion she spoke more with Maria than she did with Chuck. Which was how Maria had connected the dots between her place in Mexico, travel, and the possibility that she might be able help Patsy, if she was willing. She was. One phone call. He'd called her on Saturday morning.

"Oh my God! Are you kidding me? Chuck Reynolds? Is this really you? How are you? What's going on? Are you still a cop or did that beautiful wife of yours finally get you to retire?" Liz was still the same.

"Slow down, girl!" he laughed. It was just like old times. Like nothing had changed in all those years.

"Okay. Okay," she said. "Talk to me! Tell me how you found my number and why you are calling out of the blue and what on earth is going on in your life?"

The old friends chatted for nearly an hour. No, he and Maria never had kids. Yes, she had retired from teaching toward the end of the pandemic, but he was still on the force. Yes, Liz and her husband Miles were doing great. But he now struggled with early dementia. They were working on protocols to slow the progress. Yes, it was difficult. But life is difficult sometimes, isn't it? Yes, they still had their timeshare units in Mexico and other places around the world. No, they had not used them since the pandemic. No, he didn't get out of California very often. No, she didn't get to California very often. Only to see the kids.

Finally, he asked, "I need a favor and am wondering if you can help."

The conversation turned serious for the next thirty minutes. He laid out his dilemma and didn't hold back. If Liz was going to help, she needed to know everything.

She asked if she could spend some time with this, make a few phone calls and get back to him. She knew time and confidentiality were critical factors.

"I need to talk to Miles. Dementia or not, I need to run this past him."

Forty minutes later she called back to tell Chuck the plan. She'd already made many of the arrangements.

"Listen, we have timeshare points to use or lose. I'd rather they be used to help this woman and her kid because you believe so strongly about this and because we can. And your house? Oh my God? Are you sure Maria and her mother are safe? They can come here. I'm not close, but it's safe."

How do you thank someone like that? he thought.

She had called her daughter and son-in-law. Chuck was to leave Patsy and Alicea with them in the town of Fallbrook, northeast of San Diego. From there, the two Marines would drive them to a small local airport, where they'd be met by another friend and all flown on a private jet to Puerta Vallarta, Mexico. They would then check into the Miller's resort, Vidanta at Nuevo Vallarta, for a one-week stay. During this time, Patsy and Alicea would practice using their new names and Patsy would get a crash course in working hospitality at a major resort. Madeleine and Bret Collier, Liz Davidson's daughter and son-in-law, would stay to ensure all went well and enjoy a much-deserved vacation for themselves. Liz suggested this to keep Patsy from being blind-sided by the vacation ownership sales team. She believed Maddie could help Patsy adjust to her new life working at a world-class resort. Madeleine and Bret were also trained to watch for trouble. If there was an issue of security or danger, they could intervene. It seemed like a good plan.

From there, with the new names supplied by Chuck, they would fly overseas to their final destination. They'd spend their first month with a retired policewoman who would acclimate them to their new home in Ibiza, Spain. That part of the plan had already been arranged by Chuck.

"Meanwhile, my son-in-law will be on standby if they need help."

She talked so fast, and Chuck was trying to write it all down.

"Wait. Wait," he said. "Liz, how can you do all this? Don't you need their passports and other information? I don't have that yet. I don't have their new names yet. Not for sure anyway."

"It doesn't matter. Get them to my daughter. Bret will make the arrangements on military cyber-secure computers. My son-in-law still works for the Corps, but now as a civilian. He won't use federal time or money, but he can help facilitate things. I've already checked on commercial flights out of Puerto Vallarta. There is room available. Enough empty seats that they'll be able to make the connections. My kids will take care of everything the day after you arrive and catch that private jet a day or two after that. That way we make certain all is ready before sending the jet to pick them up," she told him.

"How did you do this? Make these arrangements? Do you seriously have a private jet at your disposal?" Chuck asked his old friend.

"Oh, heavens no! But I do have a good friend who owns a private air charter service. It truly is one of those amazing laws of the universe that you reap what you sow. I don't call in favors very often, but I have given a lot of time and energy to helping others over the years. Not ever do I have a single regret about that.

"Back to Maddie and Bret. They're good kids. But they really aren't kids anymore, Chuck. They're on the back side of forty already and excited to know they can help. Between you and me, I think they miss the whole excitement and drama that is part of being in the military or law enforcement. You know what I mean. There is a certain sense of accomplishment when you put bad guys behind bars or protect the innocent and keep them safe. That's why you haven't retired. Am I right?"

"Damn, girl. You might be right," was all he said.

"How'd we get this old, my friend? Seems like we were just kids," she mused.

"Liz, too many of our friends didn't make it this long. I've seen too much. I've watched them taken by drugs, accidents, suicide, homicide, obesity, and just plain stupidity. We may not ever be rich or famous, but we're the lucky ones. We did manage to get this old. I hope to keep growing old, too. And don't you dare tell Maria, but I am thinking about retiring. I'm just not sure when. I think this life is getting too dangerous for me and the people I love. Please promise me that your daughter and son-in-law will be extremely cautious, and you will, too."

"I promise."

His conversation with Liz had taken place after Maria suggested that she might be able to help. He'd called her on Saturday morning. Now it was Monday, and he was implementing the plan. Driving Patsy and Alicea to hand them over to Maddie and Bret Collier.

Two and a half hours later, Officer Reynolds pulled up to the Veterans of Foreign Wars Post 1924 in Fallbrook, California.

Blanca

The angel rode with them through the great Central Valley of California, around the perimeter of greater Los Angeles, and finally to their destination at the VFW Post.

As they drove, she listened to the rhythm of the road and examined the minds of the occupants, she knew the dilemmas that plagued each of them. Jeff was right. There would be no easy decisions ahead.

"God give me strength," she prayed.

I am here.

Chuck

When Chuck pulled up to the Post, there were only a few cars in the parking lot. He'd been instructed to drive down the left side of the building out of sight from the main road and enter through a side door.

Patsy was not about to wait in the car without him. The three of them got out and approached the door. Chuck knocked and tried the handle. It opened. They entered a dimly lit bar decorated with Marine Corps and other military service memorabilia. One grizzled old veteran sat at the bar with a fresh drink in front of him. A regular, thought Chuck.

The friendly blonde behind the bar greeted them with a smile. "Hi. I'm Dory. I don't recognize you. First time here?"

Before Chuck could reply, she said, "Oh wait! I'll bet you're here to see the Commander. He told me to expect you about this time. Yes?" Chuck nodded.

"Have a seat at a table or at the horseshoe. We're pretty casual here, but I can't have a kid at this bar, okay? I'll get them for you. Hey, Bret! Maddie!" she called through the pass window to the kitchen. "Your friends are here."

"Now, can I get you something to drink? They're working on dinner. We have Burger Night on Mondays. That's later tonight, but the bar is open. I have soda, too."

"No, thank you," Chuck answered.

"How about you, ladies?" she asked.

"Nothing for me," answered Patsy.

"Mom, can I have a soda?" Alicea asked her mother.

"Do you have any Coke Zero?" Patsy asked.

Dory responded with another happy smile, "Of course! We keep it here because too many of the kids get amped on caffeine. We have several members who still have kids at home."

Just then a man and woman came around the corner and introduced themselves.

"Hi, I'm Liz's daughter, Maddie."

"And I'm Bret," said the clean-cut handsome man who stuck out his hand and spoke directly to Chuck Reynolds. A beautiful chocolate Labrador Retriever was at his side. "And this is Mattis. He's my service dog. Goes everywhere with me. Nice to meet you and glad we can help."

Chuck was curious but wasn't about to ask about why Bret needed a service dog. Bret was used to the unasked question he read on the faces of those who met Mattis for the first time. Normally, he ignored it. This time, he didn't.

"Six combat tours. Mattis helps with the PTSD," Bret said.

Chuck nodded. He understood. "Thank you," was all he said.

The old man at the bar watched this encounter without a word, but now he chimed in. "Hey, Commander, do we got us a new member?" He took another sip of his drink. "Welcome to the Post. It's a pretty good place, but that Dory there waters down my drinks. You gotta keep an eye on her."

All eyes turned to the old veteran with sad eyes. A brief pall fell over the room as everyone except Alicea felt the sadness in his gravelly voice. War and military service to preserve the freedoms in the United States takes a toll. Alcohol is just one of the ways former service members tend to cope. Suicide rates among veterans are way too high. Help is too often not available or timely or simply not wanted. Bret and Maddie are a few of the many veterans who continue to serve by volunteering at VFW and American Legion Posts around the country. They give our veterans a safe place to land. Without the help of dedicated volunteers, these posts will eventually close.

On this day, Bret and Maddie were also coming to the rescue of a young woman and her child, who were complete strangers to them. But a call had come from Maddie's mom. Of course, they would help.

"Ah, Bill, are you complaining about me again?" Dory put her hands on her hips and stood directly across the bar from the old man.

"You water my drinks," he said. "As a matter of fact, you do."

His words were deliberate and concise. Dory could hardly hold back a laugh. At the same time, it hurt her heart to watch this man who had once been in the prime of his life reduced to his four o'clock trip to the VFW to get smashed. He had no one and nowhere else to go. His wife had passed on two years earlier. This was the only place he felt at home. Here, he was with Marines. As they say, once a Marine, always a Marine.

Dory made sure he would not die of alcohol poisoning, and she'd make sure he had a ride home later that night. She'd make sure he ate something, too. This is the esprit de corps among America's military members. It does not matter who, which branch of the service, skin color, height, weight, sex, or age. No one gets left behind. At least that is the way it's supposed to work. Usually, that is exactly the way it works. Spirited banter and competition between services will always be part of the common thread. But deep down, they are connected by their call to service.

Dory winked at Bill and let him know that his next drink was on the house, if he drank a glass of pure water first.

"Oh Lordy, girl! Do you know what fish do in that terrible stuff? Water? I nearly drowned in water out there in the Pacific. And you want me to drink it?" He laughed at the line he used every time she made the offer. He rarely drank water.

"Listen, the regulars will start coming in soon. How about we get out of here?" Maddie offered, then turned to Dory, the bartender. "Bret and I have the kitchen prepped for the crew who should be here soon. All is ready. Hold down the fort and call if you need us."

"Officer Reynolds, I think this is where we part company. Ladies, are you okay with that? If so, I will take you home and get you some dinner and you can rest. Does that work for everyone?" Maddie kept her voice low. She did not need Bill or Dory hearing this part of the conversation.

Patsy gave Chuck an imploring look. "Are you sure?" she asked directly.

"I'm sure," he said.

They hugged and she thanked him profusely. Alicea, too, was reluctant to let him go.

"It's okay, girls. You have my number if you need me. I'm sticking around tonight, but not going with you. It's safer that way. Be strong."

Maddie said she'd meet them by Chuck's car to get their gear and left by another door to get her minivan. Bret went with Chuck, as they led Patsy and Alicea back the way they'd come in.

"I'll be back in a few minutes," Bret told Dory. "Bill, you don't be giving Dory any sass. You hear me?"

Chuck smiled at the easy fellowship among these new acquaintances. He'd only been around them for a few minutes but believed in his heart they were good people. They would take care of Patsy and Alicea.

Outside, he opened the trunk and eyed the minivan as it came around the corner. Maddie pulled her van up next to his car. She put it in park and left the motor running. She opened the door and jumped out to help grab their backpacks and load them into the van. This was a woman who got things done. She did not sit in her car waiting for the men to load it or for Patsy to get her own things. It's little actions that tell a lot about a person and their personality.

"Does that box go with them?" Maddie asked.

"No," said Chuck, and turned to face Bret, who had come outside with them. "Is there a place we can talk that's private? I need some advice and a witness."

Maddie was already back in the van. More hugs, goodbyes, and thank yous were exchanged between Officer Reynolds, Patsy, and Alicea. Then the doors closed, and Maddie pulled out of the parking lot, heading toward the home she and Bret shared that was only a few blocks away.

"What's up? How can I help?" Bret asked.

"I need to open this box and I need a witness. I'm not sure what's inside, but it's been in my trunk for a week, and I learned today that it's not what I thought it was. I need to find out what it is, who sent it to me, and what it means." Chuck was stammering out the words.

Bret listened without saying anything. But he was getting a strange sense that something was not right. His face showed his doubts.

"Listen. I sound like an idiot," Chuck said. "I'm not. I don't think it's a bomb or anything dangerous, but I need to open it with a witness, but only one, and only in private. Can we do that now?"

Years of training and combat duty, plus the tone from Maddie's mom when she had asked them for this favor, had Bret's radar and suspicions on high alert. He eyed the parking lot again. His phone was close and instinctively he'd keep it that way in case Maddie needed to reach him. All was quiet.

"Sure. Let's go to my office," he said.

Once inside the office, Chuck set the box on the desk and Bret locked the door. The small windowless room was packed with Veteran Benefits brochures, flyers about Burger Nights, miscellaneous items for coming events, a large Marine Corps recruiting poster, an outdated computer monitor, an old rotary dial phone, and several file folders. Mattis curled up under Bret's desk.

Bret handed Chuck a box cutter, noting that the Amazon box was addressed to Officer Chuck Reynolds, the Monterey County Sheriff's Department, at an address in Salinas. There was no return address. It wasn't one of the normal labels from Amazon.

Chuck sliced through layers of tape sealing the cardboard top and sides. He was slow to lift the flaps. What did he expect to find? In the back of his mind, thoughts of Sergio's missing money kept returning. Where did this package come from?

He raised the top and the two men looked inside.

"Holy shit," said Bret.

"Crap," said Reynolds.

"Where'd you get that and does someone want it back?"

"I don't know. It was mailed to me at work. I thought it was a holster I'd ordered. It's been in my trunk for a week."

"How could you have a package with that much money in it and not know it?"

Mattis stood up and stared warily at Officer Reynolds. Leaning into Bret, the dog felt his tension. Bret rubbed an ear and let the fingers of his left hand scratch the soft skin around Mattis's collar.

Bret's doubts were rapidly expanding. Were he and Maddie getting into something far more dangerous than getting some woman and her kid out of the country for safety from some ex-boyfriend as they'd been told? Mom had made it sound like they were helping. Now it seemed more like they were trafficking or smuggling. And all that money? Was this guy trying to bribe them? And telling him this bullshit story about needing a witness, but doing it in private? Bret's mind flew through a variety of scenarios. None of the them were good.

Bret stood very still. How to get out of this? Maddie was taking that woman and her kid, if it was even her kid, to their home. He no longer looked at Chuck with the face of a friend, but as if he were now facing the enemy.

"Shit. What kind of shit are you getting us into?" Bret asked with a look of complete distrust on his face. Officer Reynolds stared back at Bret.

"This is not what you think," Reynolds said slowly.

"You don't know what I think," Bret replied. "But you better have a good explanation and it better come fast."

BOOK II

TWENTY-FOUR

Chuck

This is a mess, thought Chuck. *I know this guy doesn't trust me. I wouldn't trust me if I were in his shoes.*

"This looks bad, I know. But I can explain. First, I need to know I can trust you. Second, is it safe to talk here? No one will come through that door or can hear us?"

Bret felt naked without his own little Smith and Wesson nine-millimeter tucked in his concealed carry holster. He'd put it in the drawer to his right, before he and Maddie went to prep the kitchen for the fundraiser dinner they'd host here later tonight. The early crowd would show up soon. Bill was always the first one to arrive once the doors were unlocked.

"Are you armed? Am I or my wife in danger? Because if you've been less than honest with us or with Maddie's mom, I promise you might not live to regret it."

Chuck knew the man across the desk from him was just as dangerous as he. Trained. Cunning. Deadly serious. They could both think and react like the trained military men they were. One Marine. One Army. Both on the same side, but at the moment Bret had the advantage of age and home turf. He asked Chuck to sit down. "Let's sit here and talk. I don't think either one of us should rush to judgement just yet. Full disclosure, I'm not armed, but it's loaded and in the drawer six inches from my right hand. And then, Mattis is here, too."

Chuck smiled. "I'm armed. Three firearms. One knife. You have nothing to fear from me, but we might all be in danger because of that package. I swear to you, I did not know what was in it, but earlier today I got a phone call and learned it was not what I had thought it was, and my suspicions began to grow. Right now, I think we need to take a breath and look in that box to see if there is anything other than money. A tracking device. A note. Anything."

Bret felt the adrenaline pumping through his body begin to subside. With a slight grin he told Chuck, "Look, I've never seen that much money at once in my life. I am not touching it. You shouldn't either, although your prints are probably all over the box already. Here, use these." Bret tossed him a thin box of latex gloves that had been sitting on the shelf behind him. "We use these in the kitchen and stuff always finds a way into my office."

Chuck put on a pair of gloves, snapping them into place after years of practice at crime scenes. "Should we take pictures?" Bret asked. "Or what?"

"Not yet. For now, you and I are the only ones who know about this. The guy who sent it to me is dead. At least I think I know who sent it. But again, I'm speculating. I need to see if there's a note."

"Okay," Bret said.

Chuck began to dig through the loose stacks of bills. Bret noted that most were one-hundred-dollar bills with a few stacks of fifties and twenties. Whatever the total, there was a lot of money in the box. A lot of money.

"There!" Bret saw it first. A small corner of white paper just visible toward the bottom.

Chuck eased his latex clad fingers under the money and used his thumb and forefinger to tug at the small piece of notepaper. It came free as he gently pulled it from its hiding place among the stacks and rolled wads of cash. There was no order to the bills in the box. It was as though someone just grabbed all this money and crammed as much into the box as could fit.

Chuck continued to rummage through the bills, looking for anything else that might be hidden under there.

"I don't see or feel anything else. Nothing like a tracking device or other object. We can't dump this out here. Do you have a safe somewhere?"

"First," Bret asked, "what's on the paper?"

It was a small sheet of lined paper torn from a spiral edged pad and folded twice. The frayed edges were messy. The paper itself was dingy, as though it had been folded and refolded several times by someone with dirty hands. Like old bills, it was worn. Chuck's first assessment was that this note had been with the money for a long time. He carefully unfolded the note so Bret could see.

It held a series of numbers, written with different pens and different colored ink. There were no dollar signs, but each number was at least four figures. One entry showed *240500*, and another was *180760*. The rest ranged from *5000* to *92300*. They were not listed in numerical order, nor were there any commas, decimal points, or dollar signs. They were put down randomly, not in neat columns. There were no dates or other notes to indicate the meaning of the numbers.

It was the four words across the top of the note that told Chuck what he needed to know. Bret read them and waited for Chuck to explain.

Todo por Patsy y mí bambino.

All for Patsy and my baby.

"He stole for them," Chuck said.

"So. You seem to know something now that you didn't know before. And now you are putting this woman and her kid with me and my wife. And we are supposed to take her and the kid to Mexico on a private jet?" It was a statement Bret posed as a question. "You need to tell me now how this is going play out. Are they really who you say they are? Because I'm not trafficking anyone or smuggling anything for anybody. Friend of Mom's or not. If I don't like your answers, this mission gets aborted, now."

Bret was more comfortable with this cop dressed like a cowboy, but he was still wary. "And this?" He pointed to the box of money. "This needs to get out of my office, now. We need to go. I have a hundred people showing up here in about thirty minutes and they will all want to talk to me if I'm here. Are you safe? Does anyone know you're here? Anyone tracking you?" Bret asked.

Chuck had been going over everything in his mind. The move. The box. The woman in Chowchilla. Had they tracked him? They didn't know about the money, or it would have just been taken from his car earlier. His car? Did they track his car? Of course they did. The letter to Patsy left in the mailbox? Did they know where she lived or did they only know the area, playing the odds and hoping they'd find her? Of course they did. Things were beginning to fall into place. His intense detective skills were finally working on this case that was way too close to home.

"My car. No. No one followed me. I'd bet anything there is tracking device on it. I've got to get out of here. Away from you. Now. You keep the money." Chuck was closing up the box. He put the note back in it. "Do you have any packing tape on that shelf back there?"

"Here," Bret said as he tossed the tape to Chuck. "But I need to help you get that car out of here. We'll take it to Pendleton. It'll be safe there. You'll be safe there. We'll go over it to see if there is a tracker on it. Then leave it on base. They can't get onto the base. We can protect you there," Bret said, but knew he was going to have to call in some favors immediately. He was engaging his mind in rapid-fire mission planning, something he hadn't done since his last tour of duty.

"Let's go, then. If you agree, we'll put the box in my car. Because if they're tracking you and heading this way, we might only have a short window to get to the base. It's close, but still, we should go now. I don't want your car here. If we're lucky, they might think you stopped at the barber shop next door."

Bret could feel the adrenaline pumping again. "I'll call Madeleine on the way. Is it possible there is tracker on the mom or kid? 'Cause that would suck."

"I don't think so. I gave Patsy the new passports in the car." Chuck was feeling the strain of having put these good people in harm's way. He was also very nervous about what might lie ahead. The Norteños were not nice adversaries. But this was Sureño territory in Southern California. No telling what might happen. And Chuck was holding a million reasons they were after him. They knew. They had to know.

TWENTY-FIVE

Bret

Maddie picked up the phone on the second ring. "Hey, babe. What's up? Dinner is almost ready. Home soon or staying at the Post for Burger Night?"

Bret considered himself a lucky man. Life hadn't always been as sweet as it was now. Not by any stretch of anyone's imagination. Looking back, which he did not do often, he knew a life of hardship and hard times. He was white. Very white. Middle of Michigan, blond hair, blue eyes, Germanic heritage white. But Bret was neither privileged nor upper-middle class growing up. His parents were hard working Midwesterners who eked out a living through cold winters and hot summers. They weren't farmers or well-educated. His dad took work where he could get it. He was skilled and often had steady work, but times changed and so did jobs. His mother raised the kids doing the best she could to cook a decent meal and keep a decent home with money that came in each month.

It's a myth that every white person is privileged. Just as it is not true that every Black person has been mistreated and is due recompense. Or that all Hispanics are part of a gang or that all Asians are intellectually superior. *What nonsense our world faces these days*, Bret thought as he adjusted his rear-view mirror to make sure the cop was following him onto base. No one gets into Camp Pendleton these days without prior clearance and a pass. Bret had to make sure the guards would let Chuck enter. He was no longer a Marine, but he was a civilian employee with a certain amount of status based on both his job and the fact that he had also served. His six combat tours in the Middle East afforded him a great deal of respect among his peers and especially with his subordinates.

"Is everything okay at home? No trouble?" he asked his wife.

"Everything is great. We're just talking. What's going on?" She was intuitive enough to know there had been a glitch in the plan.

"I'm heading to the base. Taking the San Luis Rey Gate. We'll be there in a few minutes. We have a problem. I'll tell you about it later. I should be home in a few hours. Don't worry. Know that I love you, and keep them safe. But stay on guard. No one comes through our door. You got that? No one."

"Copy," was all she said.

Maddie had also been a Marine. She knew full well that her husband meant exactly what he said. She clicked off the phone, did a quick double take that doors were locked, and turned to her guests. "I need to check something in the office. Be right back," she offered and slipped down the hall.

She was back in less than thirty seconds, her Glock 43X tucked neatly into the holster hidden under an unpretentious loose-fitting blouse.

"Looks like we're on our own for dinner. My hubster has more work to do tonight. Are you ready to eat?"

The two cars rolled up to the San Luis Rey Gate at Camp Pendleton. Bret addressed the young Marine on duty, reading his name tag, but knowing him personally as well.

"Hey, Sergeant Wilborn. I've got some work to finish up tonight, but I have another concern and need your help."

Every gate guard knows the warning signs. "I need your help" is code for "Hey, I got a problem and we might need to bend the rules."

Bret Collier was one stand-up guy. The best of the best. He didn't bend rules. Ever.

Wilborn took his flashlight and looked throughout Bret's car. "Any problem here, sir?"

"No. But I need to get the guy in the car behind me onto base. Now. There's a long story and I'm not going to bore you with it, but I need to get that car to Explosive Ordinance Disposal and make sure it's clean. I have not yet cleared this with anyone, because of the hour, but you can call it in. Say it's me and let's make sure we don't have a situation that could backfire back in town. I'll wait."

On the way to the gate, Bret had already called his senior officer and EOD. He left messages, but no calls had been returned. He knew a call from the gate would get priority. He waited.

Chuck sat in his car behind Bret and prayed another car did not pull up behind him. None did.

Wilborn disappeared into the guard shack. The wait seemed interminably long. When he reappeared, he showed Bret the pass he'd already prepared for the car behind him.

"Head straight to EOD, sir. They're expecting you and Officer Reynolds. You're in good hands tonight. Be safe. I'll let him in."

"Thank you, Sergeant Wilborn. Before I go, just a warning against any strangers trying to follow us in. No one. Stay alert," Bret said.

"Copy, sir."

Bret thanked him and eased through the gate. He kept an eye on his rear-view mirror and inched forward to watch as the guard stopped Officer Reynolds. While Reynolds was still talking to Wilborn, another set of headlights appeared. Wilborn handed Reynolds the pass and told him to drive safe. Halting the third car behind them. The two cars proceeded toward EOD. This night might be longer than Bret anticipated. He did not think for a moment there was a bomb on Chuck's car, but EOD would find a tracking device if one was present, and this was the safest place for Chuck if he were being followed.

Bret did not see the third car follow them onto base. He slowed. Waiting. Watching. Chuck followed. He, too, wondered why the car behind him was not coming into view. Had that car been turned away? Not someone authorized to enter? They continued along the road, Bret leading the way. With another look in the rear-view, Bret thought, *I'm glad I'm one of the good guys and have this whole team of good guys on our side.* And then, an unbidden thought intruded on his mind, *How much money is in that box? It's in my car now. How am I going to get it safely to that woman and her kid? And with them to wherever they are going? How am I going to protect this cop from the shit show following them? How do I keep my Maddie safe on this damn dangerous little adventure Mom set us on?*

Aloud and alone in the darkness of his vehicle Bret said, "Mom, I love you, but you and I are going to have a serious talk tomorrow," as if she were in the car and could hear him.

Blanca

"I can do this!" the little angel told herself. "This is what they mean by multi-tasking. I can watch over Patsy and Alicea and still keep track of Officer Chuck." She had help. Maddie was a descendant of Hannah's. Hannah would be watching over them, too.

Blanca still marveled at the strength of Hannah. She was a formidable Warrior Guardian Angel. She had lived through a difficult era on earth. The late 1600s in the raw and untamed land known as New England. Hannah and her family fell victim when the native people were coerced to raid English settlements. Hannah and her new baby were kidnapped, but miraculously her husband and other children escaped to a nearby garrison for protection. Many others were not so fortunate. In the days and weeks that followed the March 1697 uprising, the Puritans living in Haverhill, Massachusetts, found the bodies of twenty-six of their neighbors who were taken and had resisted the raiding Abenaki.

Among the remains were those of Hannah's baby, Martha. Her tiny skull fractured as she lay naked at the base of an apple tree. Her carcass already partially eaten by wild animals. Her family devastated by the grisly discovery, they prayed against hope for Hannah's return. Her body had not been found among the others killed along the trail north.

There was no sign of Hannah, nor the midwife who had been taken with her, Mary Neff. When her child cried out like the wee babe that she was, she was silenced. Hannah and Mary watched in horror as one after the other of their neighbors who tried to escape were swiftly and quietly executed and left where they fell. Hannah cautioned Mary to stay silent. They lived. They survived a long march north following the banks of the Merrimack River. When they reached a small settlement where the families of the raiding party waited for them to return, Hannah knew that any window to escape would soon close.

In an act some called frontier heroism and others called vigilantism, Hannah Duston killed and later scalped ten members of the Abenaki natives and escaped with her midwife, Mary Neff, and another captive, young Samuel Lennardson.

Hannah made her peace with God. She is said to have later regretted her actions, which had felt justified at the time. She begged the Lord for forgiveness and prayed daily for the souls of her victims, as well as her own. When her time on earth was over, she learned her true fate and was pressed into service as an angel, watching over her many descendants over the past three hundred plus years.

Blanca rode along in Chuck's car on the way to Camp Pendleton's Explosive Ordinance Disposal. The ladies were safe in Maddie's care. She was such a good mother and protector. Blanca loved Madeleine immediately.

"She will be an amazing guardian someday," she told Hannah.

"Yes, she will. But Blanca, focus on the task at hand, not the future."

Oh dear, thought Blanca. *I'm getting chastised and this mission is only just getting started.*

When the two cars reached the San Luis Rey gate at Camp Pendleton, Officer Reynolds waited as Bret cleared the way for him. Blanca waited, too.

When she saw the third car pull up behind them, she knew it was not good. Her wings itched. And suddenly she was joined in the back seat by Chax and Mara. They sat on either side of her.

"Dear Blanca, did you think your little sword trick would eliminate us forever?" Chax said.

"And here we are. Stronger than ever. Is he your new charge? That cop in the front seat? He is so very boring. We are making absolutely no headway with him. I suppose you will get to keep him. But we're still working on the girls. Oh, dear Sergio did love them so. And oh my Satan, you got Sergio, too!

We were amazed that Jeff was able to pull that off. We haven't seen him yet. Maybe he's still in training? But that little stinker is up there with y'all.

"So, darling Blanca, we just popped in for a brief hello. By the way. Spoiler alert. No bomb in this car, darn. No one wants to blow up the money. Chuck, yes. Money, no. But they were smart enough to put a tracking device here that your people will find. I suppose congratulations are in order for finding Bret and Maddie to help. We've had both of them on our radar for years, but they continue to elude us, too. Damn those who pray! Oh dear, we've shared too much information. But it's been such fun. Good night, Blanca. And good luck. You do know we intend to win these two. Patsy and the kid. Both of them." He laughed again.

"Au revoir, sweet one," Chax gagged on the word sweet. "We have a calling in Paris now. But you are close to our thoughts, and we wanted you to know we aren't about to let you win this one."

As quick as they came, they were gone. Blanca sat in the back seat as Chuck followed Bret to the EOD auto bay. The lights were on. He pulled up to see a half dozen people in bomb squad gear. All motioned for him to exit the vehicle. He did.

Bret and Mattis were at his side in a moment. "Come with me. Your car stays here."

TWENTY-SIX

Chuck

"Hey, I don't know if this means anything, but a car pulled up behind me at the gate, but never came onto base. Do you think someone was following us? Do you know if your wife and my girls are still okay?"

"I talked to Maddie on the way here and all was fine. She'll let me know if anything goes south," Bret told him, adding, "My boss is meeting us. You're going to have to trust me on this, because, with all that cash, you have a bigger problem than just getting that mother and daughter to safety. You get that, right?"

Chuck nodded in the gathering dusk. "I do. And I'm really sorry I got you involved in this, but I have to admit that, man to man, I'm thankful for your help. I could not have done this alone."

Bret sized up the taller officer next to him. Humble. *I'll give him points for that. Older. Maybe not as much combat experience, but he's been a homicide detective and gets points for that. Not something I'd ever want to do. I saw enough death in the War on Terror to last a lifetime, but none of that was as bad as what we witnessed in Rwanda, in 1994.* Bret needed to bring his thoughts back to the present. He knew the triggers, and this was one. If he went there, he'd see them again. The bodies. The maggots. He could never eat rice again.

Stop! He chastised his mind as PTSD threatened to send him back to that hellish nightmare. Outwardly, Bret just stood there with Chuck. He had not replied to Chuck's admission of being thankful for the help. Mattis leaned into his master's leg, as if to say, "I'm here. It's okay."

Chuck watched the other man intently. He was an expert at reading people. Something was going through his head. Chuck waited to see how this was all going to play out.

Bret finally inhaled a deep and ragged breath and let it out slowly. He reached down to rub the neck of his dog. Chuck smiled as he looked at the man and his dog. Mattis wore a service dog identification vest, with several military patches sewn onto it. They represented units Bret had served with and the dog's job helping Bret with his invisible disability. *My heart is with you, man*, he thought, but said nothing. They waited. Blanca stood by and watched. Silently waiting for a cue she was needed. Bret finally broke the silence.

"Listen up. You have a couple of choices here depending what they find in your vehicle. If nothing, it might be easiest for you to take the road out to the west side of the base, over by San Clemente, and head home from there. We'll give you an escort off base, but you're on your own after that. But what about the money? If you had not showed it to me, with the note, I wouldn't know a thing about it. You could take it all and go home and figure out what to do with the rest of your life. You'd have enough to start a new life. Right?"

"You know I can't do that. Don't you?" Chuck and Bret stared at each other.

"Yeah, I didn't think so," said Bret. "I guess you really are one of the good guys. But it's blood money anyway, isn't it? The guy who stole it is dead. He stole it from worse guys. And he wants it to go to the lady and kid. I think I have this right. So, what are we supposed to do about it?"

"That's the big question. Isn't it?" Chuck asked.

Bret answered, "Look, my boss will be here soon. We need to make a decision. Right now, that money is in my car. Not yours. Not something I want a bunch of EOD guys to know about. My boss is another matter. I trust her."

Bret rocked a bit from one foot to the other. Mattis sat and waited patiently. Chuck said, "Her? Okay. Talk to me. You got an idea?"

"I do. But I need you to cooperate one hundred percent and I need you to completely agree, or I want you to take the money and the escort and head back to wherever you came from," Bret told him.

Chuck took no time to think about it. "Whatever you suggest about the money, I agree. It's not my money. I don't want it. But if it will help her get settled with a new life someplace where they can't touch her, please do what you think is best."

At that moment a tan military Humvee arrived from the opposite direction and came to a stop next to Bret and Chuck. A tall Marine in a camouflage uniform got out of the passenger seat. Bret was no longer an active-duty Marine. He was a federal employee working for the Department of Defense.

"Ma'am. Thanks for meeting me at this late hour. Colonel Phyllis Willis, I'd like you to meet Officer Chuck Reynolds of the Monterey County Sheriff's Department. Homicide."

Turning to Chuck, Bret asked, "Did I get that right? Are you addressed as Officer or Detective?"

"Either is fine. I prefer Chuck," he said, reaching out his right hand to greet the senior military officer, who happened to be African American. Chuck could see the full bird emblem on her collar. Her face remained stoic. Formidable features. Tall. Dark. Mid-fifties. Beautiful.

"Officer Reynolds. Chuck." Willis nodded an acknowledgement. Courteous, but cautious, thought Chuck.

"They are still going through your vehicle over there. No bomb, but they did find a tracking device that was active."

Chuck wondered how she knew that already, when Chuck and Bret had been watching from outside the bay doors and were told nothing. The look on his face must have given away his curiosity. Willis smiled and said simply, "They keep me informed."

"Talk to me, Collier. What's this about and what do you need from me?"

"Ma'am. We have a situation here. It's beyond my pay grade. We don't seem to have an acceptable response, but I do have an idea if you can help. We'll need to go somewhere else to talk. I need to get something out of my car and maybe we need the SCIF?"

"Hmm. You did sound serious on the phone. Let's take the Humvee. Leave your vehicles. My driver is cleared. Get the gear you need and let's go. We have about a twenty-minute drive to the SCIF."

The SCIF. A sensitive compartmented information facility, commonly pronounced "skiff," is a term for a secure room or area to discuss, process, or store sensitive information. Whatever Bret Collier had stumbled onto, Colonel Willis was a trusted leader and Bret had come to rely on her as one of the good guys. Dependable. Trustworthy. A leader who cared more about Marines than a paycheck.

Bret grabbed the box he'd had Chuck drop into the back of his SUV. He was no longer worried about his fingerprints being on the box. He was in this stink hole up to his eyeballs. If it all backfired, so be it. He knew in his heart of hearts that he was guilty of nothing other than trying to help out the friend, make that a former friend, of his mother-in-law.

Colonel Willis eyed the box. "We can't take anything into the SCIF. Certainly not that box. What's in it?"

"This is what we need to talk about, ma'am," Bret said.

"Then let's go to the NCIS office instead of the SCIF. We'll still have privacy," offered Willis.

They rode in the Humvee with minimal conversation. The driver kept his eyes on the road, only clarifying direction with Colonel Willis as to their destination. The sergeant didn't need to ask if he should wait for them when they went inside. He would stay with the vehicle and wait until the colonel dismissed him. Even if that took all night.

After passing through several guarded checkpoints, depositing their cell phones and weapons in a locked box, they entered a narrow conference room with a long table surrounded by several chairs. The colonel tossed her cover on the center of the table, grabbed one of the swivel chairs, and sprawled her lanky frame against the padded backrest. "Sergeant!" she called to the guard posted on the other side of the soundproof door.

When the sergeant didn't answer, Willis laughed at her own mistake. "Guess I should have asked for that cup of coffee before we came in here."

"You're packing quite the arsenal there, Officer. You think you need that much fire power for this operation? Talk to me. What's in the box and what the hell is going on?" Willis looked from Bret to Chuck and back again. "Bret, maybe you should start?"

"Yes, ma'am. But he might have to fill in the blanks."

"Okay, fine. Start with why there is a civilian car on my base with a tracking device on it, which we destroyed by the way, but whoever was on the other side of that tracker will likely know where it stopped working. It's a pretty sophisticated piece."

Chuck chimed in; this was, after all, a problem he created. "Ma'am, if I might, I believe the tracker was put on my car in an effort to find that box and what it contains."

"And who do you think wants to track you and that box?" Willis asked.

"The Nuestra Familia."

"That's interesting. You know this is Sureño territory around here? Those two gangs have kept the peace by staying apart from each other. The last thing anyone wants or needs is a turf war. We may be up to our necks in military warfare training, but we read the news. We know what's going on outside these gates."

Her eyes went to the box. "What's in there?"

Bret answered, "We opened it together this afternoon. There's money in there, ma'am. A lot of money."

Willis looked at Chuck. "And you didn't know there was money in that box before today? Where'd you get it?"

Chuck looked down and had the good sense to let Willis see his sheepish expression. "Ma'am, it was addressed to me at the station. No return address on the label. I had ordered a shoulder holster. It was in an Amazon box. I thought it was the holster and threw it in my trunk. Then this morning I got a call from someone at the Department that another package had arrived for me from Amazon. I had a friend open it and he told me it was the holster. That's when I started wondering what I'd find in the box in my trunk." Chuck looked up to see if Willis was still listening. She was.

"You see, ma'am," giving Willis the respect her rank earned, "a Norteño soldier called Sergio had been on my radar for years, but we could never catch him for anything. About seven years ago, a young woman worked with us to see if we could get a conviction after he threatened her. We never got enough evidence. But her talking like she did put her life in more danger. She wasn't qualified for WITSEC, but we helped her find a job and hide out in a fairly remote location. She was pregnant at the time, and we left her at a women's shelter until she had the baby. A girl. Then we moved her to the new location and thought she was safe."

"Go on." Willis was intrigued by the story. She had no plans for this Monday night, and it was poker night for her husband and his friends.

"Everything was going well until a couple of weeks ago. We aren't sure how they found her, but they did. No one had any idea about this box or the money. But we tried to move her to a safe location. In the meantime, I moved her and her kid to my house, and thank God I sent my wife away and had a female cop stay with her." Chuck swallowed hard and scraped his boots across the polished floor.

"They shot up my house that night. Neither the female cop nor the lady or her kid were hurt, but my house is a mess. The Norteños left a calling card. The body of this Sergio guy was left at the scene. Forensics determined he'd been killed elsewhere and dumped at my house. My business card was in his pocket." Chuck told her as Bret listened intently. He was hearing most of this for the first time.

"With help from friends, I got her to another safe house. We got fake passports for her and the kid and now I'm trying to get them out of the country." He nodded toward Bret and continued. "I knew Maddie's mother from years ago and she offered to help. That's how we got down here. But the box has been in my car for about ten days. I wanted to work this case because it was my house that got shot up. I felt personally attacked. As you can imagine, my boss said I was too close to the case and wanted me to take vacation time. I did. So, I am in no official capacity at this moment." Chuck was trying to get all the facts out in the shortest version possible.

"Meanwhile, one of the guys working the case told me there was a rumor that Sergio had stolen a million dollars from the NF, and they want it back. That's why he was executed. Double tap to the back of the head. Now they are scrambling to find the money."

"Wait. Is the money in that box?" Willis asked, following the story with rapt attention even as she wondered how the Corps could possibly help. But she knew they could. Bret was right to trust her with this. Nothing but trouble would come if they tried to do anything else with that much cash.

"You want to open it?" Willis asked.

"Bret, you said you had an idea. What are you thinking?" Willis was glad they'd gone to the NCIS conference room. She was glad she could help. Not once did she consider this might garner a bit of extra cash for herself. Not once.

Bret had listened as Chuck gave his explanation. He now understood more of the situation and felt himself begin to relax. Mattis lay at his feet, comforting the anxiety that sprang from post-traumatic stress and the violence of war. Just thinking about this man having his house shot up caused an uptick in his heartrate. That woman was now at his house. With his wife. Would they be safe if these jerks found their way to them? His thoughts moved over possible scenarios and his heartrate increased again. He turned to Colonel Willis.

"Yes, ma'am. I think we should entrust this to your care. Have it counted and somehow entered into the system as illegal drug money that rightly belongs to one Patsy Garcia and her daughter, Alicea. But they'll have new names by tomorrow. Maddie and I plan to meet a private plane at the airport in Fallbrook and fly with them to Puerto Vallarta, Mexico. That's why I'd asked for vacation time. We'll stay at a resort that Maddie's mom has and then put them on a commercial flight, with the new passports, and send them to a place called Ibiza. This is a plan Maddie's mom came up with because she has friends in those places. Ma'am, I never even heard of Ibiza before, but it's somewhere in the Mediterranean. We didn't know anything about the money and neither did Maddie's mother."

Willis sat up with long fingers and manicured nails steepled in front of her face, chin resting on her thumbs. She contemplated Bret's plan when the younger man added, "Once she is safe, I hope this money can be delivered to her. I don't know the logistics on currency exchange or anything else, but I know it can't go in a bank and there are all kinds of other rules. We need to act fast, ma'am. Can you help? Can you think of anything else we can do?"

Colonel Willis pondered the situation and stared intently at the box on the table.

"Reynolds, where do you go from here? Do you have anything to add to this story? Are you dumping all this on Collier and walking away? The money? The woman and her kid? Are you planning to stay and see this through or go?"

Chuck had seen his role as over once he delivered Patsy and Alicea to Fallbrook. The money changed that. Now he wasn't sure what his obligation should be or why. He didn't want to put these people in danger, but he felt he'd already done that.

He answered honestly. "Ma'am, I don't have a plan any longer. I'd planned to leave, but I will do everything I can to see this woman and her kid get to safety and get their money. I don't want to be the cause of greater danger to them, or anyone else." He looked pointedly at Bret.

Willis considered his answer carefully.

"Question for you, Chuck. Are you speculating based on the word of a questionable informant that this money was actually stolen from the cartel by this Sergio?"

"Yes. But not from a cartel. The Norteños grew up in California. From what we know, they started as a prison gang with ties to illegal immigrants. I believe most of those who started the Sureño gang in Southern California, were born in Mexico, but the Norteños were nearly all born here in California. And back to the point, yes, I believe the NF soldiers have orders to get the money back. In fact, I was worried when we pulled up to the gate and a car tried to follow us in. The guards must have turned them away because we never saw that car again."

"Hah! I'd like to see them try to get it back from the United States Marine Corps. I'll check with the gate." Willis stepped out of the conference room and barked an order to a sergeant on duty at the front desk.

"Sergeant, get me a boxcutter, two fresh boxes of rubber bands, a notepad, three pens, a calculator, and bring me two secure metal cases. I want the ones that are slightly larger than a briefcase, but not full carry-on size. And bring me a cup of coffee. Also, let my driver know we'll be here at least another hour, if he wants to get something to eat."

"Copy that, ma'am."

Within a few minutes, Willis had the requested items. Bret used the secure base telephone line to check in with Maddie. All was well at the house, and all was well at the VFW Post. Burger Night was in full swing, and everyone was having a good time. No trouble there tonight. There was nothing going on that was out of the ordinary. Bret wasn't sure what Willis had in mind, but it seemed obvious that she'd made up her mind about something.

TWENTY-SEVEN

Blanca

"Hannah, thank you for holding everything together with Patsy and Alicea. Is Maddie handling this situation well? Her husband is up to his neck in surprises but I think all is well here. I had another visit from Chax and Mara. What is it with those demons?"

Blanca went on with several questions for Hannah but gave no time to hear her answers.

"Slow down, little angel! Everything is fine here. Those two were just harassing you. I heard what you did back at the restaurant. Congratulations! We all believe in you and we're here for back up if you need us. Anytime."

"Thank you," she answered demurely as she realized how excited she must sound.

"I think they might be making a new plan," Blanca said.

"Anything can happen. Just do your best to keep them safe. Help them make the best decisions possible. You'll know." Hannah smiled and told her to get back to the conference room and keep her eyes and ears open.

Blanca watched as the trio sorted and counted the money in the box. They gave Colonel Willis the note and searched for anything other than United States currency. Nothing else was there. Once they finished sorting, they began to count. They grouped the bills into stacks of hundreds, fifties, twenties, and so on. There were far more one-hundred-dollar bills than anything else. Bret and Chuck called out numbers. Colonel Willis kept track on the yellow legal pad. She used the calculator to make the final tallies. They worked together, and even as they worked quickly, it was not a fast process. There was that much money. Blanca knew that while these were honest people, each was curious about the final tally. How much was there? The informant had said about a million were missing. How did Sergio do it? they wondered.

Bret thought of what this money could do to help the VFW Post. They were always hosting fundraisers and doing everything they could to keep the post solvent. He made a decent living, but he and Maddie weren't wealthy. They had not been able to purchase a home in Fallbrook but were thankful for the lovely home they rented. *It's not our money*, he thought. But as they counted, he wondered about the kind of difference that much money could make in a person's life. A big difference, he thought.

Colonel Willis purposefully kept herself from thinking about the power of that kind of money. People do incredibly stupid things when it comes to money. Most servicemen and women never have enough. Their wages are not the worst, but they are certainly not extravagant for putting their lives on the line. She kept track of the numbers, could not find a correlation between the odd stacks and rolls and the numbers on Sergio's piece of paper. None of them matched up. They started from scratch and kept counting.

An hour later, Willis said, "I need to take a break. Anybody else?"

"This is taking longer than I thought," Chuck said. "And I seriously need to wash my hands."

"There's a head through that door," Willis said, indicating a door in the wall opposite the entrance. There are also some vending machines at the end of the hall outside to the left. I'd guess this is going to take several more hours, but we ought to get it done as fast as possible. You two have certainly stirred up my night in a way I never could have imagined." She chuckled. "I've been thinking about your transportation problems. We might be able to do something about that, too. We might be able to make this whole thing a lot easier. But I'll need to bring in the big brass for clearance. We used to be able to do a lot more with a lot less. But everything is about being transparent these days. Although covert ops still has options. I need permission and a budget." She eyed the money stacked on the table. "And unfortunately, I need to account for where we got the money.

"Put the money already counted in the first case. We're at $450,000. Just glancing, with some of the smaller bills there, I'd say your informant was close to right. Probably right around a million. Let's take a break, I need to walk around. My joints get stiff. Use the head. Grab something to drink."

Willis went on, "I'm guesstimating we'll work for another hour or two at the most and call it a night. I'm still working out logistics in my head. Need to make a couple of calls before it gets any later.

"This room stays locked. My orders. Nothing is touched until we return," Willis told the sergeant on duty. They collected cellphones from the lockers but left their weapons.

Willis glanced at the black watch on her wrist. "Back here in twenty."

Chuck and Bret nodded in agreement and said in unison, "Yes, ma'am."

Blanca watched them file out and eyed the guard as he closed and locked the door behind them without looking inside.

As Colonel Willis strode out the door, Bret turned to Chuck. "I'm calling Maddie again. There are a few offices here we can use and have privacy if you want to call your wife or whatever. The vending machines are down that way," he said, pointing toward the end of another hall.

Bret knocked on one of the unguarded doors and stepped inside and Mattis followed him in. Chuck was hungry. It had been a long time since breakfast in Chowchilla, but he needed to wash up. He stopped at the men's room and checked his phone for missed messages. He'd call Maria in a few minutes and let her know the current situation. He was at last comfortable that he wasn't being spied on.

Blanca also felt the tension drain from her shoulders. There was something rewarding about watching these humble and honorable humans in action. They were each trying to do the right thing for Patsy and Alicea. They were a woman and child they barely knew but were willing to help. Even Chuck was not considered a close friend. Patsy was fortunate to have these three in her corner. And Maddie, too. Blanca remembered Liz Davidson Miller, from her early days of training with Hannah. Maddie's mother. She was a strong woman. She'd gone out of her way to enlist the help of Maddie and Bret to help her old friend Chuck, to help Patsy and Alicea. She'd offered to pay, too. Not that she was wealthy, but she had some assets and was willing to use them to help. Blanca liked that she had wanted to first discuss it with her husband, Miles. Even though Miles was already diagnosed with dementia, and Blanca knew the road ahead would not be easy for Liz, she admired her spirit and positive attitude.

Bret called Maddie and filled her in on the latest details, letting her know he'd be later than expected, but that they might not be flying to Mexico after all. Possible change in plans he told her. "Willis is looking at ways to help. We'll talk about it when I get home. Nothing definite, yet."

"Just keep me posted and let me know what I should do. So far, all is quiet here. Monday night is good for quiet. So much better than Fridays."

"It's still early," Bret said.

"True, but our neighbors aren't out front yet with the usual bonfire and grill already going. The mariachi music isn't cranked up. It's actually a quiet Monday night in the hood." She laughed. They'd lived in Fallbrook for a few years and were accustomed to the usual weekend festive gatherings of their Hispanic neighbors.

"I'm glad we are blessed with good neighbors, even if they get a little loud on the weekends. They're always out front, and if there are strangers around, they will notice. I'll leave the light on and see you when I see you. Love you."

Across the hall in another office, Chuck called Maria. "Hey, hon. How you doing? How's your mom?"

"Well, my love, I'm much better now that I hear your voice. We are fine. How about you? Patsy? Alicea? Are you all safe? No trouble? All went well? And are you heading back tonight or." She paused. "When?"

"First, we are all safe. That's most important. I'm actually at Camp Pendleton, Marine Corps base, right now, in Southern California. We've got some work to do here tonight. I like Liz Davidson's daughter and son-in-law. They're good people. But like I said, we've got some work to do tonight, and then I'm going to get a few hours of sleep and I should be on the road early tomorrow. I'll be there tomorrow night. Have you been staying alert? No strange activity? Nothing out of the ordinary?"

She heard the concern in his voice. "No. Nothing." She waited. If he wanted to say more, he would. After a long pause when neither spoke, she said, "Chuck, I'm scared. I don't want to lose you." She wasn't whining. She wasn't crying. She was, matter of fact, telling him what she wanted in life. She wanted him. Alive. Whole. Healthy. With her.

"I know," he said. "We'll talk when I get home. I've been thinking a lot lately. I love you, Maria. Now don't get too excited, but it's probably time for me to think more seriously about hanging up my spurs. We'll talk later. But in the meantime, the thought is crossing my mind that if I'm going to retire, we need to move far away from Salinas. Have you checked out any places?"

"But the ranch?" she asked, "How can we leave?"

"My sister is still there. We can fix up the house and rent it out. Rent out the whole of it. Since we inherited it, and there is no debt, we could probably borrow enough to go wherever we want. Wherever you want."

"Chuck. What are you saying?" She knew his voice. His subtleties. This was new and not just talk like the other day. He was seriously thinking about retirement. Soon. Her intuition told her what he wouldn't: Something had happened. Something scared him. Something more than just getting their home shot up. As if that wasn't bad enough, she thought.

He lightened the moment with a laugh. "Hey, I'm just saying that if you have some free time, you and your mother might want to think about places you want to live. Faraway places."

"Seems like we had this conversation recently," she said.

"Or was that a dream I had?" She didn't know where this conversation was going, but she'd keep him on the phone for as long as possible.

"Too much on my mind, love. We'll talk tomorrow night. I promise. I gotta go," he said. "I love you, Maria."

"I love you, too, Chuck."

She said a silent prayer and looked heavenward with a smile. "Yes. You come home. We'll talk," is what she said.

Both Chuck and Bret finished up their conversations and stopped at the vending machines. Bret put in some bills and pulled out two bags of sea salt and vinegar chips, then grabbed two cans of Mountain Dew from the soda machine. Chuck settled on a stale roast beef sandwich on white bread and a Diet Pepsi.

Bret took Mattis outside to relieve himself, which gave him time to stretch his four legs, too. Back inside Bret joined Chuck at a small table in the central area of the building, Mattis curled up on the floor next to Bret, and they waited for Colonel Willis to return. It had been seventeen minutes since she walked out the door. It was three minutes before nine at night on Monday evening. It had been ten days since Chuck's trip to Paso Robles to pick up Patsy and Alicea. It had only been two days since Bret first heard the name Chuck Reynolds. A lot had happened in the ten days and a lot more in the last twenty-four hours.

The men sat in silence. Two veterans now back on a military base; they trusted their instincts and training and relied once more on the brotherhood of servicemen and women to help in a time of crisis. Bret wondered, not for the first time, if his mother-in-law had stopped to think about what she was really asking. If she knew the depth of where this little operation might lead. He wanted to help. He really did. But he also needed to be out of this environment. The intensity of this drama brought back too many bad memories. Mattis sat at his feet and felt Bret's tension. He raised his large chocolate-colored head and put it in Bret's lap, as if to say again, "No worries, Dad, I'm here."

"I'm here, too," Blanca whispered.

A minute later the exterior door buzzed open, and Colonel Willis strode inside. Bret marveled once more that his boss never just walked anywhere, her long legs stretched out before her in a fast pace with purpose. She never looked like she was marching but moved with a gliding stride and erect posture. Always. *She has the walk of a leader*, Bret thought. *She gets things done, too.*

Blanca entered the conference room in the NCIS building with others and perched on the back of one of the chairs. She waited to see if there was more news from Willis. She already knew the minds of Bret and Chuck had been with their wives. Both were concerned about how and where this adventure was going.

They each returned to the same seats they'd occupied earlier. Colonel Phyllis Willis spoke first.

"First of all, Bret, you're a civilian. I can't stop you from going to Mexico. I can deny your personal time off, now that I'm aware of why you're taking time off work and what you're planning to do. But I'm not going to do that. This is your decision and, quite frankly, I'm proud of you for trying to help."

"You!" she said and pointed to Chuck. "Are a loose cannon. Someone tracked you to *my* base and you come here with a million dollars or so in unmarked bills and want our help to get this money and these women, who now apparently have false passports, out of the country. You, an upstanding, law enforcement officer, have the *cojones* to ask for help in an illegal criminal activity. I think I have that right. Don't I?"

The look she gave Chuck was decidedly accusatory. Bret kept a neutral face. Chuck looked directly at Willis. "Yes, ma'am. I'd say that's the gist of it."

"And this is because...?" Willis drew out the word because and droned on cauuuse.

"Because a woman and her kid are in danger. If I do nothing, they are facing certain death, dismemberment, rape, trafficking, and or any other horrible fate you can think of. They did nothing wrong, but they will be blamed for stealing a million dollars of drug money, turning Sergio Sanchez against the NF, and they will be used to set an example. I've seen this all too often."

"And so, you are the knight in shining armor? Rescue the damsel? Save the day? Take home a million dollars for your effort? Is that your plan?" Willis asked.

It took every ounce of restraint for Chuck not to respond to the bait Willis was dropping. Why was she doing this? Chuck wondered.

"Nothing else to say?" Willis asked, as Bret watched and also wondered what Willis was up to. He wondered what Willis had discovered in those twenty minutes they were apart.

"Ma'am, begging your pardon, but I don't know what else to say or what it is you hope to hear. I told you I didn't know about the money until today. I did my best to not hide it, but to find a way to get it to the rightful owner. I do not believe it should be returned to the NF, to be used to purchase more drugs and send more people to early graves," Chuck said.

His face now had a deep red undertone. It was a hint to his half-Cherokee mother and an indication that he might also be dealing with high blood pressure. He'd been under a lot of stress, so that wasn't surprising, thought Willis.

"Officer Reynolds, you're here. Your car has been cleared of the tracking device and it was destroyed. There is no bomb planted on your vehicle." She turned to Bret. "Or yours. We checked it thoroughly just to be sure.

"Officer Reynolds, do you trust us?" she asked the cop.

"What?" Chuck was taken aback for a moment by this change of subject and the Colonel's tone. But he shouldn't have been, he thought, this was Interrogation 101. Start talking down one line of questioning and switch gears mid-stream.

"Yes, yes, I trust you. But really, I don't have a choice, do I? These people shot up my house. They think I have something to do with this, and apparently, I do. I was just trying to protect the woman and her kid. Now, I want to do that, and still protect my own wife and family and, frankly, myself." He looked up at Willis with eyes that told of his willingness to turn this entire situation over to someone else.

"I've always been the strong one. Able to figure it out. Fight the bad guy and win. I get to know them here." He tapped the side of his head. "But now? Honestly, ma'am, I would like nothing better than to know I left Patsy and her kid and all that money in good hands who will do the right thing by her, and I want to go home to my wife.

"Yes, I trust you. I don't have a choice," Reynolds added.

"We all have choices," Willis said.

Bret had remained silent. Blanca watched and listened and was elated. She knew Chuck was making the right decision. He did have a choice. He actually had several choices. But his choice to let someone else take over was the best one in this situation.

"Listen up," Willis addressed them both. "We're going to keep at this task until eleven. All the money is going in these two cases. Whatever is left uncounted at that time, we'll bundle together and put in a third case." She turned to Reynolds. "At eleven, you will be driven to your vehicle, and you will be escorted off base using the San Onofre entrance. Go get some rest. Go home. You aren't being read into the rest of this operation for your own good. I suggest you retire. Get the hell out of Salinas, and away from the gangs and La Familia. You are not going to be the Lone Ranger and stop these people without assistance. Understood?"

Chuck stared at Colonel Willis. "But you want me to stay and count money for two hours? Why don't I just leave now? Why give them time to get someone to the other gate? Or is there another reason for the delay?"

There was, but Willis wasn't about to share that bit of information with Reynolds.

Blanca watched and waited. There was a lot of posturing in the room. Only Mattis, the dog, seemed calm since they'd returned. Bret was feeling the angst of PTSD and regretted that he'd ever agreed to get involved. *It's a good thing I really love Maddie and her mother*, he thought. Liz Davidson Miller had certainly stirred up a lot of drama.

Willis said, "I don't want to bring anyone else in here with this money and I want to get as much done as we can before you go. Do you have a place to get some sleep? There are a few berths for emergencies at the other end of the hall. You can catch some sleep there, if you want to wait until morning to leave."

Chuck thought about the offer and agreed he'd work until eleven and take the room to crash. He'd leave early in the morning and still get home before dark. He asked Willis if he needed to get his car tonight or if someone could bring it to this building in the morning. He wanted to leave early.

"I'll have it here by five in the morning. Does that work for you?" Willis was happy for the extra time.

"Sure. And you promise me you'll take care of Patsy and Alicea, and they will get this money, or at least most of it?" Chuck was feeling a sense of walking out on the woman and her daughter. He didn't like that feeling. He needed to assure himself he was leaving her in safe hands and not turning her from one bad situation to another.

"Absolutely." Willis had a plan.

Blanca smiled. The Colonel had a good plan.

They continued to count the money without any further conversation.

Willis made another notation on the notepad and checked her watch.

"Let's stop. It's ten minutes to eleven and we're at $980,000. Judging from the bills left, there is more than a million here."

She'd already ordered a third case that was delivered earlier. They stood and stretched. Willis stepped out and called to the sergeant at the desk.

"Ma'am?"

"Anyone else in the building?" Willis asked.

"Ma'am. Yes, ma'am. Three sergeants in the break room and your driver. All ready for duty within five minutes, ma'am."

"Good. Tell my driver to be on standby in ten. Get an escort to take Officer Reynolds here to a private berth and get him anything he needs. His car will be delivered here later tonight. He'll need a zero four thirty wake up and he needs an escort off base via San Onofre at five. Understood?"

"Ma'am. Yes, ma'am. Anything else?"

"Yes. Collier and I need this room for a few more minutes, but I want two more escorts to report here ASAP. That's all."

Chuck stood and realized he was being dismissed, but they weren't all leaving together. He turned to Bret and stuck out his hand to shake. "Thank you. And thank your wife and Liz. I don't know what I'd have done without you."

Bret put his knuckles forward for a fist bump rather than a handshake as had become the greeting in the wake of COVID-19. Chuck realized he was not being snubbed. This was the new norm in America. Handshakes replaced by fist bumps. He fleetingly wondered if a man's word was still considered his bond with a fist bump.

Willis told Officer Reynolds to sleep well and that he'd get a wake-up call at zero four thirty. His car would be ready as would his escort off base.

Chuck wondered briefly if Willis thought he couldn't hear the directives she'd just given the guard.

"Got it. Thank you, ma'am, for your help. Take care of them. Please."

"No worries, Officer. They are safe and will continue to be safe, and the less you know, the better. I wish you safe travels. Here is my card. There is a number on it. If you have any trouble or blow back from all of this, call this number and use the reference code La Niña. Got it?"

Chuck looked down at the card. It was a normal-looking business card with the name Colonel Phyllis Willis. He wondered how many jokes she'd heard about her name.

"Thank you again. Ma'am. For everything," he said.

Another staff sergeant appeared and asked if Reynolds was ready.

"Right this way, sir," he said, and led Reynolds toward the far end of hall.

Willis closed the door, telling the guard, "We're almost done here."

She turned to Bret. "How you holding up, Collier? You okay? Mattis?"

"Yes, ma'am. We're fine. I'm sorry I got you all involved in this, but I'm thankful for the help. I truly thought this was some simple little thing of helping get a woman away from an ex-boyfriend with ties to a gang, until Reynolds showed up with that money. Then I didn't know what to do. Calling you was my best option, but I hate that I laid this on you."

"Collier, I hope you will always call me when you face a dilemma. That's what we're here for. My God, I may have more years as an officer and leader in the Corps, but you're the one who paid the dues and took the shots and put your life on the line more times than I can count. Do not think for a moment that I don't know exactly what is in your service record.

"It's men and women like you that make this old woman happy to still serve. And for the record, I may be your boss, but I am well aware of who knows far more than me about our department. I don't want to lose you under my command. Got that?"

"Thank you, ma'am."

"Which means, I really do not want you in harm's way, or in Mexico, or moving around with a bunch of cash and a woman and kid with fake IDs. Capeesh?"

Blanca sat on the edge of her seat, listening. She could not believe it was all working out so well. Patsy and Alicea now had the backing of the United States Marine Corps to help. She was feeling a sense of accomplishment in a job well done, when she was suddenly and immediately caught up in the web of her own making.

She was there. But she didn't orchestrate any of this. She was not responsible for getting the girls to Fallbrook, for getting the help of the Marines, for putting Chuck or the other cops at risk or for whatever was coming next. She had protected them in the closet. She had pushed the demons away and protected them at the restaurant, but mostly, she was there for emotional support and to help guide their thoughts and actions. There was a power much higher than hers at work here. It was a brief moment in time, but Blanca recognized the lesson being taught. There was no room for pride in her thoughts and actions. She was working as ordered by God.

It's okay to get excited when you are happy.

"I understand, ma'am. But I now have an obligation to Officer Reynolds, my mother-in-law, and most especially to this woman and her child. I gave them my word. Do you have another plan? Something you didn't want to tell Reynolds?"

"I do. Sit down, Collier. I'll give you the gist of it. All verbal. And if you agree, we'll take care of paperwork tomorrow and this woman will be on her way to safety on Wednesday. Thursday at the latest. If you don't agree, I'll grant your leave time, you will take that money with you, and you can do this on your own."

"I'm listening."

Blanca was listening, too. Would Bret agree to let others help? Or would he be stubborn as was often the case with men and insist he do it on his own? This was a dilemma faced by many guardians. These humans have free will. Blanca waited and prayed.

"It's unofficial pending your agreement. You have the deciding vote whether we go ahead with a joint agency top-secret operation. They want your decision by first thing tomorrow. As of this moment, there are no documents, emails, or texts. But there is verbal agreement between the brass on all sides that we open an official joint agency task force and highly classified operation. Eyes only. Need-to-know only. The ultimate goal of the operation is two-fold. Are you with me so far?"

Bret repeated himself, "I'm listening."

"We'll work with DOJ, FBI, DEA, and the Corps. All are on board, if you are."

"Why me? What about Reynolds?"

"You. Your combat skills. Your intuition. Mattis. And Maddie."

Bret let that last bit sit on his brain for a few seconds. "Maddie and Mattis?" he asked.

"I don't get it. What are you getting at, ma'am? Just tell me. I'm tired and I want to go home."

"Collier, my first thought was to reinstate both you and Maddie back in the Corps for this operation, but on reflection and discussion with others, that's not feasible. Now, I'd like to loan you to the DEA, but you will still report directly to me. I will lead Operation La Niña. We want to get this mother and her kid safely out of the country and preferably somewhere far away. But we'd also like to know who is coming after that money and if there is any way we can use it to draw out some of the big players from the NF."

"Do you plan to use them as bait?" Bret asked. "And me? My wife? My dog?"

"We think we can help you with this," said Willis.

"Excuse me, Colonel, but how? How do you see this going down?"

Bret stood up again. He didn't like where the Colonel was taking this conversation. He began to pace. Mattis was with him step for step.

Blanca watched. She had thought this was all very good. The Marines to the rescue, but now she was having doubts herself.

"Oh Lord, what is your plan? What are they to do? What am I to do? Please, please guide me," Blanca prayed.

"Look, Collier. You called this in. You asked EOD to check a civilian vehicle for a bomb. No bomb, but a sophisticated tracking device was attached. You bring in a law enforcement officer, who checked out, but you also bring in more than a million dollars in unmarked bills and ask for my help. In turn, I went up the chain of command. Help is out there, but they want something in return, too. They want a link to the drugs coming out of Mexico. Or at least to those operating in California, and they want their counterparts around the world. A million is probably just a pittance to them, but they want it back and that cop down the hall who seems to be their only lead to that girl, who is apparently the legitimate heir to this stolen money, unless it goes back to its rightful owners, and no one wants that, or to the United States Government. Not sure why the feds should get it, but there you have it."

"Ma'am. With all due respect, I was asked to help out this woman and her kid. We didn't know a thing about the money until tonight. I said that before. I'm saying it again. And that girl doesn't know a thing about the money. So, you tell me what is right? I risk my life, my wife, my dog." He glanced at Mattis. "And the life of that woman and kid that are sleeping at my house right now, so DEA might be able to bust a few middling gangbangers and you get a feather in your cap on your way to a star on your collar?"

Bret knew he was being insubordinate. But he was a still a civilian as long as Willis didn't decide to reinstate him. This had not gone as well as he'd hoped. He felt betrayed by his boss. He'd admired Willis. She was an easy woman to work for, a good woman, and was known for her no-nonsense, but affable leadership style. Bret liked and trusted her. But now? Now he was questioning her motives. Just as he had questioned the situation when he first met Chuck and they opened the box of money together.

"Careful, Collier," Willis said.

"Ma'am, I came to you for help. You offered it. I appreciate that. You know all the particulars on my end. I'm trusting the word of that cop and you. I've got a lot to lose and nothing to gain in this situation. I'm caught in the middle trying to help. I've got two fugitives running from drug dealers asleep under my roof with only my wife to protect them. I'm no longer in the military. I have Mattis because the PTSD from my tours threatened to ruin my life. I got my life back and my act together. I serve as commander of the VFW Post in Fallbrook and do my best to be a good citizen. Dammit, I am a good citizen. And now this? Ma'am, please, in all honesty, what should I do? I will gladly bring the mother and kid here and leave them and the money with you. At least the Familia couldn't get to them on base."

"Collier, you're a genius. Why didn't I think of that? Let's go get them."

Willis was up and heading for the door.

"Ma'am? What just happened? What are you doing?" Bret was confused.

Blanca's eyes were wide. "Lord? Help?" she asked in a feeble voice.

I am here.

TWENTY-EIGHT

Bret

"Let's go, Collier. Call your wife. Make sure they're up and ready to go."

"Ma'am? Talk to me. I'm not a child, and I may work for you, but I am no longer one of your Marines." Bret had not raised his voice, but his tone commanded attention.

"We're taking these cases to a secure lock-up. Then you and I are going to get that woman and her daughter and bring them here, on base. There is another private room right here at NCIS where they can stay until we can get them safely wherever you or that law enforcement officer in there want them to go. I figured out a safe way to execute this entire operation with minimal risk, utmost security, and I think it's a win-win situation all the way around. Come on, Collier. We'll leave your vehicle on base. If they followed you from the VFW, they'll know your SUV. We're taking the Humvee. My driver is also my aide and has full security clearance, but you already know that. Grab that heavy case. I've got these two."

With that brief information from Willis, they locked the cases in a secure vault using a two-key system. One key stayed with the sergeant of the guard, the other was kept by Colonel Willis. They retrieved their weapons and exited the building.

The driver held open the passenger door for Willis and the rear door for Collier. "We'll both ride in the back this trip," Willis said and climbed in first.

Bret sat next to the Colonel and Mattis climbed in to sit on the floor at his feet. Bret still felt uneasy and unsure about what was happening. Although Willis seemed quite sure of herself. Bret waited. He knew the Colonel would fill him in, in time.

Blanca was flying along on this whirlwind of activity and simply trusted the Lord.

"I wish Hannah was here. She's always so calm and reassuring when emotions start building and drama increases," Blanca whispered.

"I'm here, Blanca. But I need to stay with the girls, too. This entire crew will be together soon. Just hold on and trust God."

Blanca smiled. *Yes,* she thought, *everything will be all right. Doubt comes from the dark side. I have no need to doubt, only to do as instructed and trust the Lord. Always.*

Willis asked Bret to give the driver his home address.

Once they were on the road back to Fallbrook, Willis turned to Bret.

"Look, Collier, I don't want to abort your mission, but you asked for help, and frankly, I think you've gotten yourself in a sticky situation that could cost you dearly in the long run. It's one thing to secretly move people around. But you do realize that this could be considered trafficking. It's another to move that money. That could be considered smuggling. All in all, if you are caught, you are not coming out of this looking good. I get that your mother-in-law wanted to help a friend, but did she really understand what she was asking you to do?"

"Probably not," Bret admitted. "She's a good woman and always trying to help the underdog. My Maddie didn't fall far from that tree." He smiled in the dark vehicle.

"Okay, but now you brought the Corps into this mess. You brought *me* into this mess." And maybe I can see better than you what might lie ahead for everyone. I have no vested interest in that cop back there, but I do in you. And I can't, in all good consciousness, let you make a mistake that might ruin your life."

Bret had not thought of it that way until they opened the box of money.

"Ma'am, are you going to help that woman and her kid or not? Will you share your plan with me or leave me in the dark?"

"I'm leaving all of you in the dark, for now. But yes, I will get her to safety. I'll ask you the same thing I asked Reynolds. Do you trust me?"

"I do. But I also know that not every military operation is a success. This one seems to have trouble written all over it." Bret was skeptical.

"Ah, Collier, that's one thing I admire about you. You say what's on your mind and you don't mince words. You've been there, done that on too many occasions, and you know full well that too often you are your own best resource. I rely on you every day at work and I'm glad you're on our team."

"Thank you, Ma'am, but that doesn't make me feel any better about the outcome of this mission."

From the front seat came the driver's voice, "Nearing the gate, ma'am. We're going directly out the Fallbrook Gate. We'll be on public roads shortly. Anything to report to the guard? Anything to watch for out there?"

"Yes. Stop at the gate. I'll talk to the duty guard," Willis replied.

"Hold that thought, Collier," he said as the driver dimmed the lights on the Humvee and slowed to a stop at the gate.

"Sir?" came the question from the gate guard, not used to military vehicles leaving at this late hour, or stopping at the gate.

"Colonel Phyllis Willis here. First Intel Battalion. We'll be off base for about an hour. Returning with two female civilians through the San Luis Rey Gate. Preauthorized. Code name, Operation La Niña. Identification papers forthcoming on our return. Highly classified. Colonel Willis and General Frank Thompson are your contacts. This is eyes-and-ears-only mission. Reference One Marine Expeditionary Force. Inform San Luis Rey Gate to be ready for us. Copy?"

"Copy that, Colonel Willis." He proffered a sharp salute, thinking the conversation was over and acknowledging the senior officer.

Willis snapped a quick answering salute and added, "Keep an eye out and send an alert directly to me or General Thompson if any unauthorized personnel or civilians try to gain entry until this alert is over. An official memo will go out tomorrow. Inform all gates."

With that the Colonel closed her window and the sand-colored Humvee rolled onto the streets of Fallbrook, California. It was nearly midnight. Traffic was light. The driver eyed the GPS on the dash and followed directions to the Collier home.

Bret noted that Maddie was correct, the neighbors were quiet. On most Friday nights, they'd still have a bonfire roaring and music playing with anywhere from five to twenty-five adults and a half dozen kids sitting around the fire on the large concrete patio that was their front yard. Shouts of laughter would explode at random, and sometimes they danced, but always they seemed to have a good time. Tonight, the house was dark, and all were either in bed or gone somewhere else for the evening.

The porch light lit up the entry to the Colliers' front door. Bret could see light coming through the few windows that faced the front of the house. He knew Maddie would wait up for him. He wondered what the woman Patsy was thinking. This had not been the plan explained to her by the cop. Would she go with them? Or would she feel threatened? Bret couldn't begin to try to get inside her head. But he felt Willis might have to call the cop and have him talk her through this change of plans.

He opened the door to the Humvee, not waiting for the driver. Mattis jumped out, recognized that he was home, relieved himself, and trotted to the front door.

Blanca

Blanca continued to pray and was happy to see Hannah again. She was also happy to see Patsy and Alicea up, dressed and wearing smiles. Whatever Maddie had said to them, they didn't seem concerned about this new set of circumstances. Blanca prayed the Colonel was being truthful and this was not a plan to hurt these women. She thought of the many Jews who boarded trains bound for places like Auschwitz and Dachau, where they thought they were going to safety.

"Please, Lord, help me protect them."

You do not know my plans. They are protected. You are with them.

Blanca wondered if she was being chastised or praised.

"Yes, dear Blanca," Hannah said. "You are doing fine. Do not doubt yourself. We are given the information we need for the job to be done."

Maddie opened the front door and Mattis was the first inside. She recognized Colonel Willis and immediately saw the concerned look on her husband's face. Whatever he was thinking, it wasn't good. After these many years, she knew her man's dark side; his anger, worry, frustrations, and anxieties. She knew when he was relaxed and comfortable and when he wasn't. He was definitely not relaxed and comfortable at this moment. But Maddie was also wise enough to keep her own counsel and not say anything until Bret gave her an indication of where this was going and what was troubling him. She invited the Colonel inside and waited.

The driver stayed outside with the vehicle.

Introductions were made. Alicea rubbed her eyes and asked if she could go back to bed. Mattis grabbed a bite to eat from his dinner bowl, and Blanca and Hannah waited to see how this would play out. Suddenly, the two angels were no longer alone with the humans.

"Jeff? Why are you here?" Blanca asked. "I didn't even call for help."

"I did," Hannah said.

"Hey, Blanca, Hannah. How are they doing?" Jeff already knew what was going on but made conversation with his peers. "Any demons hanging around?"

Hannah answered with the authority of her more than three hundred years as a guardian. She also had a well-deserved reputation as a badass Warrior Guardian Angel and trainer, too.

"Jeff, is Sergio ready to step in for training? I know it's early, but sometimes we need to make an exception and put new angels into service right away. What do you think?"

Jeff stood still in a moment of surprise. Was Hannah really asking his opinion? This was epic. "Wow, Hannah." He pondered the question. This was not a time for a flippant answer. She was serious and asking his opinion. "Yes. I think so. He went through Hell on earth. He had personally battled many demons while he was still alive and I'm convinced he wants to do right by Patsy and their daughter, Alicea. He doesn't have a sword. He's still in training and not a full-fledged guardian, but if God is calling him to help here, then we all know he's right for the job. Isn't that what you told me once? Or something like that?"

Hannah smiled as she, too, noticed the emotional growth in Jeff.

"He hasn't been on any missions yet, but there is always a first, isn't there?" Jeff didn't wait for an answer.

"And knowing him like I do, I'd say that looking after Patsy and Alicea will give him the confidence he needs as well as show him the evil deeds of his former friends. He knows them well. He'll know what they are thinking and probably what they plan to do, what they know or don't know, and how to protect against the demons now working on Jorge and the NF."

Jeff paused and looked at Hannah and back at Blanca. "That's what I think, but you know that's really way above my pay grade. It doesn't matter what I think. It only matters what God the Father wants, right?"

"Right," Hannah agreed. "He wants Sergio. But I wanted your opinion. We might have a problem with Patsy feeling scared about going with those Marines and not staying where Officer Reynolds told her to stay."

She smiled at Jeff. "Thank you for the vote of confidence. You are correct, it's not our job to second-guess God, but He asked me to ask you. I would say it's all part of ongoing training for all of us. We need to gather the facts and offer help as best we can with the tools provided."

"Does anyone want anything to eat or drink?" Maddie asked the room in general. "Should we sit and talk about why you're here and what's happening? I'm sure Patsy has some questions as this was not part of the original plan."

"Nothing for me," came murmurs from all. No one was hungry or thirsty. Although Bret did hear his stomach growl. The salt-and-vinegar chips had worn off hours ago. No one moved to sit. They stood in a circle in the small foyer.

Maddie turned her attention back to her husband. The Colonel might be the highest-ranking Marine in the room, but this was her husband's domain. She was not about to let the good Colonel forget that.

"Bret? We're listening," she said.

The three angels were immediately joined by a fourth. Sergio took in the scene with a bewildered look on his face.

"*Hombre*, do things keep getting strange up here or what?"

Jeff laughed and made introductions with Hannah and Blanca.

"Welcome to your first training session, Serg," Jeff said.

"Dios mío!" Sergio whispered. "Is that Patsy? Is that my daughter? Where am I? What is happening?"

"Relax," Jeff said. "All will be clear soon. You were asked to join us at the last minute, and you will soon understand everything that is happening. For now, watch and listen. Stay focused."

Blanca again marveled at Jeff's emotional development. Hannah stayed quiet while she watched and waited. At least there were no demons in the room.

Bret took the lead. "Maddie, why don't you take Alicea to the office and wait for us there. Maybe some television time?"

Maddie knew he'd fill her in later, but this was probably not going to be a good conversation to share with a child. She smiled at Alicea and said, "Hey, let's go watch a movie or something on Netflix or Disney while these grownups talk about boring grown up stuff."

Alicea gave her mother a questioning look. "Can't I just go back to bed? I'm tired."

"It's all right, mija. Go with Miss Maddie. I'll be right here." Patsy turned to Madeleine. "Maybe you could read her a story?"

With her mother's blessing, Maddie led the way down the hall.

Bret continued once he heard the door close. "Patsy, Chuck was worried you might have been followed here. We took his car to the Marine Corps base and had it checked. There was a tracking device on it. That's probably how they found you when you stopped for breakfast. Then either they followed you here, or they simply followed the tracking device. Most of those work within a certain range or distance. If the tracker gets too far away, he loses the connection. This device was different. It could be tracked from anywhere. At any rate, we took it to a secure location on base and destroyed it. They can no longer track him, but we believe they do know what his vehicle looks like. Chuck is still on base and so is his car. If they were following him, we want to be sure he doesn't exit Pendleton the same way he went in. He's resting now and plans to leave early tomorrow to return to Salinas. We are working to get a loaner vehicle for him and return his car at a later date."

Bret hesitated, but knew he had to go on. He glanced once at Willis for confirmation. Willis nodded. "Go on."

"Once Reynolds leaves Pendleton, he's on his own. We have only so much authority when it comes to civilians, but we do have ways to help. We are pretty sure that since they haven't come here yet, they don't have a tracker on you. We don't know who is after you or why. Reynolds seemed to think it was related to the Familia and Alicea's biological father, a man named Sergio Sanchez, who is reported to have stolen over a million dollars from the NF and was subsequently executed by the gang."

Patsy knew Sergio was dead. She had not known why.

"What?" she asked.

"A million dollars? Sergio wouldn't do that. He idolized the NF. He would never steal from them. He knew the consequences of something like that. He was an idiot in many ways. So was I for threatening him when I wanted him to get out, but he didn't. He couldn't. He knew the price he'd pay. He may have almost killed me once, but he didn't. I've been hiding with my daughter for all of her life. I thought he found me and was coming to finally kill us. But again. He didn't. He died. He was murdered. And now I'm hearing that he stole from the gang? None of this makes sense to me. None of it. I don't believe it. I need to talk to the Cowboy Cop. Can I do that?"

"Yes, of course," Bret answered. "But first I need to tell you the rest. Then we will share a plan to get you to safety and you can decide how you want to proceed. The choice is yours. Completely."

"Okay, fine," she said. Sounding anything but fine.

The angels listened in silence. Hannah was glad Sergio was present. That would eliminate speculation on their part, making it easier to influence the humans.

Bret went on. "Patsy, a plain brown box was delivered to the sheriff's department, in care of Officer Reynolds. Inside there was over a million dollars in unmarked bills. There was also a note that this money was meant for you and Alicea."

He paused to let that sink in. Her face paled. She started to tremble. "I need to sit down," she said and moved toward the sofa. Bret and the Colonel moved with her and took up seats across from her. Mattis jumped up on the sofa and settled in next to Bret. The angels stayed against the back wall. Watching. Listening. Waiting.

"What does this mean?" she asked. "What am I supposed to do with a million dollars of drug money? Blood money! I don't want it." Patsy stared at her feet. She said the first thing that came to mind, but she was also thinking about her daughter and that Sergio had died for this. For them. To give them a better life. To maybe help them get away?

Colonel Willis spoke for the first time since the introductions were made.

"Ma'am, I know you're distraught. I realize this is all a shock to you. Based on the word of Officer Reynolds, we believe you and your daughter are still in danger. We want to help. Will you let us do that?" she asked.

"Let you?" she asked. Her eyes flashed at Willis. "I let the Cowboy Cop help me and look where it got him. Look where it got us. I saw that woman at the restaurant. I know she was looking for me. Why didn't Chuck tell me about this money? Why didn't he warn me?"

"Because he didn't know," Bret said. "Not until you arrived at the VFW and we checked the box that was in his trunk."

"That box back there in his trunk? All that time that box had money in it that Sergio stole and wanted to give it to me? They kill for way less. You know that. What am I supposed to do now? Where can we go that is safe? They will find me. And how can I hide that much money? It's impossible. And it's not my money!"

She was on the verge of hysteria but keeping it together. She hadn't raised her voice. She was protecting her daughter. She knew the walls in this house were not thick or soundproof. Even with the television on or Maddie reading a story out loud, Alicea might hear the shrill tone in her mother's voice and come running.

Colonel Willis moved to sit next to Patsy on the sofa. Bret and Mattis were on the other sofa, perpendicular to the one where Patsy sat. Mattis lifted his head and watched Willis with interest.

The angels continued to watch and wait. Sergio longed to go to Patsy and comfort her. He'd caused all this pain in her life. He'd brought her to this edge of fear and uncertainty. He'd paid a high price to the Norteños. They wanted more. They wanted him to kill her. He couldn't do it. Not then. Not later. When he found out where she was hiding at that ranch down by Paso Robles, he kept silent. When the cowboy cop told him he thought she went to Las Vegas, he knew Reynolds was lying. He stole the money bit by bit. Not all at once. He knew stealing was a sin, but he'd felt a bit like Robin Hood. He was not stealing from the rich to give to the poor. He was stealing from evil to give for good. It didn't make it right, but somehow his mind justified his actions. In his heart he knew it didn't. *Lord, forgive me*, he'd prayed. *My actions got me killed. Are my actions going to the be the death of this woman I loved so much and my niña, Alicea?* He was too new at the business of being an angel to know that Hannah, Blanca, and Jeff all knew what he was thinking.

I know, too.

Sergio looked around at the other angels. "Why am I here? How can I help? What am I to do?"

"Listen," Hannah said. "We'll all know soon."

Willis put her hand on Patsy's shoulder in a gesture that was meant to be caring and supportive. She reacted with a sharp shrug. She removed her hand immediately. This was not a woman wanting to cry and be consoled. This was a woman determined to do the right thing and protect her daughter. She'd been doing that for nearly seven years now. This was the first Willis had ever had contact with her. From the conversations earlier that night, Willis had pictured this woman as a victim, but she no longer saw her that way. She was strong. She would do whatever it took to protect her daughter. Of that Willis was sure.

"Ms. Garcia, we want to help you," Willis said.

"Why?"

"Because it's what we do. We don't just rescue important people or rich people. We have sworn an oath to protect this country from enemies, both foreign and domestic. Right now, you are in the middle of both. You've got both home grown and foreign enemies trying to hurt you. We are convinced that it true."

"Would you be helping me if I didn't have a million dollars in cash?"

She was not falling for the smooth-talking lines of the Colonel. She was going to have to convince her that the United States Marine Corps really did have her best interest at heart, and not their own.

"Yes, ma'am," Willis said.

"In fact, the money is a huge problem, but it's currently locked in a safe place at Camp Pendleton. I need to level with you and share an idea and see what you think. The final choice is yours, but I'm afraid your options are limited. La Familia has resources far and wide. From what we've learned, we think it's a matter of time before they catch up with you, and also with Officer Reynolds and his family. Next on their list will be the Colliers. I'm not sure how far this will go. I understand Maddie's mother was also involved. Sergio's grandmother. They won't stop. It's what they do. They can be ruthless toward anyone they believe is against them or in their way." Willis didn't want to scare her, but she did want her to understand the gravity of the situation.

"How can you help? I don't want any of these people to get hurt because of me. I wish I'd never met Sergio. But at the same time, I adore my little Alicea, and if it weren't for Sergio, I wouldn't have her. What is it you want me to do and where do you want me to go?"

Willis breathed a sigh of relief. She was letting down her walls. She knew she could protect her, but not without her permission and agreement. This would be an interagency operation with full cooperation and a deeply satisfying humanitarian effort. She'd already gotten buy-in from all of the agencies ready to be involved. A few details needed to be worked out, but with luck, they'd have time and resources, thanks to Sergio.

"The first thing we have to do," Willis said, "is get you out of here and to a safe place. We need to leave Bret and Maddie and wait to see if there is any move made toward them. Most likely not. But Reynolds did stop at the VFW, and they know he ended up at Pendleton. We don't know what action they will take from there. But the longer you stay here, the more dangerous this becomes for all of you. I'm asking you to come with me to a secure location at Camp Pendleton and let us keep you safe. We have a comfortable place for you to stay."

"Wait. Not jail," she said.

"No. Not jail."

"And Alicea will be with me?"

"Yes, but until we can get you safely away from California and at a safe location, you will not be able to come and go at will. We will make sure you have good meals, clothes, and all that you need, but we don't want you to use cellphones or anything to give yourself away. It might sound like prison, but trust me, it's not. And I promise you, as I'm promising Bret here, and Officer Reynolds, who is currently at the place where I'll take you, that you can talk to him, and you will be safe there. He can even stay with you until we have made a plan to transfer you." Willis paused. "But Patsy, we need to go now. Reynolds is planning to leave at five in the morning. It's already after midnight and he'll want to know the situation and plan. He was ready to walk away and leave it to us, but I'm a good judge of human character and I'll bet my last dollar he won't rest until he knows you're really safe."

Patsy stared at Willis. Her mind a jumble of thoughts. She looked over at Bret and his dog. "I'll be right back," she said.

Without another word, she rose and walked down the hall and knocked on the closed door, before opening it and going inside where Madeleine Collier was reading a Karen Kingsbury novel to Alicea. Maddie looked up when the door opened and said, "I didn't have many options for books. Everything okay?"

All four angels crowded into the room with them.

Alicea looked up from the huge beanbag chair where she'd nearly gone back to sleep. Almost. "Hi, Mama," she said.

Maddie smiled at Patsy. "All done?"

Patsy walked over to Maddie, who stayed seated on the floor next to Alicea. When Patsy leaned down to give her a hug, Maddie stood up and the women embraced. "Is everything all right?" Maddie whispered in her ear.

"Everything is great." Patsy replied softly. As they pulled apart, Maddie noticed tears threatening to spill. "You're sure?" she asked again.

"I'm sure," Patsy said. "Change of plans. We're going now. We're going to a safe place on the base. Apparently, it's better for us there and the last thing I want to do is put you in danger. You've been so kind to us. Thank you."

Maddie didn't know what or why things had changed. But they had. She was surprised to see Colonel Willis at their home, but she knew Bret respected her and she trusted they would do right by this woman and her adorable little girl.

"I'm glad we could help even if we didn't do very much," Maddie told her.

"You've done far more than you realize. And please, thank your mother, too. Apparently, my Cowboy Cop knew her in high school."

"Yeah. That's what they said." Maddie was anxious to talk with Bret and find out what was going on and if they were still on for the trip to Mexico.

"Hey kiddo." Patsy looked at Alicea. "We're heading out again. Sorry for interrupting the story, but we need to go."

Alicea got up, gave Madeleine a hug, and thanked her. "Bye, Miss Maddie."

"Goodbye, Miss Alicea. You be good. It's awfully late. Way past your bedtime I'd imagine."

Maddie smiled and hugged her back. She loved being around kids. She prayed for the best for this one, and Patsy, too.

Mother and daughter walked out first, followed by Maddie and the four angels.

Colonel Willis, Bret, and Mattis were standing by the front door. Bret did not put the vest on Mattis. They would not be heading back to Pendleton on this trip.

"Be safe," he told them. "Ma'am, please call if there is anything I can do."

"Just keep a low profile this week and keep your eyes open for anything out of the ordinary. Especially at the Post. His car was parked there for a short while. They might connect the dots. Make sure your people there know better than to chat with strangers." Willis gave Bret a knowing look. "I can either have someone return your car tonight or you can pick it up yourself tomorrow if Maddie can drive you into work. You know how to reach me, regardless."

Willis escorted Patsy and Alicea to the Humvee and opened the back door for them, not waiting for her driver to do it.

"We get to ride in that?" Alicea had already forgotten all about the story Madeleine had been reading. As tired as she was, she was excited about this next leg of their adventure.

With the door closed, Willis turned to Bret, who had walked outside with them. "I'll keep you in the loop. We'll set up everything tomorrow. This is officially Operation La Niña. If Reynolds wants to see this through, I'll read him in tomorrow. Meanwhile, I mean it about you and Maddie keeping a low profile and your eyes open."

"Thank you, Colonel. For everything."

She climbed into the front passenger seat of the Humvee and the driver backed out onto the street, made the turn, and they were gone.

Bret noticed the neighbors had returned home. A few mingled out in front. The firepit was lit, and he heard the faint strains of Latino music drifting softly across the street. They were watching him. They had watched the Humvee pull out of his driveway. From their vantage point, he did not think they could have seen the mother and daughter get inside.

Bret raised an arm and waved to his neighbors. Several waved back. They'd watched the interesting scene unfold with the military vehicle at the Colliers' house. *So much for a midnight rendezvous without witnesses*, thought Bret.

He started back inside to share the news with Maddie and threw one last glance across the street, when he heard a beer can open and smiled to himself. *My neighbors are not spies or gang members. They're just good people enjoying the start of the week*. Bret smiled. An uncomplicated life is a good thing to embrace.

Sergio

Hannah felt the love between Bret and Maddie and was happy to be a part of their life.

Blanca was on her way to Camp Pendleton with Patsy and Alicea.

Jeff was back in Salinas.

Sergio was not sure what he was supposed to be doing. There were questions he could answer, but no one had asked. Maybe he was supposed to return and get more training? His confusion at being an angel was troubling. *I feel like I'm now one of the good guys, but for a long time I was one of the bad guys.* He looked around the sparse room and realized he wasn't alone. There was a man sleeping on the twin bed. It was his old nemesis, Officer Chuck Reynolds. The Cowboy Cop.

"I guess I'll just wait here and see what happens," Sergio whispered into the night. "Besides, I don't know where to go or how to get there. Anywhere."

All in due time, Sergio. All in due time.

TWENTY-NINE

Blanca

She was glad the drama from earlier tonight had dissipated. There was a change of plans and it seemed to her that all would work out, but Blanca was not getting a clear message on what she should do. She knew the answers would come, but she was getting impatient, and that was not considered a virtue. She stopped to pray and ponder.

"Dear Lord, our Father, please let me know your wisdom and guide me to do the right thing by Patsy and Alicea. I have this fear I'm not helping them make the right decisions. I thought it was all worked out, and then this Colonel came along and changed the plan. Lord, at first I thought that was good. Now I'm concerned I made a mistake. I guess I'm asking for your blessed assurance that I'm doing what is right in your sight. Amen."

Blanca blessed herself, making the sign of the cross. *In the name of the Father, the Son, and the Holy Spirit.* She sat in the stillness of the night. Would He answer her?

Do not be fearful. You will never know my wisdom.

I will always guide you. I don't make mistakes.

For the second time in less than twenty-four hours, Blanca knew she was being chastised. But she also felt loved. Just as a parent must provide discipline to a child, she, too, needed discipline and direction.

"Thank you, Father. I will rest now as they rest. You will guide me. In time. Your time. Not our time."

Patsy

Patsy lay in the dark and felt the warmth of her little girl lying next to her on the bed. Alicea had fallen asleep as soon as her head hit the pillow. She'd actually nodded off while they were still in the Humvee but woke as they made their way to these temporary quarters, as Colonel Willis had called it.

She even posted a guard outside their door. She wondered again if this was for her safety or if she really was being held prisoner. She wanted to see Officer Reynolds. He'd been her rock and the only person she'd trusted since she threatened to go to the cops about the NF. But none of that mattered anymore.

Nothing she told them was new. The police had already known everything she had to share. They knew as much as she did. But she knew she was still a threat to La Familia, because she had threatened them and not been made to pay for those threats. You do not threaten La Familia. She'd loved Sergio. She had loved his grandmother, too. But he turned out to be as bad as the rest. Or was he?

She lay in the darkened room, but sleep didn't come. Her mind kept returning to what she learned tonight. Sergio had stolen money from his Norteño family and had planned to give it to her and Alicea. Her mind couldn't grasp that as a reality. Why would he do that for a woman and child he didn't care about? Or want.

He'd wanted her to have an abortion. That's when her hot temper got the best of her. She'd been so happy to learn of the pregnancy. Sergio had not. Did he die for her? Was he killed because of the money? Or just his bad luck? Who killed him? she wondered. And who might be after her now? Whoever it was seemed to now be on the radar of the United States Military. This couldn't be good. Her mind twisted with the ins and outs of the dilemma and possibilities.

Surely, she'd never be allowed to keep the money. She didn't want it anyway, she told herself. She still had money from the sale of her mother's house. It was put away safe. No one knew about it except that lawyer. She could get it and use it when she knew where she was going. Somewhere far away.

"Far, far away," she whispered in the dark.

Alicea stirred and went back to sleep. Patsy closed her eyes and tried to do the same. It would soon be dawn and she needed to talk with Chuck before he left.

Blanca listened to her thoughts and prayed again. "Dear Lord, thank you for all you've done to keep them safe. All praise and glory to you. I promise to do my job and be the best Guardian I can be. I trust and believe with all my heart and soul that You know best."

Blanca, too, closed her eyes, and then had another random thought. "I don't have a heart anymore. Hmmm. But that's okay, Lord. My soul is happy being part of your team. Amen."

Bret

"Come here, my precious wife. I need a hug." Bret fell into Madeleine's arms as he crossed the threshold back into their home. Maddie had waited for him just inside the door.

"That's usually my line," she said, and held him tight.

"I know. But tonight was hell. I'm glad Mattis was with me. The tension got pretty high. I like to think I'm not triggered anymore, but that's not completely true. What would I ever do without you?" he whispered into her long dark hair.

"Good thing you don't have to," she returned and kissed his neck.

Mattis wedged his nose between their legs and made it a family hug. They backed up from each other and laughed.

"Okay, Mattis, come on. Let's all sit on the couch for some family lovin' time." Maddie knew Bret wanted to talk about what had happened. Eventually she'd let her mother know there had been a change in plans. It now looked like her friend Chuck Reynolds and his problems were being handled by the Marine Corps. But that could wait. For now, she sat with Bret and waited for him to talk. Mattis climbed up between them again. His favorite place in the world.

Bret began by taking a deep breath and slowly let it out. Maddie thought it sounded like a giant sigh of relief. She waited.

"Well," he began, "this is officially out of our hands for now. I don't think we'll have anything more to do with any of them, but I can't be completely sure. You'll have to let your mother know, but not yet. We'll have to call back that jet before it heads down here."

He paused and reflected on all that had happened since the cop had arrived at the Post, plus the instructions Maddie's mom had given them earlier.

"Okay, babe, to recap for you and to be sure I have this all straight in my head as well, here's what went down and the way I see it and remember it. Let me know if you saw or heard anything different."

"Copy that," she said.

"First, your mom calls with this crazy plan for us to take a week or two off work. She wants us to meet some friend of hers from high school. That was, what? Forty or fifty years ago? The dude's got to be pretty old, right?" He didn't expect an answer. Maddie waited.

"So, she tells us he's bringing a woman and her kid. They're getting fake passports, because they're running from the Norteños. She wants to send a private jet that belongs to one of her rich friends to the little airport here in Fallbrook and we're supposed to get on board with this woman and her kid and fly to Puerto Vallarta. Then we check into this fancy resort and wait a week. They are expecting us, and during that time we are supposed to help the woman and kid practice using their new names, and she's supposed to get a crash course in working at a nice resort. And we are supposed to help with that and also keep an eye out for gang members who might find her and still want to hurt her. Oh, and they might now have it in for us because we helped her, too." He paused. Maddie stayed quiet.

"Oh, I forgot the part where I'm supposed to use the Marine Corps system to make flight reservations for her out of Mexico, too. How could I do that? Don't answer. I'm working through this." She didn't say a word.

"And then we are supposed to get them on a plane using the new passports, which someone else is supplying, and send them off to some island called Ibiza that I've never heard of, but your mom has friends there, too. And she wanted you to fly with them to Europe to make sure they got there safely."

Bret turned to face his wife and stared into her beautiful gemstone blue eyes. "Maddie, so far is this what you and I actually agreed to?" Maddie nodded and realized how dangerous this was for them and how utterly stupid it would be for them to do this. The risk was not worth the reward. Especially to help someone they didn't even know.

Maddie squeezed his thigh. "Yeah, pretty dumb. But we've done dumb before to help someone who needs it."

"True enough. But so far, is that about how you have seen this going down?"

"You are spot on. Except I was pretty iffy about what I was supposed to do once I got them to Europe. I figured the cop was going to help."

"Yeah, me too. But wait until you hear the rest."

"I'm listening. And truthfully feeling relieved they aren't still here."

"When they got to the Post and you brought the woman and kid here, he tells me he needs my help with something else. He wants to know if we can talk in private. I say, 'Sure. Let's go to my office.'

"Then he tells me he needs to get a box out of his car, and he needs a witness when he opens it." Bret paused.

"A witness?" Maddie asked.

"Yes. That's what he said. So, I'm getting nervous about this dude. Your mom hasn't seen him in forever and we don't know squat about him. And we don't really know anything about this woman or her kid. For all we know he could be trafficking. She could have kidnapped the kid from an ex. Anything is possible. So yeah, I was nervous. That started my whole PTSD stuff acting up. I could feel my insides going nuts. Mattis knew it, too. He stuck to me like glue."

Mattis heard his name and moved his head onto Bret's lap. "Yeah, I'm talking about you, good dog."

"What was in the box?" Maddie asked.

"Holy shit, babe. It was full of money. More money than I've ever seen. Mostly hundreds, but plenty of fifties and twenties, too. Not neat stacks from the bank. It was used money. If that's what it's called. Not like all neat like we see on TV or in the movies when someone opens a case of money. That's when

I knew we couldn't go through with helping them get out of the country. We could go to jail for that kind of stuff."

Maddie sat up and stared at her husband. "Are you kidding me?"

"Of course I'm *not* kidding you!" Bret could feel the adrenaline kicking in again just talking about it.

"What did you do? How did Willis get involved?" she asked,

"I called her. This was not something I could deal with. This Chuck guy was worried he'd been followed. I immediately thought of some of the trackers we've pulled off of vehicles. I needed to know. I called in for a request from EOD to check a civilian car for a bomb or trackers."

"You did what?" Maddie couldn't believe what she'd just heard.

"I know. I know," he said. "But I needed help and I've got the whole effing Corps at my disposal. Not really, but I've given so much in service to this country, and I just had to believe in my gut that Willis would help. And she did. But it wasn't without some drama and macho posturing about all this. We counted most of the money. I was surprised how long it takes to sort and count that much money. We didn't even finish, but I know there is more than a million dollars there. And the real kicker? Wait until you hear this. Maddie, there was a note in the box that the money was for Patsy and her kid. But then the cop tells me there is a 'rumor' from an informant that the kid's bio dad is the one who stole the money from the Norteños to give to her. His name was Sergio and I guess he was popped a couple of weeks ago, and now the gang wants their money back. That's why they were tracking the cop. He is their only link to the mom and kid. They even left this Sergio's body at the cop's house way out in the country and shot up the house with Patsy and the kid and another cop inside. It's a miracle none of them were killed. So, no. I don't want any part of this. I'm already fearful just being as connected as we are. This sucks. And what about your mom? I hope this Reynolds guy didn't leave any connection to her lying around for them to find. We need to warn her, I think."

Maddie stared at Bret. "Is that all? What is Willis going to do? What is going to happen to them? The Corps can't protect them forever or get them out of the country legally, can they? And what about the money? Holy shit, Bret, this is bad, isn't it?"

"It is. It's damn bad all the way around. But honey, Willis is smart. She's got the money locked up and secure. She's been in touch with a couple of other agencies. Not sure if you know, because we don't talk about it, but several other law enforcement agencies now work out of Pendleton, too. So, Willis was in touch with DEA and FBI and probably another one of the alphabet agencies and they're setting up a joint task force. Operation La Niña, she called it. Eyes and ears only."

Maddie stared at Bret, waiting for him to continue. She could feel her heart pounding. "Any idea what they're going to do?"

"Not exact details, but they're going to funnel the cash into one of the non profits set up to help victims. It's not going back to the gang, and it's not rightfully Patsy's either. But they will use it to get her and the kid to safety. They can do whatever the hell they want. You know that. It'll probably go down as a training exercise, and the fewest people possible will know about it. For now, we need to lie low and watch for anyone who might be watching us. We need to be super careful everywhere we go. And especially at the Post. Agreed?"

"Of course. What about the Post? Do you think they followed him there? Us? Could there be trouble or danger at the Post?"

As soon as she asked the question, Maddie laughed. "What am I saying? The Norteños would be nuts to show up on Sureño turf, and then go to our VFW Post with our veterans, most of whom have concealed-carry permits and take no shit from anybody. They wouldn't have a chance." She laughed again. "Sometimes I forget how badass we are down here in little old Fallbrook."

Bret smiled at her observation. "Chuck thought someone followed us up to the gate at Pendleton, but never came through. Willis warned the duty guard to be on the lookout. For once I'm glad there's a barber shop and a bar close to the Post. They might have thought that is where the cop stopped."

Bret went on, "I called Dory earlier and warned her to keep her eyes and ears open, too. I hate the thought of racial profiling, but this is a case of being pretty sure that whoever is after them or us is Hispanic."

"How are you feeling now? Still running on nerves? Feeling any better talking about it?" Maddie asked him.

Bret stared at his wife for so long she thought he might not answer. She waited.

"I'm okay. Yes, I still feel the adrenaline. It felt very much like waiting for an IUD to hit. I knew shit was coming, but not from where. Then I was worried about you. There were too many what-if's in every scenario. Then I started to turn on the cop and even Willis. But mostly I held it in check. Even now, you're the only one I trust."

He paused again, then studied her face and told her, "Willis might be using us, you, me, and Mattis, in part of this scenario and whatever she plans to have happen. I agreed, but told her I needed your buy-in, too."

"Doing what?" she asked.

"That's just it. I don't know. But she's got something up her sleeve and swears we won't be in danger." Bret and Maddie stared at each other. Neither said anything more. Each knew what the other thought without words. Soft smiles played about their lips. They knew they were already all-in on whatever Colonel Willis was planning. Their service hearts would not let them do otherwise.

Maddie put her head on his shoulder, and they sat together quietly. Neither spoke for several minutes. Mattis was determined to keep his eighty-pound body snuggled between them, his big head still in Bret's lap. The only sound in the room was the ticking of the dining room clock and the faint strands of Hispanic music from across the street. A car drove by. Slowed. Turned. Picked up speed and was gone.

"Your mother owes us." Bret laughed. It was good to hear him laugh. That was the first step in easing back from a PTSD episode.

"Well, at least we aren't sitting in a Mexican jail and calling her to bail us out." Maddie laughed, too.

"You do realize that might have been our fate if we went through with this?"

"Listening to you tonight, I have no doubt. Or an American jail. I'm so thankful I'm married to such a great guy. My Marine with special skills and the talent and smarts to know when it's time to call in the Cavalry."

"Well, thanks for the credit, my badass wife, but the truth is I was scared shitless tonight."

They laughed. He was exaggerating, but they both felt they were far better off for not taking the risk and running with the plan as outlined by the ever resourceful and creative Liz Davidson Miller.

"Will they be all right? Do you think? What about my mom's friend? Is he in danger?" Maddie thought about all she'd learned tonight and felt a weight had been lifted from their shoulders, but it had landed somewhere else. Would her mother take it on herself to help if the Marines couldn't?

"Oh Lord, no," Maddie said as her thoughts turned south.

"Lord no, what?" Bret repeated. "What are you thinking?"

"My mom," she said. "If Willis can't get them out, and she ends up going back to the cop for help, do you think my mom might try to take them on her own?"

"Well, we both know she's stubborn enough to try. We need to make sure she doesn't."

THIRTY

Chuck

He woke with a start. He'd not slept in his own bed with his dear wife Maria since the night before his call from Patsy. They treasured the few nights at the hotel in Monterey, but that seemed like ages ago.

He managed to get a few hours of restless sleep but woke with a start and needed a few seconds to orient himself and realize where he was. That must be what woke him, he thought. The unfamiliarity of this place. He lay alone in the darkness, closed his eyes again, and felt a sense of loss. Had he really just abandoned Patsy Garcia and her daughter? Had he really just turned them over, along with more than a million dollars in unmarked bills, to some Marine Corps Colonel he didn't even know? Chuck wrestled with his own ethics and morals over what had happened tonight.

"Fuck," he whispered aloud. It was a word he didn't use often, or lightly. "I can't do this to her. I need to be sure they are safe."

"*Si, será mejor que hagas eso.*"

Chuck threw back the dark green wool blanket and coarse sheet and leapt to his feet. His Sig Sauer already in hand and pointed into the darkened room where he'd clearly heard the Spanish-speaking man tell him he'd better do as he said.

"I'm armed and have a bullet with your name on it aimed center mass. Who are you and what the fuck are you doing in my room?"

Willis had told him this was a safe room and guards were posted outside. His mind raced as he wondered how this guy got inside. He kept his gun pointed in the direction from which he'd heard the voice. The room was small. He heard no movement. No breathing. No swish of fabric. Nothing.

"Look. You obviously aren't here to kill me or you'd have done it while I was asleep." He paused. Listened again. Heard nothing. "This is ridiculous. I know you're there. Turn on the light and let's talk."

Chuck could feel his heart beating at his back. He felt sweat break out on his forehead and armpits. He waited. No sound. No light. Did he imagine the voice? Was Willis playing tricks on him? Was this a dream? No. This was real. He stood very still in his boxers and tee shirt.

Then it came again. In English, with a Spanish accent this time.

"You can hear me?" whispered the voice across the room. He sounded surprised.

"I hear you," Chuck replied. "I'm going to turn on the light. Whoever you are, let's talk about why you're here." The voice seemed oddly familiar, but Chuck couldn't place it.

He reached toward the small reading lamp next to the bed. Without taking his eyes off the opposite wall, or moving the aim of his Sig Sauer, he switched on the light.

The room was empty.

"What the hell?"

He checked the small closet and bathroom. He looked under the bed. He was alone. He tried the door to the hall. It opened easily when he turned the handle. He hadn't been locked in from the outside. An armed Marine stood watch.

"Everything all right, sir? Can I get you anything?" the staff sergeant asked.

"Was someone in my room?" Chuck asked. "Just now."

"Uh. Sir? No, sir. I've been here all night. You're the only one in there. This door has stayed closed per orders." The sergeant was trained not to show emotion, but Chuck could see the strange look on his face.

"Maybe a dream, sir?" he asked, giving Chuck a plausible excuse for thinking someone had been in his room.

"Do you have any word on two female civilians who might also be here tonight? They'd have come in after me. With Colonel Willis." Chuck had wondered if Willis might move them to the base for safety.

"Sir, in this building I'm not at liberty to say anything about what I see or hear, but Colonel Willis gave orders to let you know the civilians are safe and here at NCIS, if you wish to see them before you leave. I have orders to wake you at zero four thirty."

The NCO consulted his watch. "That's almost two hours from now."

"Okay. That's all for now. Thanks." Chuck ducked back into the room, closed and locked the door from the inside. He needed to think. He wondered briefly if the stress was causing him to have delusions. He'd heard that voice as real as if the person was standing at the foot of his bed. The first time it was loud. As if the voice was answering the questions Chuck had only thought in his half-asleep state. But when the voice asked if he could be heard, it was a mere whisper. In Spanish the first time. English with an accent the next. *Was I really just dreaming?* he wondered again. It had seemed so real.

"I heard you. I know I did," he said quietly to the empty room.

He crawled back into bed and his thoughts turned to Patsy and Alicea. *I need to be sure they're safe. Maybe that was my subconscious telling me to do right by them.* He turned off the lamp, pulled up the sheet, turned to his side, and closed his eyes in the darkened room.

"Mira. Cowboy Cop. I don't know how this works. This is me, Sergio. *Estoy muerto*. But not. Can you still hear me?"

Chuck lay very still. His Sig Sauer now under the pillow. He inched his fingers around the grip. Kept the safety on. Waited. The door had not opened. He knew in his mind there was no one else in the room. *Sergio? What in God's name is happening to me?* he wondered and didn't say a word.

"Ah, *bien*. Maybe you cannot hear me after all. They didn't tell me what to expect. Maybe it is like my life. I must figure this out on my own. *Dios mis, ayúdame a entender*. My God, help me understand."

Chuck felt his heartrate quicken. He had trouble breathing. *Am I having a heart attack? Am I losing it? Why am I imagining that Sergio is here talking to me? I know there is no one here. No one but me. All common sense tells me this. If I'm imagining this shit, or dreaming it, I am absolutely ready to retire. This is not normal. I am too rational to be thinking this.* Then he began to pray in earnest.

Quietly he whispered, "Dear God, our Father in Heaven. Hallowed be thy name. Thy kingdom come, thy will be done, on earth as it is in Heaven. Give us this day our daily bread and forgive us our trespasses as we forgive those who trespass against us. Lead us not into temptation but deliver us from evil. Amen."

A small laugh came from across the room. Chuck made the sign of the cross. Why was he hearing that voice? Had Sergio come to haunt him? He sat up again and turned on the light.

"I didn't take you for a praying man, Cowboy Cop. But you probably didn't think I was either. Did you?"

Chuck stared in disbelief. He was afraid of nothing. But he was afraid at this moment. He was afraid he was losing his mind. Because he heard Sergio. And now he could see him. Sitting in the only chair in the room. Not dead. Not with two gunshot wounds to the head and a body riddled with postmortem gunshots. He looked great. He was smiling.

Sergio and Chuck locked eyes. "Ah, so you can see me now, too!" Sergio whispered.

"Dear Lord, what is happening to me?" Chuck was afraid. This seemed too real. He was losing his mind.

"Don't be afraid, Chuck. I'm not here to hurt you. I ended up going to the good guys. Can you believe I made it to Heaven? God really does forgive us through our faith and belief in Jesus. Mí abuela prayed for me, too. In secret I prayed for me. I tried to help Patsy and the kid I wasn't sure I had. I did help them. But they killed me for it. My own good friend Jorge ordered it. Can you believe that? We were altar boys together back in the day. I remember it clearly. How did we make so many bad choices later in life?" He shook his head. Chuck stared in disbelief.

"Our amigos. Bad influences. Greed. We always wanted more." Sergio kept talking.

Chuck watched and listened from the bed. He didn't try to move. He could see Sergio's lips move. Heard his words, but he still did not believe he was really there. *If I don't talk to him or give credence to this dream, maybe it will go away,* Chuck thought. *I'll just close my eyes. He will go away.*

"Don't be afraid of me, Cowboy Cop. I'm not here to hurt you. I'm no longer controlled by the bad guys. And I will tell you, there are some really bad demons out there, too. I'm here to help you because I'm here to watch over my little girl. I'm here to protect them from the demons who want to destroy her."

Chuck's eyes were closed. When Sergio stopped talking, he cautiously opened one eye.

"I'm still here," said the angel.

Chuck opened both eyes and stared at the apparition in front of him. No doubt it was Sergio. "But you're dead," Chuck said.

"I am," Sergio confirmed. "*Muy muerto.* My body is very dead, but my soul is alive and with the Lord in Heaven. I only recently learned I'm even an angel, but without all the training I'm supposed to get. I guess this is an emergency, and they sent me out to help. But I didn't think you were supposed to be able to hear me or see me."

"All right, Mr. Angel, what is going on? How are you here? Am I going nuts?" Chuck was always the ever-confident, stereotypical tough cop. He was the kind of law enforcement officer that people either loved or hated. There wasn't much middle ground or gray area with Chuck Reynolds. And here he was talking to a dead man like the guy was actually sitting in the chair across from him. He'd seen the body at the morgue. Sergio Sanchez was dead.

Sergio laughed. "You aren't crazy. I have a message for you. God loves you, and He loves Patsy and He loves my little Alicea, too. I've learned that my kid is God's child. A girl! He has plans for her. He's got a bunch of angels watching over them. That's pretty cool, isn't it? And He let me into Heaven. Can you believe it? And now, I'm here to help you."

"How?" What is it I'm supposed to do?" Chuck asked. "You really messed things up for her when you stole that money and made it worse by sending it to me."

"No. That was the best thing I could do to protect it."

Chuck ran a hand through his hair. "Am I seriously having a conversation with a ghost?"

"I'm not a ghost," Sergio declared defensively. "I'm an angel."

"Where are your wings?"

"I haven't got them yet."

"What?" Chuck laughed. "Are you like Clarence in that movie, *It's a Wonderful Life?*"

"I loved that movie! I did. Yeah, I guess so. I need to help you save Alicea and Patsy. So, Cowboy Cop, how are you going to do that?" Chuck stared at Sergio.

"Apparently, they are in another room in this building. Why don't you go talk to them? Because I guarantee she is not going to believe me, nor is anyone else if I try to tell them about you. Sergio Sanchez is an Angel from God. Right?"

"You are right about that. They won't believe you. But I wasn't sent to them. I was sent to you. Go back to sleep. Rest. I will help you figure this out. The Lord and many more angels are here to help. When you wake, you will know the right thing to do."

Chuck was suddenly extremely tired. He took a deep breath and looked up again at the angel, but he was gone as quietly as he'd appeared. *Gone. I'm losing mind*, thought Chuck.

He turned off the lamp and closed his eyes. Sleep was immediate.

"Sleep, mí amigo. You will soon see clearly." Sergio kept vigil in the darkened room. No demons would enter this building tonight.

THIRTY-ONE

Willis

It was after two in the morning when Willis crawled into bed, feeling good about the call from Collier and her ability to help. Since the government now seemed more concerned with which bathrooms people should use or whether certain individual rights were being violated or that someone should or should not be elected or appointed to some of the most important positions in the free world based on the color of their skin or which sex they identified with, than actual qualifications, Willis and other military leaders were taking a back seat. There was chaos in the world with Russia and the Ukraine, China and North Korea; and with former President Trump's half-finished wall at the southern border of the United States, immigrants were pouring illegally into North America in unprecedented numbers; Texas, New Mexico, Arizona, and California were taking on the burden of helping individuals and families they could neither control nor afford.

The military lost considerable resources left in the Middle East after the War on Terrorism. More equipment was then sent to help Ukraine in its fight against Russia. Money was allocated by the current administration to replace equipment and restore military readiness in the United States, but the fact remained that a drawdown had lessened American military readiness. Veteran suicide rates were up, and esprit de corps had waned. Yet Colonel Phyllis Willis put together a top-notch team in record time.

All were one hundred percent on board and ready to make this happen. Willis promised to take the heat if anything went sideways. She was either going to make that leap to one-star general and keep going or she would retire. The Corps was her life. But if the government would not support the mission of the Marines in support of our own country, she didn't care anymore either. It was time to do or die. Willis and others needed a project to make them feel like the service men and women they were. They needed to help others. She smiled, then closed her eyes and felt sleep come immediately. She'd be up again in less than three hours.

They began arriving shortly before five in the morning. As usual, Colonel Willis was first. The NCOs on duty had made a fresh pot of coffee, and bottles of water were already on ice. Gone were the days of jelly donuts and bear claw pastries. All was ready in the conference room as attendees placed cellphones and weapons in lockers, to be retrieved later.

Willis took the lead once the door was closed. They were in the same room she'd spent half the night counting money with Reynolds and Collier.

"Thank you for taking my unified communications call. This meeting shouldn't take long. We've all got things to do. Let's confirm what we discussed and answer any questions you might have. First question, does anyone foresee any problems?"

She paused and looked around the room. No one put up a hand.

"Next, is everyone clear that your department is on board and not in violation of any government, military, or civilian protocol or laws?" Nods around the table.

"Three, do any of you have any problems with any part of this operation? Are you all still willing to participate? Time is of the essence."

She waited and watched the expressions on the faces of her team. The others looked around as well. All agreed. All were on board. No one other than the colonel had said a word.

Willis waited a heartbeat.

"No? Good. That means we've done it right.

"Now I want to introduce you to the people you're protecting, and the law enforcement officer involved. If they don't agree to the plan, we abort immediately. Agreed?"

Eight heads around the table nodded. These were senior officers and department heads. Decisionmakers from different law enforcement agencies. They were not all US Marines. Six men and two women who could authorize flights, expenditures, training plans, top-secret missions and more. But even these top officials had to answer to someone higher up the chain of command. All had already made late-night phones calls to superiors. Too often the wheels turn slowly, but with the possibility of taking down at least a portion of one of the major drug-related gangs in the country, and protecting the United States from foreign enemies at a time when they weren't otherwise engaged in the wages of war, authority was granted all the way around. Approval came from the highest authority when a call returned from the White House and Operation La Niña was quietly, officially sanctioned.

BOOK III

THIRTY-TWO

Jorge

"How the hell did you lose him?" Jorge spoke quietly into the phone, but there was an edge to his voice. Those sitting near enough to hear felt relief not to be on the other end of the conversation.

"He did what?" Jorge listened as the man he'd sent to follow Chuck Reynolds tried to explain that he'd driven to a military base near San Diego, and they were stopped by the guards. He could not follow him into Camp Pendleton.

"He didn't stop anywhere else that you could have taken care of business?" he asked. Jorge listened a bit longer then shouted into the phone. "*¡Cállate la boca!* Stop talking. Get back here now. Come see me mañana."

He pressed his right thumb against the red button on his phone to end the call. He could feel anger rise in his chest. He wanted to slam the phone down. Throw it against the wall. Punch a hole in something. Shoot something. He didn't.

He sat quietly and waited to get control of his emotions. He needed to keep control of this situation. He needed to find that damn cop. Sergio's old girlfriend, who he was supposed to have killed years ago, and that damn kid were the biggest problems of all. Because of the money. Most of all, Jorge needed to find the money Sergio stole, and Jorge had to get it back before they put a bullet in his head, too.

His men waited and watched. No one said a word. They knew Jorge's moods. He had to answer to those in power, but Jorge was the boss here. He'd taken over from Sergio. Things were different now. Where Sergio was fairly easygoing and even laughed with them sometimes, Jorge was always on edge and ready to have someone killed at the least little slip. The whole organization had been feeling the pressure for months, but from the night Jorge gave the order to kill Sergio, and then they went out and shot up that house, nothing was the same.

Everyone seemed to be waiting for something worse to happen. They had to lie low from the cops, but also from any retaliation that might follow from either the big bosses or those still loyal to Sergio. No one knew who could be trusted. Least of all Jorge.

He looked around Diego's garage, eyeing each man. No women here today. Good. He took a deep breath and eyed the spot where they'd pulled the trigger on Sergio. The heavy plastic collected all the DNA and blood evidence of the kill. Forensics wouldn't find anything in the garage to lead them to Sergio's killers. Jorge was confident that no cop or CSI could ever prove this was a crime scene.

"We're pretty sure Sergio's baby momma is still alive and so is the kid. We know she was somewhere down by Paso Robles out in the country, but we didn't find her. That Cowboy Cop said she moved to Las Vegas, but he was lying. We know she's not there." Jorge held up a hand to silence one of the men who started to ask a question.

"I'm not done," he said with a look that nearly froze the man's heart.

"We've waited for a week and a half to find out who was killed in that house, and we've got nothing. Either no one was there, or they somehow hid so well that all of our bullets missed them. I'm telling you it's impossible, but if anyone died, they are keeping that news completely under wraps. We must continue to maintain silence, too. No one says anything to anyone. You're signing your own death warrant if you do. Got it?"

He individually eyed every man in the garage. Each nodded in agreement as Jorge's eyes met his own.

"We must find that money. I don't have it. None of you have it. Sergio took it. We know he did. No one else could have. But what did he do with it? We searched his grandma's house when she was at church. Not in her bank account nor in any of Sergio's accounts. We searched his house, too. Not there and no trace of it. The boss thinks he took it for the bitch and the kid. Our best bet was following the cop.

"We messed up by not searching his car when he was in Monterey. Something is up with him. The guys I sent after him are on their way back. They lost him. I guess he found the tracker and drove to a military base and destroyed it. They didn't pick him up until he was right outside of the facility, but they said they didn't see any woman or kid with him. No one has seen his car since then. Before he went to Southern California, we had him over in the Valley. He got away there, too. Now we start over. I will not go down alone if we don't get that money back."

Jorge went on talking to his soldiers. "We go back to the start. Keep your eyes open and keep your reports coming in. If she gets on a plane or a bus, I want to know about it. She's probably going to try to run if she has money. Chuck Reynolds will eventually come back here. He's still a local cop. If we didn't kill his wife at the house, he'll come back for her. But we aren't making any moves in that direction. We stay low. Keep the money coming in and keep selling but keep it quiet. No one gets busted. Nothing leads back here.

"Stay armed. Stay alert. Keep as clean as you can. They're watching us. All law enforcement eyes are on us. I'm meeting with the boss this week and will do what I can to convince him that we'll find the money and the bitch," Jorge said and added, "Meeting over. Everyone, back to work. Eyes open."

Jorge left the garage and headed toward Sergio's grandmother's house. He parked in the driveway and sauntered toward the front door. The grass was dry and brown. Her once pretty flower bed along the cracked sidewalk held a few dead flowers. Even the weeds were dead. *This drought sucks*, he thought, and knocked on the door.

He heard her shuffle toward the door, and a moment later she opened it a crack, but left the chain up on the inside.

"Ah, Jorge. You come to see me? You want me to fix you some lunch? I was just heating up a tamale."

She closed the door and took off the chain, opening the door wide for Jorge to enter. She'd known him since he and Sergio were best friends playing together as youngsters.

"No thank you, *Señora*. I just wanted to come by and visit and tell you how sorry I am about Serg."

She led him to the kitchen table. The aroma of her tamales made his stomach grumble. But he wasn't there to eat.

"So terrible," she said. "I worry now about you, too. There are bad people out there. This used to be such a safe neighborhood and town. I don't know how it changed or why, but it makes me sad. I miss my Sergio, but nothing I can do will bring him back." She looked deep into Jorge's dark eyes. "Do you know anything? Who did this or why? The police don't seem to know anything. Or maybe they just don't care because our skin is brown."

Jorge leaned over the table and gave her a small hug.

"*Mamacita*, I haven't heard anything. Who would want to do that to our Sergio? He was a good man. You know that. He was always the one trying to please people. Just like when we were kids. You remember those good times? You remember when we were altar boys together?"

"Oh. *Sí. Sí.* You were such good boys. Now you are all grown up. I still can't believe my Sergio is gone." She started to cry and reached out to hold Jorge.

"You be careful out there, Jorge. I don't want anything to happen to you, either."

"Yeah, well. We do the best we can. Right?"

"Yes. You do that," she said reflectively. "What are you doing for work now? Are you still working for that big produce company? Is there a woman in your life?"

Jorge smiled at Sergio's grandmother. She'd just given him the opening he needed.

"Sí, Abuelita. I'm now a foreman at a major produce company here," he lied.

"And I do have a girlfriend. We might get married next year," he lied again and gave her his best grin. "Will you come to my wedding?"

"Ah, Jorge. Of course, I will. I always thought I'd live to see Sergio marry Patsy someday. But I guess that wasn't meant to be." And there it was.

"What ever happened to Patsy?" he asked casually.

"I don't know. She just was gone one day, and he never talked about her again. But there was never anyone else, either. At least not that I knew about," she said.

"Mamacita," Jorge continued to use one term of endearment after another to keep Grandma at ease. The last thing he wanted was for her to become suspicious of his visit. "Did Sergio leave anything here for me? Maybe a suitcase or a box or something like that?"

She sat a little straighter in her chair. Or did he imagine that?

"Not that I can think of. Why do you ask? Were you expecting him to leave something for you? Did he have something of yours?"

Jorge could sense the change of her tone. She was more guarded now. Cautious. *Careful, Jorge*, he told himself.

"Yeah, well, it's no big deal, but I left something with him that I'd like to get back. I'm just not sure if he still had it."

"What was it?" she asked.

"Uh. Well. Uh. Abuelita. You see. Uh. I'm embarrassed. It was guy stuff," he offered.

"Guy stuff?"

"Yeah. Guy stuff."

"Young man. I did not get this old without knowing when someone is lying to me." She looked him straight in the eye, her tone serious. No more tears.

"You tell me right now what he had of yours that you call, guy stuff."

Jorge's mind had been racing along. "Girlie magazines. I'm sorry, Abuela. Maybe you found them and threw them out? If so, they weren't Sergio's, they were mine and I take full blame."

She stared at him and then began to laugh.

"Oh, you boys! Is that all? I was worried it might be drugs." She continued to giggle and took a hold of his hand across the table.

He could feel the dryness of her skin against the dampness of his own that was beginning to perspire.

"Did you find anything like that?"

"Maybe. But you're going to laugh when you hear what I did with it," she said.

Sergio removed his hand from hers. He could feel sweat breaking out on his upper lip now. He wiped it with the back of his hand, forced an endearing smile, and said, "Tell me."

"Sergio left an Amazon box hidden behind the sofa. It was all sealed up and addressed to an officer at the sheriff's department. I had no idea what was inside and didn't want to know. Sergio didn't put a return address on it, and I didn't either. I didn't want to have to explain anything if it was drugs or something and I didn't want it here in the house. I took it to the post office and mailed it. That was right after they found my sweet Sergio."

Her eyes were getting misty again.

"But I can't imagine why he'd want to send those kinds of books to the sheriff's department. Maybe as a joke?" She laughed.

Jorge no longer felt cold and clammy with sweat and fear. He was beginning to seethe with new anger. At least he was pretty sure he knew who had the money.

"Do you remember the name of the cop Sergio put on the box?" he asked.

"I think it was Reynolds," she said.

There was nothing more he could do here. He wasn't going to hurt Sergio's grandmother. She didn't know anything and while it seemed like she had unwittingly sent over a million dollars to the cops, he wasn't going to out her to the boss. Hurting her would solve nothing. They knew where the money went. Now, more than ever, he had to find that cop. There was only one reason Sergio would send the money to him. He was the one he'd talked to on the street that day. He was the cop that bitch went to see all those years ago. That damn Cowboy Cop. Sergio was trying to find his kid, and that Reynolds had to know where they were hiding. Jorge was sure of it.

Jorge pushed back from the table and stood up.

"You're sure you don't want to stay for tamales?" she asked.

"No, Abuelita. I need to go. It smells good. You take care of yourself and call me if you need anything."

He gave her a brief hug and kissed her cheek. His actions belied the anger and frustration welling inside.

"Thank you, Jorge. Sergio was lucky to have such a good friend as you. You take care of yourself, too."

Jorge drove away with a new action plan coming together in his head. He hit the call button on the steering wheel. A man answered.

"I know where the money is," Jorge said. "But we'll need time and a lot of luck to get it back."

THIRTY-THREE

Chuck

He opened the door to the aroma of fresh coffee and saw a new guard posted at his door. A female sergeant stood outside another door down the hall, and a third was positioned at the closed door to the conference room. It was still dark out, but there was a hum of activity coming from the kitchen and common area. Chuck was dressed and ready to go. However, he was no longer planning to go home this morning. He'd changed his mind about leaving without Patsy and her kid. He had to see this through.

"Do you know if my car is here yet?" Chuck asked the sergeant at the front desk.

"It's out front, sir," came the short answer. "Colonel Willis and the others arrived a few minutes ago. They're in the conference room. The female and child are here, too. They're awake and getting ready. Colonel Willis will be out shortly to meet you. You can wait here if you like. We've got coffee and water, but I'm afraid that's it other than the vending machines down the hall."

"Coffee's fine," Chuck said and filled a paper cup. Taking a sip of the black coffee he wondered why coffee always seemed to smell better than it actually tasted.

The door at the end of the hall opened and Patsy emerged, dressed and ready. Alicea was right behind her. They each had their backpacks on and Chuck thought again how sad it was that they had so few possessions with them. The Walther had been removed from Patsy's pack after the shooting at the ranch. Chuck forgot to ask about it. It was probably still locked up in the evidence room.

"Good morning. Did you two sleep okay?" he asked Patsy.

"Hi!" Alicea was first to respond. "I didn't think we'd get to see you again. Do you know we're at a real army place?"

"Marine Corps," Patsy corrected and smiled at Chuck.

"I'm glad to see you. I'm not sure what's happening, but you're the only one I trust right now. Did you hear about the money, and do you know what's going on?" she asked.

She was talking loud enough for the NCOs to hear. "There was this colonel woman who brought us here last night, but I thought she said you were leaving this morning. Are you leaving? Do you know what's going to happen to us?" she asked. Agitation and anxiety edged her voice.

"I'm not going anywhere until I know you're safe. Let's just sit tight and not talk about this here. Okay?" His eyes traveled to the Marines on duty and back to lock with hers. He was sure they were all very trustworthy, but there were also a million reasons to be cautious.

Patsy picked up two bottles of water and gave one to Alicea.

"Well," she said, "we're as ready as we'll ever be for whatever happens next."

The conference room door opened a few minutes later and Colonel Willis came out. Chuck and Patsy got a brief glimpse of several people inside.

"Good. You're both here. Ma'am, would you be willing to let my Marines keep your daughter company while we have a brief meeting? I promise she'll be in good hands. She won't leave the building, but we have some adult things we need to discuss."

Chuck could see the fear in her eyes. She glanced at Alicea, then back to Chuck for confirmation. He nodded. She bit down her maternal instinct to keep her daughter within sight at all times. Chuck could almost see the emotions play out across her face as she reached a decision.

"Hey, mija. How about you visit with these nice Marines while Mommy and Officer Reynolds have a grown-up meeting? I'll bet you have lots of questions for them."

Alicea took a sip of water and dropped her backpack to the floor. "Sure." Turning to the female Marine who had been posted outside their bedroom she asked, "What's your name?"

Willis went through the ritual of securing phones and weapons again. Then she escorted them both into the conference room and closed the door behind them.

"Have a seat." She gestured toward two empty seats next to each other at the center of the table.

Out of habit, Chuck quickly assessed the nine people in the room and made snap judgements. In addition to Willis, he and Patsy faced six men, three white, two Hispanic, and one Black. There were two other women in the room. One Black and fairly young, the other white and mid-forties. Skin color is of no consequence here. Some wore a uniform, others were in civvies. All were Americans. Chuck knew in a heartbeat these were powerful decisionmakers. These were leaders from several law enforcement agencies, not just the United States Marine Corps. *How did she get them all here so quickly?* Chuck wondered, but said nothing.

Willis began the conversation. "Team, I'd like you to meet Officer Chuck Reynolds and Patsy Garcia. You've been briefed on the situation." Then she turned to Chuck and Patsy. "I'm going to dispense with the introduction of my team. I will tell you only that we pulled together several organizations in order to help you find a safe haven and place for you and your daughter to live." This last she spoke directly to Patsy.

"But." Her tone softened, became less military like. "We agree that our plan might not be to your liking. You are civilians. You are not obligated to do what we think is in your best interest, but we hope you will see the benefit of our plan. It's a plan to help you escape the NF, have a home and a job, and live without fear, once and for all. But it's also a plan to help us capture some high-level drug dealers and fight our own war against crime."

She paused and looked around the room, then back to Chuck and Patsy. "If you don't like the plan, you will immediately be given back what was brought here last night, along with your vehicle, minus the tracking device, and you can determine your own future in any way you see fit." She paused again. The others used their individual keen senses of perception as they studied the faces of Chuck and Patsy for telltale signs of emotion.

"Okay," Patsy said cautiously.

"Shall I continue?" Willis asked.

"Yes. I want to know what you're thinking. If my daughter and I can live without fear, that would be a dream come true."

Chuck kept silent and nodded to Willis. He was glad she didn't say anything about not wanting the money. Chuck knew it would come into play, but he had yet to figure out what Willis was up to. Whatever it was, it was no small matter. You don't assemble a team like this to change a name and put someone on a plane for Timbuktu.

Colonel Willis took a deep breath. Heads nodded around the room.

"First, we put our own sources to work and confirmed the money here in our safe was stolen from the NF. Our sources confirmed the belief that it was stolen by one Sergio Sanchez, and he was killed for it. A high-level foot soldier named Jorge Salazar is leading the ground operation to get the money back. The general belief is that the money was stolen for one Patsy Garcia, in order to secure a future for Sergio's biological daughter, Alicea."

Willis continued. "But we also know that it was not given to her, it was mailed through the United States Post Office to Officer Chuck Reynolds at the Monterey County Sheriff's Department in Salinas, California. The Norteños want the money back. And they're willing to do just about anything short of breaking into a military installation to get it. Everyone still with me?"

More nods around the room. "We also know that they have access to public flight manifests and have somehow tapped into the FAA data systems. They know who is flying and where they are going. This is no small feat. These people have intel at the highest levels and are not to be underestimated. To make this operation work, we need to do four things." She paused again and looked at her watch. It was twenty after five on a Tuesday morning in early September.

"One. We need to make them believe Patsy and her daughter are dead. Two. We need to lure them out of hiding to chase the money. Three. We need to take down as many as possible at the highest levels of the organization. And finally, we need to make sure the charges stick and can be prosecuted."

Patsy took an audible quick breath when Willis mentioned her name and the word dead in the same sentence. "Uh." She raised her hand like she was back in grade school.

"But not really dead, dead. And you aren't going to make me meet with them, are you?" she asked with eyes wide.

"No. Of course not," Willis continued. "We'd like to supply you with new identities, not the ones you picked up in Modesto. But we'd also like to use your real identification to book flights and lure the Norteños after a look-a-like operative. We'll plant chatter online and through our sources. We'll even let the information slip through the walls of our maximum-security prisons where many of the gang leaders are currently housed." Willis looked at Chuck this time.

"We need to be convincing, and we'd like you to stay involved. They will eventually discover that the money went to you, if they haven't already. They shot up your home. They aren't going to stop unless they get some money and think you are out of the picture as well."

Willis dropped her eyes to the table and back to Chuck. She knew a lot was riding on her next words. "As you know, plans can change, but to protect your family, we think you should retire and find a quiet safe place to live, far away from Salinas. You'll have to make a new life, too. You are too known and too visible. We believe it's only a matter of time before they come after you again. And your family. You got yourself into this mess by nature of your job. You can keep doing as you see fit, but we all agree that will only lead to your early death. You won't stop them forever."

"I need to talk to my wife," Chuck said.

"With your permission, we'll have someone from the Naval Postgraduate School in Monterey pick up your wife and mother-in-law this morning and bring them here. Is there anyone else that needs our protection? Other family members? Pets?"

Chuck thought of his sister and her family. They lived up the canyon beyond his home. The siblings were years apart in age and had never been overly close. They shared family time, but never socialized together. They had different names. Plus, his sister and her husband were card carrying NRA members. He had no doubt they could hold off a small army if necessary. She'd have a fit if the United States Marines showed up to "protect" her.

"No," he said. "There's no one else they will threaten to get to me. My wife has the dog with her, and my sister can take the horses and livestock."

"What about you? We know about the loss of your mother, but is there anyone else close to you? Anyone who was close to Sergio?" she asked Patsy.

Patsy looked at the Colonel and glanced at the faces around the table. Her eyes took on the shimmer of unshed tears. "No. Me and Alicea are all alone. My employer where we lived won't want anything to do with this, but I'd like to get our stuff out of our house. Sergio had a grandmother in Salinas, but I don't know if she's still alive. I don't think they'd hurt her, though. Uh, can you tell me where we are going to go?"

"First of all. I need an answer. Do you want our help, and do you agree to work with us and help us, in return for a new life? I'm not disclosing a location at this time but will tell you that we will make you as comfortable as possible. You will be able to live without fear, and you may not be rich, but we can ensure you get a portion of the money for Alicea's education and living expenses." Willis looked at the Black woman on the panel. She nodded.

"I need both of you to agree and I need you to agree now. If you walk out the door, you will keep going and we will all forget this meeting ever took place." She checked her watch again and waited.

Chuck sat very still. He thought about the dream. It had seemed so real. And now, dream or not, the message from Sergio was clear. He knew what to do. They really had no other choice.

THIRTY-FOUR

Blanca

The angels were also in the conference room. Sergio was restless. He wanted his Cowboy Cop to accept the offer and convince Patsy to do the same. He knew the Norteños would never stop hunting for the money or his kid. They'd hurt her. He knew in his heart he'd hurt them bad enough already. He wasn't there for them when they needed him. He nearly got them killed by mouthing off to Jorge Salazar. "Oh God. I did so many bad things when I was alive. Help me, so I can help them now," he prayed.

Blanca raised a large wing and smiled. "We do what we can. They'll make the choice they are supposed to make, and we will stay with them until they, too, are called home."

"Am I supposed to get nervous like this?" he asked.

Blanca laughed. "Sometimes we do. That's usually when I call for reinforcements. But they are already here. Can't you feel them?"

Sergio didn't know what he was feeling. "Maybe I'm too new at this. I feel very unsure about most everything."

"That's normal," she said. "Just keep praying. Your energy is guiding Chuck. I've watched him take care of Patsy and Alicea since she called him about the letter in her mailbox. He cares. He's gone above and beyond to keep them safe. He's put himself and his family in danger for them. He needs you now. He needs an angel in his court. God chose you for the job. What a privilege!"

Boosted by her pep talk, Sergio prayed on Chuck's behalf. "Lord, thy will be done. Please take care of this man and help him as he helps others. Please keep them safe."

Sergio thought he heard laughter.

That's why I sent you, my son.

Patsy

"Chuck?" She looked at him with a question in her voice. "I'm sorry. You had a life before all this. Now you're in danger, too. And your sweet Maria. I feel so bad. But I can't go back to my house and always be looking over my shoulder. I can't do that. I can't take the money and try to buy my way to safety. They'll find me. I need to agree. But if you don't, I understand."

Chuck looked at the silent faces around the room. "Looks like we're in. I've been thinking about retirement anyway. I guess it's time. You just gotta promise me that you aren't going to drop me a city somewhere."

There was an inaudible release of tension in the room. Patsy felt it as much as anyone. She'd been so afraid Chuck would say no.

"So now what?" she asked.

"Now we go to work," Willis said. She stood and opened the door. The meeting was over.

Alicea sat at a small table in the kitchen with the female sergeant and wore her uniform cap on her small head. Her dark hair was pulled back into a tight bun at the nape of her neck to look just like the young NCOs.

"Mommy! Look what Miss Barb did to my hair? She said I could call her Miss Barb, even though the men call her Gittens. That's her last name. Everybody calls everyone by their last names, not their first names. Isn't that weird?"

Patsy smiled as her daughter shared what she had learned about Marine Corps life in the last few minutes. "You look very pretty and very grown up with your hair like that," she said.

"Thank you, ma'am." Alicea gave a short bow, proud of this new information. She was at that impressionable age when children are like sponges, soaking up everything they can, before they become teenagers and insist they already know everything there is to know.

Colonel Willis went with the others to retrieve cellphones and weapons, then escorted them out the front door. Chuck's car was there, too.

"I guess we'll know soon enough what we've gotten ourselves into," Patsy said.

"Mama, I'm ready to go home." Alicea pulled on her mother's sleeve. "Will you fix my hair like this for school?"

Willis returned to the small group of people in the kitchen. "Okay, folks. Grab your gear. Let's get some breakfast. We've got a big day ahead."

Blanca

"Have you figured out where they're going?" Blanca asked.

"I haven't a clue," said Sergio.

"Me either," she said and added, "But we've got the good guys in charge and it looks like they have a plan to help everyone."

Thinking back to the day she first met Patsy and became her guardian, Blanca shared what she knew with Sergio.

"Do you remember the day Patsy told you she was pregnant?"

"How could I forget?" he asked in return. "I was so angry with her I almost killed her then and there. She got mad back at me, and everything escalated. We talked about this not too long ago. I went to my friend Jorge's house to cool off and that's when I opened my mouth complaining about her, and they ended up ordering me to kill her." He shook his head.

"Me? Kill the woman I loved? It would not have been the first time they ordered something like that, nor the last. You had to prove yourself. Loyalty above all. Blood in. Blood out.

"Anyway, I was consumed by that anger back then. It fed me. I was probably capable of anything. But you know what?" He didn't wait for an answer. "I changed after that. I thought about being a father. I wanted to be a better father than my dad had been. I didn't want anyone to hurt Patsy or the kid." He looked at the floor, remembering. "Yeah, I remember that day. It was a bad day."

"You're right, Sergio. It was a bad day. I was there, too. Several of us were there. We stopped you from killing her. We stopped you from killing that precious little girl. We stopped you because God asked us to stop you. Alicea needed to be born. She is part of a much greater plan to help your people and the people of Salinas. The gangs and the violence need to stop. Your best friend ordered your execution. My heart breaks just thinking about that. I don't know her role as an adult, but your daughter holds a key that will someday unlock a world of peace and possibilities for goodness to prevail."

He stared at Blanca. "You were there? Nobody was there. Just me and her."

"You couldn't see us then, but we were there. Do you remember breaking the cookie jar? Remember your hands around her throat? Remember that voice in your head telling you to let her go?" Blanca spoke softly, letting her words sink in for him to realize she knew things that no one else did.

"Were you that voice?" he asked.

"No. That was Jeff. He was your guardian."

"Where is he now?"

"Jeff isn't a trainer, and he got a new assignment when you passed. He could not prevent Jorge from killing you, but he did get you to Heaven, and he did save your little girl and Patsy. That's a win in our book." She smiled and her whole face lit up.

"Whoa! You're glowing!"

"That happens sometimes when we are really happy. It's always best when we're happy for someone else or another angel. I'm happy for both Jeff and for you. Oh, wait until you meet the Love Angels! They are so very delightful! Lots of energy and light," she told him.

"There's a lot to learn in this Angel business, isn't there?" Just when Sergio thought he was figuring things out, they hit him with something else. There seemed to be a lot of rules and regulations and then they changed. Or did they? Maybe it wasn't a one-size-fits-all sort of deal.

"Hey," he said. "Can they see us sometimes?"

"I think sometimes, yes. It depends," she said.

"On what?"

Blanca laughed. "I don't even know. I don't think anyone has ever seen me, but I know my friend Roy has been seen, and Hannah turns into an owl whenever she wants to."

"Hannah was the other angel with us earlier. Roy? I don't think I've met him," Sergio said.

"No? You will. Those two are as different as night and day. Hannah is a Warrior and Roy was a Church of the Brethren, God-fearing farmer from Ohio. He's the quiet one, but he gets things done. At any rate, God gives us what we need when we need it. We don't do anything without His word."

"We, collectively and individually, are simply soldiers for God. We're angels. We aren't in charge. We don't make policy. We can't enforce anything. We can only be there and try to keep them safe and help them find eternal life with God in Heaven. The demons, those bad guys from down below, are doing everything they can to persuade humans to make bad choices. We do what we can. We save a lot. But we don't save them all."

Blanca looked lovingly at the humans. "Let's go. It looks like they're heading out."

Chuck

He drove his own car and followed Willis and the girls who were back in the Humvee. It was just after six on Tuesday morning. Maria would be up soon. He needed his wife. He needed to hear her voice. He needed to know she was okay and let her know what was happening.

She picked up on the second ring.

THIRTY-FIVE

Two weeks later
Jorge

"How do we get on that fucking military base?" Jorge Salazar was livid. His people had gone back down to Sureño country, trying to find that asshole cop and Sergio's baby momma who had their money. Nothing was going as planned. He listened for a few more minutes to the man on the other end of the burner phone.

"What?! You're sure?"

The three other men in the black SUV listened to the one-sided conversation.

"Yes, sir," Jorge said. "I'm on it." He was riding in the back seat and Diego was driving.

"Fuck," he said after clicking off the phone.

Monterey County Sheriff's Department

Sheriff Mike Foster leaned back in his chair and smiled. Alone in his office, he read the news report again.

The Associated Press

CAMP PENDLETON, CA. — Five civilians were killed and two Marines were injured in a fiery vehicle crash at Camp Pendleton Marine Corps Base in Southern California.

The two-vehicle explosion Sunday night killed a recently retired Monterey County Deputy Sheriff, his wife and mother-in-law, along with another civilian woman and her six-year-old daughter, who were all in the same vehicle. Two Marines from the 1st Marine Division at Camp Pendleton were also injured.

Division Colonel Phyllis Willis said Wednesday that the cause of the accident was under investigation but that both vehicles were traveling at a high rate of speed and were completely destroyed in the fiery explosion.

Willis would not release the names of those involved and did not have details about the extent of the injuries. She did not give any reason for the civilians being at Camp Pendleton.

A spokesperson for the Monterey County Sheriff's Department would not comment or provide any other information.

Foster leaned forward and picked up the file still on his desk. Chuck Reynolds' retirement application and confirmation. He hoped the news out of Camp Pendleton would work. He had no idea where Chuck went or how he pulled this off, but it had his fingerprints all over it. Foster knew in his heart there would be no official death certificate for any of them.

Coming on the heels of the huge Norteño/Sureño bust last week, Sheriff Foster knew Chuck had something to do with it. He didn't work Vice, but somehow always managed to weed out the troublemakers in his county. How on earth the feds got involved and set them up, Foster had no idea. They had not been in touch with his office until they made the arrests. Jorge Salazar and those lower-level dealers were lying low again.

Foster never understood the posturing between agencies about who was in charge or who got credit for a bust. His concern was always to get the job done. Weed out the bad guys, get illegal drugs off the streets, and keep his county safe. It was a beautiful county. He loved it here.

"I'll miss you, Chuck. You were one of a kind," he said aloud in the stillness of his private office. "Wherever you are, wherever you go, I wish you all the best."

Jorge
"Talk to us," said Diego. "What's going on?"

"El Jefe and four others got busted. I guess they met up with some of the Sureños and some of them got busted, too. They're all being held by the feds, and I guess they got the money Sergio took and the last cocaine shipment, too. We got to get Francisco and Roberto back here. Pronto. Call them right now. Then I'll tell you the rest."

Diego made the call to the two men who had been searching in vain for Chuck Reynolds in all of the small towns surrounding Camp Pendleton.

"Patrone says come home," Diego repeated the four words when he was asked for more information by Roberto. "Patrone says come home." Diego hit the off button on his phone.

"So, what else?" he asked Jorge. "You got more bad news?"

"Yes and no. In a way, it's good news. We don't have to worry about the asshole Cowboy Cop or Sergio's baby momma no more. They all got killed down there at that fucking Marine Corps Base."

The air in Jorge's voice had gone flat.

"It's like we had this whole job to get the bitch and the kid. Get the money. Set up the cop and get rid of him once and for all, too. We didn't do anything. And it's all done."

Jorge started to laugh. "It's fucking done!"

"Let's go get a *cervesa*. We got no orders and nothing to do for a while. As long as they can't pin Sergio on us, we're good."

Diego turned up the music, and the men were in high spirits once again.

Chuck

He parked the rental car and took his first look at the ranch from the road.

"This is it," Maria said. "What do you think?"

"Looks beautiful," Chuck said.

"I think we need to drive in there and see the house and the land. Don't you?"

"The realtor will be here in a few minutes. I just want to get a sense of it first." He had the window down and could feel a touch of fall in the air.

"Winter comes earlier here," he said.

Maria slid her hand across the console and caressed his muscular thigh.

"Good. I'm looking forward to some cool evenings and a warm fire with my husband at home, instead of off chasing bad guys."

Sergio
"I thought since I was with the Cowboy Cop, maybe I'd still be in Salinas," Sergio said to no one in particular. He looked around at the countryside out here in the middle-of-nowhere America and wondered again how he got there.

"Am I going to eventually get some training for this job?" he asked aloud and watched as Chuck paused, and a strange look passed over his face.

"You can hear me again, can't you?" he asked with excitement.

"What did you say?" Chuck asked.

Maria answered, "I said I'm looking forward to some evenings with my husband and a warm fire.

"Chuck. What's going on? You have that deer-in-the-headlights look you get sometimes when I know you are working out some scenario in your head." Maria knew her husband well.

He came out of it immediately and gave her his best smile.

"Nothing. Yes. I was just thinking. It could be nice living here."

"You can hear me! I know you can! Listen, man. I'm not a ghost. You aren't crazy. I'm your new Guardian Angel! It's me, Sergio Sanchez! Can you believe it?"

"No," Chuck said.

"No what?" Maria asked.

"No." He regained his composure. "I'm not sorry I retired. We belong in a place like this. Away from death and violence."

"Amen," came the voice of Maria's mother in the back seat. She had no idea there was a very real Guardian Angel sitting next to her on the seat. Although she'd always believed in God, and she believed in Guardian Angels, too, the thought of one actually being with them through all of their choices and actions was not something any of them ever consciously thought about.

"Amen," Chuck and Maria added. As did Sergio. The angel was ecstatic that Chuck could hear him.

"I know you can hear me," he said again, with a sing-song lilt to his Spanish accent.

Chuck wondered if the stress was causing him to imagine things.

I don't make mistakes.

Patsy

She had just finished brushing Alicea's hair and put the clips in to hold it back on either side. Patsy smiled and gave her daughter a hug.

"This is exciting! Your first day of school here and my first day at my new job."

"And our new names, too," Alicea reminded her.

"You remembered! Good."

"We are lucky to be here. And to have Señora Sophia here all the time to watch over us and help us get settled is really good, too."

"I like her," Alicea said. "She's nice."

They had been on the island of Ibiza for five days. Patsy was still getting acclimated to the many changes they'd experienced recently. She shuddered thinking about the night they escaped through the field. Now, she and Alicea were living temporarily with Señora Sophia, a retired officer with the Ibiza Policía.

She had a new job as a hostess at the prestigious TRS Resort in Sant Antoní. All of this, her whole new life in this beautiful place, had been arranged by unseen forces, as had their new living arrangement with Señora Sophia. Everything had been done for her. For them. How could she ever thank them?

She wondered where Cowboy Chuck was now. Had he gone back to Salinas? She didn't think so. She knew it was dangerous for him to be there now. Because of her. Not for the first time, she felt a tear threaten to spill. Her emotions had been getting the best of her recently.

As if reading her mind, Alicea asked, "Mommy, is Officer Chuck coming here, too?"

"No, sweetie. I don't think so. He was talking about retiring and taking his wife to a place she loves. It's just you and me. But we can have a good life here. We'll be speaking more Spanish than English, too."

"Are you ready to go?" Señora Sophia called from the kitchen.

"Yes!" they answered in unison.

As Sophia pulled the car out from under the carport and started down the hill, the sun danced off the Mediterranean like a sea of diamonds. Patsy silently made the sign of the cross, blessing herself and thanking God for delivering them from evil.

Blanca

The angel felt Patsy's prayer and love for the Lord. "He holds you and He is always there for you. All you have to do is ask for Him." Blanca made the sign of the cross, too. "Thank you, Lord, for giving me these two to watch over and protect. It has been my joy to be with them on this journey. Whatever future, time without end, in my eternal journey as an angel, I will forever feel blessed for having been here for these two."

I don't make mistakes. Your journey with them is not yet complete.

Bret and Maddie

"Have you talked to your mom?" Bret asked.

Maddie laughed. "We've both been so busy that I forgot to tell you, but yes, I've talked with her several times." Maddie put the finishing edge on a trophy she'd just engraved.

In addition to Bret's job at Camp Pendleton and volunteer work at the VFW, Maddie worked part-time in accounting for a local construction firm, and the couple owned an online engraving company.

"She was relieved to know we didn't have to go to Mexico and that all her plans were appreciated, but most were not needed in the end. The worst is that she is dying to know how they are doing in Ibiza and where Chuck Reynolds went. And of course, what our role ended up being in all this. And we can't tell her."

"I know. That sucks. Maybe I can talk to Willis and let her in on a need-to-know basis."

"Bret, we can't do that. Don't even ask. The less she knows, the better. For everyone's sake, including her own. It bothers me that she knows Patsy is in Ibiza, but that was part of her plan in the beginning because of her connection and friendship with Señora Sophia. I'm glad the operation went that route for Patsy. Mom said that place is beautiful."

"You're right. But we should think of something to tell her so she stops asking more questions. If she sees the report that they all died, you know she's going to flip out." Bret seemed more concerned about his mother-in-law than Maddie did.

"This time, you're the one who is right. Let's call her now. But you know I can't lie to her. I have to let her know they're safe, but she can't know anything more. And we can't stop her friend Chuck from calling her if he decides to do that. But after all these years, and for her safety, I doubt he will contact her again."

Maddie set the trophy on the counter and picked up her cellphone.

"Hey, Mom. Gotta few minutes?"

BOOK IV

THIRTY-SIX

Six months later
Ibiza, Spain

The young waiter's eyes lingered over the hostess a little too long. He'd flirted with her when she first started work, but she didn't seem interested. He hadn't given up. He was biding his time. There were plenty of other girls to keep him busy. His tall, lean body; dark eyes; and handsome facial features served him well in life, and especially with the ladies.

He turned his back to her and wondered what it was about her that intrigued him so much. She was pretty. But no more so than most of the women he met. She had a nice voice. He liked her American accent. *I will add her to my list*, he thought. *Someday.*

Joshe Jimenez had worked at the TRS Hotel for more than a year. He began cleaning tables at the poolside café and had worked his way up to be a waiter at one of the nicer restaurants on the property. That's where Alejandra Tur worked, at the hostess station. Her Spanish had improved since she first started to work at the resort and she was finally beginning to understand the difference between the Spanish she knew from the States, and the Catalan or Ibicenco spoken by locals in Ibiza. He wondered about her back story. Where had she come from? She was definitely from America. He thought he heard from someone that she was from California. Someday he wanted to visit there. He'd lived in Sant Antoní for all of his twenty-eight years. He loved Ibiza. The Americans pronounce it eye-bee-za, but locals say eye-be-tha. The vibrant bohemian lifestyle was the only way of life he knew. He wanted to travel, but he never wanted to live anywhere else.

His job as a waiter at the TRS put him in touch with a lot of wealthy European travelers, but the hotel had a strict policy about not getting involved with guests. But management was far less concerned about those employees who got involved with each other. That only became a problem if the relationship didn't last and someone got upset, and then it did become a problem. He'd had two of those. No more, he told himself. But then he'd feel that spark every time he was in close proximity to Alejandra. He kept telling himself that he preferred girls who were obvious and loose with their bodies. They didn't cause emotional problems for him.

It was a way of life here in Ibiza. People sunbathed and swam in the nude. Bodies were lathered with oil. There were few inhibitions on the island in general. The resort was different in that respect. Guests here were from all over Europe, and some came from America or Australia. A few even visited from Asia, Africa, South America, and the Middle East, but not many. TRS guests were more reserved than locals or those who'd found the island years earlier. It had been a haven for hippies back in the sixties. Hippies and wealthy actors seemed to gravitate to Ibiza. The TRS itself was considered a very respectful, cosmopolitan all-inclusive resort. Upscale.

Joshe sensed that Alejandra was like the resort. Upscale, with a respect for herself that meant she wasn't inclined to have indiscriminate sex. Like the resort, she was different, too. She would not be loose with sexual favors. At least he didn't think so. He wanted her, though. The devil danced through his thoughts about her and made him think of all sorts of delicious games they could play together. Maybe it was time to start dropping a few hints. He could always hope.

All this went through his head as he took an order for a Galician T-bone steak and lamb ribs from a nice couple visiting from Edinburgh, Scotland. Joshe's engaging smile, easy banter with guests, and flirtatious manner with older women ensured his tips were always generous.

Patsy/Alejandra

It had taken some time to get used to using the name Alejandra Tur. Alejandra and Alicea Tur. Their new names for their new life. She liked her job. She was learning the hospitality business at a posh resort here in San Antonio Abad on one of the Balearic Islands. Locals called it Sant Antoní.

It had been six months since she and Alicea stepped off the jet that had flown them from Ramstein Air Base in Germany to Ibiza. Alejandra didn't know how they did it. She didn't want to know how they did it. But the fact remained that she had a bank account with money in it. She'd finally received the money that had been held for her from her mother's estate, and apparently some of Sergio's stolen money had been put there, too. She had more money than she'd ever had in her life but was warned to be extremely cautious about spending too much. No worries there. She was used to being frugal.

When a small apartment next to Sophia became available at the start of the new year, Alejandra jumped at the chance to rent it. She and Sophia had become instant friends, even though Sophia was twenty years older. The dear woman had grown to love Alicea, too. She watched her when Alejandra had to work and often fixed meals for mother and daughter, too. Alicea and Alejandra were rapidly increasing their command of the Catalan language spoken in Ibiza and slowly losing their heavy American accents.

Castilian Spanish is spoken throughout Spain, but many regions have developed individual languages and dialects. Those who live in Ibiza speak Catalan, but with a dialect known as Ibicenco.

Alejandra had spent weeks having Sophia work with her to change her distinctive California Spanglish into the beautiful language of Ibicenco. Her first lesson had been to stop thinking of her new home as being in San Antonio, and begin calling this beautiful city Sant Antoní.

"Sophia." Alejandra sat at her friend's kitchen table as the two chatted over coffee one morning. "Do you think it would be possible for me to someday open my own small bed and breakfast here in Ibiza?"

"Of course, Alejandra! Anything is possible." She looked at the younger woman and her face took on a more serious expression. "But you should remember there is always a chance they will find you. I worry even as you are hostess at TRS."

Alejandra sighed.

"I know you're right. And I do make enough money to be happy, and I ask myself why would I want that extra work anyway?"

Sophia nodded. "But there is something of the American in you, isn't there? You yearn for making it on your own. Being your own boss. Beholding to no one. Am I right about that?"

"Something like that, I suppose," Alejandra mused. "It just keeps stirring in the back of my head to have something of my own someday that I can leave for Alicea. A legacy. Something more than having had a drug dealer for a father who was never there for her."

Blanca

"We're together again!" Blanca said as she looked around at the other angels. "What is the occasion?"

"I asked to bring you together because even angels need a pep talk now and then. None of our humans are in crisis mode right now, either," Hannah said with a grin.

"We've all been working long and hard to keep them safe, and our work has been rewarded. We have saved a lot of souls. Our work is never over, and I'm still amazed that we've been able to reach so very many lives through prayer and effort. Even though we lose those who refuse to listen to us or to accept the Lord, our work is never in vain. We move on and save the next one."

Many of the Warrior Guardian Angels had lived as humans at one time. They were not necessarily the most righteous on earth, but they all believed in God and trusted Him completely. Hannah had once been Hannah Duston. She'd lived in the New England colony known as Haverhill, north of Boston, in the late 1600s. After she passed from the earth, her story was told and retold. She was made famous by one early historian named Cotton Mather, who wrote about her being kidnapped by Abenaki Natives and her subsequent escape. Fearing for her life as a slave or being killed if she resisted, she killed ten of her captors and scalped them to prove what she had done, and for the bounty being paid for those scalps.

It was a brutal time in history. She'd already seen her younger sister found guilty in the court of public opinion, sent to prison, and hung. She lived her later years in fear of retaliation by God, by the Abenaki, or both, for her brave act to save herself and two others. Even today, there are those who condemn her actions and those who call her a hero. She has faithfully watched over her descendants and many others for nearly three hundred years. She is a fierce Warrior Guardian Angel, protector of the innocent. She's also a trainer. Her story has been retold thousands of times. She is legendary, even among the hundreds of thousands of angels who serve God.

Blanca was happy to see the two angels she'd worked with to seal the Demon Portal before she was assigned to protect Patsy and Alicea. Roy had been a farmer in Ohio. He was truly a righteous man. He was also mentored by Hannah. Blanca knew Roy had been tasked to return and watch over his own family and descendants in Ohio.

Jeff was there, too. He'd been Sergio's Guardian since Patsy first confirmed her pregnancy with Alicea. Oh, what a day that was. It was high drama for all the Guardians. Jeff helped Blanca and Roy seal the portal and then stayed with Sergio throughout the rest of his short life.

Most had expected Sergio to go the other way. He'd turned away from God too many times and made bad choices because too often he listened to the demons. They were strong in him. But Jeff was stronger. His grandmother helped, too. Her prayers were constant. Sergio never forgot his early lessons about God. He never forgot his days as an altar boy at St. Mary of the Nativity. At the end, he died praying and asking God to forgive him. Jesus died on the cross for our sins. When Jorge Salazar ordered Sergio's execution, the Lord brought one of His lost sheep home—for good.

Blanca turned to Bambico, the red-skinned angel, with long dark hair. "I remember seeing you when we gathered on the hill to send Chax, Mara, and Abaddon back to Hell."

"Yes. I help Hannah sometimes, too. And she helps me. We come from different tribes, but God does not see those differences. He sees our faith."

Bambico nodded towards Hannah and acknowledged their relationship as teammates now working on the same side. He continued to watch over his own descendants, too.

Hannah spread her wings wide and felt the love of these Warriors. They worked well together.

"The lives of our people are interwoven. You'll pick up other assignments, as those you currently help become stronger and closer to God. They'll need you less often. But they will also call on you regularly for help and you will always be there for them."

"Sergio, I understand you were actually heard and seen by the cop." Hannah's statement turned all eyes toward the newcomer.

"Yeah, I think so. But he didn't believe it. I tried to tell him I was an angel and not a ghost. He didn't buy that, either. But I'm starting to get used to this. I'm still not sure how I got here. Is there some sort of training manual that comes with the job?"

The angels looked back at Hannah. Roy spoke first. "I guess it's different for all of us. Hannah, didn't Sergio go through Orientation?"

"Orientation?" asked Sergio.

"It was an emergency situation, and he was needed immediately," Hannah said.

"Sergio, now that Chuck Reynolds is retired and living his life in peace with his wife and her mother on their new ranch, far away from those who wish him ill, it's time for you to catch up. You'll be heading to Orientation now, but I thought you'd like to meet Jeff and those of us who've been involved behind the scenes in your life for the past six years. Blanca here has been protecting Patsy and your little Alicea. Your daughter has an important role to play in the future. She needed to be born, and she needs to live long enough to become an adult."

Sergio stared at Hannah. "She does? What? Why?" he asked. Confused.

"That is knowledge I don't have," Hannah said. "We only know we need to protect them both. Someday they will know you helped save them, too. Someday."

With that, Sergio was gone.

Blanca felt that itch begin again between her wings. She turned to Hannah. "Is there something else going on? I have that itch I get whenever the demons are near or trouble is coming."

"There will always be trouble, and there will always be demons to fight. We each have our individual warning systems. It must be time for you to return. The Lord is with you. We'll be there when you need us," Hannah told her.

THIRTY-SEVEN

Joshe

"Hey, Alejandra. Do you want to go dancing one night? Or just come and hang out with some of my friends? We usually go to the O Beach Club or the Highlander Scottish Bar. It's a lot of fun." Joshe tried to sound casual but worried she might detect the small shake of nerves in his voice. Why was he nervous? He'd asked a hundred girls out before. What was it about this one that made him feel all weird inside?

"Gosh, Joshe. I haven't been out with friends or on a date in like forever. Are you asking me on a date? Or just inviting me to join your group of friends for a night out?"

Well, she's direct, he thought.

"Whatever you're comfortable with," he answered. They were the only two in the hostess area, but that would change soon. The restaurant was due to open in another fifteen minutes. He felt himself blush. *This is new*, he thought.

"Uh, I think I just want to get to know you better. We've been working together for a few months now and I don't know anything about you," he said.

"Yeah, I'm not much of a party person. And you seem to be all about the parties. So, I don't know. I'd probably have to say no. But on the other hand, I'd like to know more about you, too. I don't have any real friends here. Only my neighbor and she's a lot older than me."

Alejandra laughed and realized that she enjoyed this easy conversation, despite the hesitation she felt inside. She thought of Alicea. Her daughter had been the entire focus of her world since before she was born. Now, she found that she enjoyed the attention Joshe paid to her. She'd noticed the looks he'd sent her way in the past. There was chemistry between them. She knew they both felt it.

"So, we got to go to work, but think about it. Okay?" he said.

"I will." She smiled, and her face lit up with a radiance he hadn't noticed before.

She's even prettier than I thought. He wanted her. He'd have to take this slow, if he was to get beyond second base. But he would. Of that, he was sure. He knew how to play the game with those who said they didn't want to play. They all want to play. He knew the right buttons to push, too.

Chax, Mara, and Abaddon celebrated a small victory.

"Can you believe we're still trying to win this one?"

"He is so close! But now we have to deal with that little bitch again."

"Right? That Blanca is more formidable than we thought."

"Her pulling that stunt with the sword back in the restaurant was ballsy for an angel."

"Yeah, but Joshe has that sexy Latin charm. He'll disarm this one and we can step in again."

"No need to hurry. We've got years to work on turning that kid to our side."

Blanca watched the demons melt into the night. She knew that itch was back for a reason.

"Not on my watch," she said into the darkness.

Alejandra

She tossed and turned in bed that night, restless with thoughts that kept returning to Joshe Jimenez, her co-worker. What was it about him that made her feel like she hadn't felt since Sergio? *Maybe I'm just lonely*, she thought.

She wondered for the umpteenth time since the day they met if he was really the womanizing player he seemed to be, or if there was something deeper beneath the surface. She had too much at stake to spend time with anyone who wasn't long-term-husband and father material. Namely, Alicea.

She vowed the day she discovered she was pregnant to protect that child with her life and everything in her. And she would. They'd just escaped all sorts of trouble back in California, and she sure didn't want to risk more problems here in Ibiza. *Maybe I can talk to Sophia about this*, she thought. *She's become my friend, and I like having her close. She's almost like a mom to me.*

Alejandra said a short prayer, asked God to guide her, turned over once more, fell immediately into a deep sleep, and began to dream.

She was standing near the water. Above it. Looking down on the beautiful blue Mediterranean Sea. The sun was warm on her face. A soft breeze caressed her cheek. She lifted her hand a tucked a loose strand of hair behind her ear. It was warm here. Not hot like summer in Central California. She felt peace as she breathed slowly in and out. Deep breaths. She held each breath for a count of seven.

The dream began to fade in and out. She was on the shore. Then she was breathing in and out and thought of the friend who had told her years ago that breathing in for a count of seven, holding for seven, then releasing for seven and doing that seven times would help her relax and rejuvenate her oxygen, lungs, blood, and would do a host of other good things for her body.

She had no idea whether that was true, but she practiced the exercise often. Then she was back in Salinas. In the dream, she and Sergio were lying together on the bed in the small apartment they shared. He brushed the hair from her eyes and told her how beautiful she was. He said she would always be his woman. They were meant to be together forever.

The image faded and she was once again looking out over the water. She felt someone next to her. Someone took hold of her hand. She swayed in the sunshine and closed her eyes. Who was there? She couldn't see him. Her? But the presence was comforting. Calming.

She stirred and felt the ground shift. Where was she now? Moving. A boat? Rocking. She thought of rocking her little Alicea to sleep years ago. Someone was rocking her now. She smiled in her sleep. And as quickly as it had begun, the dream was over. She went back to sleep.

When her alarm went off two hours later, Alejandra woke refreshed and ready to take on the day. She had showered and was putting on her make-up when she remembered the dream. She stared at her reflection in the mirror and stopped moving. She sat down the tube of mascara she'd been holding, about to apply it to already long and beautiful lashes. She stared at herself in the mirror.

It was Sergio, she thought. *He was with me in the dream. He held me again. He made me feel beautiful and wonderful and loved. I believed him. But it wasn't true.* Her eyes began to fill with tears. "Dammit," she said out loud to herself. "Why do I get weepy-eyed over that creep?"

"But I did love you, Patsy."

She heard it as clear as if he were standing next to her while she was in the bathroom, putting on her make up. She froze. It was his voice. A voice she hadn't heard since the day she found out she was pregnant and he wanted her to get an abortion. She hated that voice she'd heard that day. That awful, harsh voice had replaced the gentle one he first used with her. It was Sergio's soft voice she'd just heard again. But that was impossible.

Alejandra stared hard at her image in the mirror.

"You've been through a lot. Don't start losing it now," she said to herself.

"Find someone to love you and help you raise our daughter. She needs a father, too. Joshe Jimenez is a good man. I was not. Forgive me. I'm sorry."

Alejandra sat very still in front of the mirror. There was no one else in the bathroom. In fact, there was no one else in the apartment. Alicea had already eaten breakfast and gone off to school. This was Alejandra's time to get ready for the day, do some housework, and maybe run errands. This was not the time to daydream about an old lover, even if he was Alicea's baby daddy, and especially bad was that she was imaging him telling her to date Joshe!

She stared hard at herself, took another deep breath, and began to laugh.

"You are losing it!" She laughed again, talking to herself in earnest now.

"God, are you playing tricks on me? I think I'm losing my mind, but I feel perfectly normal and sane. Why would I now, after all these years, find myself thinking about the love Sergio and I shared and thinking he is telling me to explore a possible relationship with Joshe Jimenez?"

"And he apologized." She thought about the money he left for her. He was killed for that money. He'd made a plan to get it to her before they killed him. He wanted her to have it. For Alicea.

Maybe he did love us after all, she thought. She picked up the mascara and finished her eyes. She added a soft smear of lip gloss and decided to go in early for work. She and Joshe were working the lunch shift today. Alicea would be with Sophia this afternoon. Maybe she could take Joshe up on his offer to visit after work today.

As she locked the door behind her and walked down the path toward her new car, that was used but new to her, Alejandra's step was lighter. Her head was high, and a smile played across her face. Anyone looking would see a radiant and vibrant young woman. Strong. Confident. Energetic. She looked like the kind of woman you wanted to get to know. Because whatever she had going for her, you wanted some of that, too.

THIRTY-EIGHT

Joshe

"Hey, God. It's me. Joshe." He couldn't believe he was actually on his knees and praying to the God he knew was there but the God he'd avoided for a lot of years.

"Yeah, I know. It's been a long time. But I need you. I really need you."

He paused and wondered how to go on. What did God already know and what did God not know? Anything? Or is God really all-knowing and all-seeing? Joshe didn't know. He knew a lot of people who believed in God figured He already knew everything, and we didn't have much say about what happened in our lives. At least he'd heard that somewhere. But Joshe did. He knew full well that he had the freedom of choice when it came to decisions between right and wrong in his life. He had not always chosen right.

In my defense, he thought, *I've never intentionally hurt anyone. I've never stolen anything, and I don't get in fights or anything like that. I got a good mom and dad. I love my family.*

"But God, here is the deal. I have spent most of my adult life getting laid. Because I like it. I'm good at it. I make women happy, too. But some of them have wanted more and some I know felt bad when I was not able, or wouldn't, be there for them. Oh, the tears and the pleading. God. It was really awful. You know I began to stay away from those 'good' girls. The 'bad' girls are much more fun. Easier to deal with. Really, they are. But God. I don't want any of them to ever be my wife." He began to feel the dull pain of being on his knees on the hard terrazzo floor.

"So, God, I have this big question for you. Why did you put it on my heart to want to know Alejandra? And what am I to do about it? Am I really ready to think about stopping my way of life and finally deciding on one woman? One woman? Lord, what is happening to me?"

Joshe looked up to the ceiling in his small bedroom. He shared a three-bedroom apartment with two guys he'd gone to school with back in the day. They were all hard working, but all also enjoyed a cold beer at the end of the day and hanging out with each other. The fact that one of his roommates was gay did little to deter the friendship. It didn't matter to them. This was Ibiza. No one cared who you loved. What mattered most was one's happiness. You love who you love. Joshe didn't think about it much. But now he was thinking about it. He was being intentional with his thoughts. He knew something was changing within him. He knew he didn't want the hedonistic lifestyle forever. He wanted one woman. A good woman. One who would stay by his side and love him as much as he loved her.

He wanted children, too. He saw a future of love and joy. Sharing and caring and laughing and making beautiful love with the mother of his children. This was the life he wanted, and what was going through his thoughts lately, was that he was nearing the time to start with the next phase of his life. And for whatever reason that he still didn't understand, Alejandra seemed to be the one he wanted to find that life with. Would she want the same with him? Would he still want to be with her and make her his bride once he got to know her?

"Well, God, there's a lot going on in my head right now. But maybe you put these thoughts there. Maybe they come from somewhere else. But I'm thinking that I'll never know if I don't get started and get to know her. I guess if it's meant to be, she'll agree to go out with me. That's a start. Right?"

Joshe stood up and stretched. He made the sign of the cross, smiled, and said, "Thank you, God. Amen."

He saw her immediately when he got to work. She was early today, too.

"Hey, Alejandra. How's it going?"

"Hi, Joshe. Good. You?"

"I'm good, too. Have you given any more thought to maybe going out?"

"I have," she answered with a shy smile. "What are you doing after work today?"

"Today?" He tried to keep the excitement out of his voice.

"Uh. Yeah. That works. What do you want to do?" he asked. Her smile grew and he almost melted. *Why am I all tingly inside?* he wondered.

"I'll leave that up to you. I'm still not familiar with Ibiza, other than our resort. I'd love for you to show me around, or we can just sit and talk and get to know one another. Your choice."

Joshe smiled back. *Oh God*, he thought, *I hope I'm not turning red.* He felt all hot inside.

"Great," he said. "Do we both get off at three today?"

"I do. So, I guess that's a yes," she answered. "I need to be home by eight, but that gives us plenty of time for whatever you decide we should do. And Joshe," she added quietly, "you do know that I have a six-year-old daughter, right?"

Was it his imagination or was she blushing, too?

"Yes, I know. I think you mentioned something about her when you first started working here. I'm guessing that is why you need to be home by eight, and I promise to have you home on time." He smiled and his heart did a little happy dance when she smiled in return.

"Guess we better get to work. We're getting the eye from the boss," Joshe said and turned his attention to clocking in, washing up, and ensuring all the tables were properly set.

Blanca

She sat at the beautifully appointed table, though no one could see her or her companions at the Gaucho Restaurant at the TRS Resort in Ibiza. She recalled the day she sat on a scratched and faded bench near the edge of the playground, waiting for Alicea. Had that really been less than a year earlier?

The storm had come. Just as she knew it would. "All praise and glory to God," she told the other guardians. "The Lord used us to help stop the demons yet again. They'll always be out there, but the worst is over here. Patsy and Alicea are safe."

They are.

"Thank you for bringing me here to see this," Sergio said.

"Me too," this from Jeff.

"You were all part of this small miracle from the beginning," Hannah offered.

"Though Blanca had the lead role and questioned herself a time or two, we all learned and grew from this experience. And now, we know we've also pulled sweet Joshe from the clutches of those who tried to steal him from us," she said.

The angels grinned as they looked across the room at Joshe. There was no dark cloud above him. They could see the radiant light of his heart. He had nothing but good intentions for their beautiful Patsy and her daughter. It was a good fit.

"Those two can take it from here," Blanca said, then asked Hannah, "But will I be able to stay with them or do I only come back when needed?"

"Ah, dear girl. You will always be there when needed, but because the danger has passed here, you are needed elsewhere, too."

"Where will I go?" she asked.

"We'll have that conversation later." Hannah turned her attention to Sergio.

"I believe we have some unfinished business for you as well."

"What's that? I went through Orientation. I learned a lot, too," he said.

"Yes. But there is still the matter of your wings and sword. You are now ready to become a full-fledged Warrior Guardian Angel for God."

There was a smattering of applause from the others. Everyone seemed quite happy. Sergio had never felt like this in life. He was overcome with emotion. "Is this normal?" he asked. "That I should be emotional about this?"

"Quite," said Roy, the farmer from Ohio. "If you feel even one-tenth as close to the happy as I felt when I was assigned to look after my family in Ohio, I know exactly how happy you are."

"Where will I be sent?" Sergio asked. "Can I watch over Patsy and Alicea, or do I have to stay with the cop?"

Hannah gave him a guarded look. "We don't get to pick and choose, Sergio. Or trade. For now, you will stay with Chuck and Maria. When the time comes that they, too, are safe and on the right path, you, like Blanca, will receive another assignment. You all know I'm not in charge of those decisions."

I am. And I don't make mistakes. My love for all of you knows no bounds. You are mine. I know the plans I have for you in this eternal life. You are my Warriors. You will continue to fight the demons and save my people from eternal damnation.

THIRTY-NINE

Chuck

"Want to run to town with me? I need to pick up more hay and a few sacks of grain. We're getting low and it looks like another storm will be coming in before spring shows up," Chuck asked Maria. "Anything you need?"

"We should probably stock up on a few staples if another storm is coming. I'll check with Mom, too. She might need something. Weather seems pretty good today," Maria answered. "How soon are you leaving?"

"Whenever works for you." He glanced at his watch. "About an hour? We could hit the feed store, grab some lunch, then get the groceries and whatever else and be back by early afternoon. Does that work for you?" he asked.

She set the small paint brush down, careful not to spill or drip. She'd been working on a new art project and liked the way it was taking shape. Maria looked at her husband and thought again how lucky she was to be married to such a good guy. He was always thoughtful and caring, generous and loving. In the early years she wondered if being around so many evil people would harden his heart against humanity. Her deepest fear was that he might become one of those people who was always negative and looking for the worst in people. But the opposite was true.

He found good in everyone. They'd only been in their new home for a few months, but he'd already made friends with several neighbors and a few people in their new hometown through membership in the local farmer cooperative. They made their final decision late last fall and purchased a sixty-acre farm, where they planned to grow barley and potatoes and have a small herd of beef cattle. They talked about doing the work themselves and selling the crops to the local co-op or leasing the farming rights to others. They'd already been approached by a neighbor with a good offer to lease the forty acres of farmland, leaving them the large barn and twenty acres for cattle. The figures from the seller showed a small and profitable farm in good repair. The lease offer was good enough to pay the mortgage and since they weren't getting any younger, it might be just as well to consider that offer. Either way, they were excited about their new life.

The home was nice and had a lovely apartment over a three-car garage attached to the main house. Maria's mother loved it. "I'd be very happy here," she had said when they came to look at this place. It was the third one on the list she'd created from her online search.

"If this isn't too close for your comfort, or mine," she'd added.

Maria loved the large windows in the attic studio and knew she'd found the perfect spot for her painting hobby. There was an office they could share, a guest room and bath, with a large primary bedroom with huge windows that faced west, offering gorgeous sunset views every night. It was the floor-to-ceiling massive rock fireplace that left all three of them in awe of this particular home and ranch.

The sellers had built the home twenty-five years earlier, so it wasn't new, but they had led happy lives here and had reached an age where they could no longer live without full-time assistance. They did not want to sell, but life and aging had forced it on them. Chuck and Maria had several conversations about their own aging. Were they taking on more than they should? They weren't getting any younger, either.

But after a great deal of discussing the pros and cons, they agreed it was the best move for them if the seller would accept their offer. If time and health caused them to later sell it, so be it. It was going to be home for now. When their offer was accepted, they felt it was a sign they had made the right decision.

"Absolutely," she said. "That'll be a good break for me, too."

Maria glanced down at the paint-stained overalls she wore when working in her studio and opted to clean up and change, deciding this was as good a time as any to break for the day. She hadn't gotten much work done, but then, there was no time schedule anyway. She painted for her own enjoyment.

After getting a short list of needs from her mother, she changed into a clean pair of jeans, warm fur-lined boots, and a butter-soft sweatshirt. She tied a pretty scarf around her neck to keep out the cold and grabbed her down jacket. It might not be snowing, but it was still only thirty-eight degrees out there on this chilly day in late March.

Chuck and Maria climbed into the ranch truck and headed toward town. The fifteen-mile trip took them past beautiful farmland, country houses large and small, a rural school, and a small church, with a large white steeple, along with a few stands of Ponderosa pines and Douglas fir trees. On occasion one could catch glimpses of the river that ran through the valley. There was still snow on the ground from the last storm, but much of it was melting in the sunshine today. The road was clear, but wet.

"Maria, do you ever think about the day I asked you to pull out a map and start looking for a place for us?"

"Of course I do! That was a great day for me, you know. It was the day I could actually envision what we have now. You know I love you, and I loved that you loved your life as a cop, but darling, I'm so happy to have you alive and unharmed and all to myself."

She paused and unbuckled her seat belt. She slid across the split bench seat to the center and re-buckled, leaning slightly against her husband's right side.

"You are happy here, aren't you?" she asked.

He raised his right arm and put it around her diminutive figure and gave her a squeeze.

"I am. More than you know. And more than I thought I'd be."

"I think we had fun narrowing our choices from the internet down to the four we went to see. Don't you?"

"I do," he answered. "And I think we made the right choice here, too. This is beginning to feel like home. After living in the same house on the same ranch for most all of my life, I admit to you that this was uncomfortable at first. But after they shot up the house and all the drama with Patsy, I know we did the right thing. And yes, my love, this was the right move."

"Where do you want to have lunch?" he asked as he pulled up to the feed store.

"Thank you for taking care of Patsy and Alicea." He heard that voice in his head again.

It haunted him. He never told anyone about the voice. He didn't hear it all the time but felt reassured whenever it popped up. He wondered about the thought he'd had back when he first heard the voice and thought he was being haunted. Had Sergio really made it to Heaven and was he now a Guardian Angel?

The thought seemed preposterous, but in the back of his mind, he hoped it was true. He kept Patsy and her kid in his prayers. Chuck still believed in God and prayed often now. He made it a point to pray when he didn't need a favor. He didn't know for sure if God was out there or if He listened to anyone. But in his heart, he hoped it was true. He needed God. He needed to believe. Without God, there's no hope, he thought.

He had no idea where Patsy and the kid were living, but he trusted Colonel Willis, who assured him they were safe and doing well. She had access to the money. She had a job and friends who had her back. They had new names and no connection to the Norteños, who thought they were all dead.

Several were captured in a major sting operation, but others were rising to lead. Some things don't change.

His retirement checks were automatically deposited into a bank account each month. He hadn't changed his name. He supposed they could find him if they wanted. But he was no longer a priority for them. His name was common enough. They believed he was dead, and no one wanted to take the time or effort to prove anything different. Let sleeping dogs lie was a good adage. Someday he'd give Foster a call. He should call Joe Medeiros, too. Someday. *They both know I'm alive. That's all they need to know for now.*

"I got your back, *mí hermano*."

There it was again. It even sounded like Sergio Sanchez, Chuck thought.

"Let's eat at that new place over by the river," Maria suggested and was pleased to see the smile on his face.

Author's Note

This novel is a work of fiction. References to real events, businesses, organizations, and notable landmarks are intended only to give the fiction a sense of reality and authenticity. I appreciate the time I spent at each of these places. Those include but are not limited to Farnesi's Restaurant in Chowchilla, CA; Camp Pendleton Marine Corps Base, CA; the VFW Post 1924, in Fallbrook, CA; and the TRS Resort in Sant Antoní, Ibiza, Spain.

The food and service at Farnesi's will satisfy any appetite. It's awesome. My eldest granddaughter, Jessie Evans, was actually born at the Camp Pendleton Hospital thirty years ago, and my daughter and son-in-law, Marti and Chris Ingraham, are both former United States Marines and former Commanders of the American Legion and Veterans of Foreign Wars Organizations in Fallbrook, respectively. They were the inspiration for the characters of Maddie and Bret. Dory Maddock Fullen is the very real and adorable bartender at the VFW Post. The scene at the VFW and other characters portrayed are all fiction. I am honored to include a fictional account of action by the US Marine Corps that never happened and likely never will. But as the Marines often joke, "If I told you the truth, I'd have to kill you."

Hannah Duston was also a real person who lived in New England in the late 1600s. I am a tenth-generation descendant of Hannah's and used her as the inspiration for the Warrior Guardian Angel called Hannah throughout this series. You can learn more about the history of Hannah Duston and the Abenaki Tribe in *Fate of the Sisters*. Several other authors have written non-fiction accounts of Hannah's life, and I'm told there is also a major motion picture about her life and that of the Abenaki Tribe in the making.

I am most grateful to my wonderful friend from Salinas High School, Charles Bardin. Chuck served in the US Army and made his career in law enforcement. He was the inspiration for the character of Detective Chuck Reynolds, but any other similarities are purely coincidental. The characters portrayed as members of the Norteños or Nuestra Familia are complete fabrications based on newspaper and other accounts of gang activity in California. Any resemblance to any actual persons, living or dead, is entirely coincidental.

I made them up for the sake of a story about good and evil. Choices. Any errors in this book are mine and mine alone. It's fiction.

Believe what you will about angels and demons. I believe there are angels who protect and guide us. I also believe there are demons who work to destroy us and condemn us to eternal damnation. I am not a theologian, although I am an ordained minister with the Universal Life Church. I was raised Catholic, and enjoy services at Catholic, Methodist, Lutheran, and non-denominational churches wherever I happen to be on any given day.

I'm a woman who loves to write and I believe that God put it on my heart to write this series. These books are written for you, my dear readers. If you are feeling lost or hopeless in difficult times, I pray you will find hope in these books. There is hope. You can have it. Just ask Him. He'll send a Hannah or a Blanca. He'll send a Sergio or a Jeff. Or a Roy. Or another angel. Your very own angel. You most likely won't see or hear your angel, but rest assured, they've got you covered.

I took great literary license and combined it with actual locations and events involving the City of Salinas, a city dear to my heart, where I was raised and attended Sacred Heart Elementary School, Notre Dame High School, and Salinas High School. All else is attributed to a vivid imagination and a calling by God to write.

I have called you by name. Write the next book.

For anyone facing physical or emotional abuse, help is available.
Domestic Violence Abuse: 1-800-799-7233
Sexual Abuse: 1-800-656-4673

Acknowledgements

This series would not be possible without the help of many people. First and foremost, I thank my sister, Cheri Saunders, who inspired me to write *Fate of the Sisters*, which led to *Fate of La Niña*. There are now at least three more books in the series yet to come. Next, I must publicly thank my children and grandchildren. I love you all to Heaven and back. When we lost Dad, my husband David, last year, I, too, was lost for a time. Your encouragement and love gave me the wings necessary to return to writing and find a new purpose for my life. And so, I did.

Thank you to the team at Dorrance Publishing Company who took *Fate of the Sisters* and made it better. I look forward to working with you as we continue with *Fate of La Niña* and the next three books in line.

Thank you to my wonderful neighbors and friends for lending your names to a variety of characters in my novels. While visiting the island of Ibiza in the Mediterranean last year and working on the start of this novel, I met a waiter at the beautiful TRS Resort, named Joshe Jimenez. He asked what I was working on and then asked to be included in the book. I laughed and asked if he wanted to be an angel or a demon. His response inspired the end of this novel.

"I'm an angel by day. A demon at night."

We laughed, and I included another waitress in the novel, Alejandra Tur. Thank you both for serving me lunch and a daily glass of wine while I feverishly worked on this novel.

Special thanks to the following wonderful people in my life. I treasure all of you.

My children and bonus children and their spouses, from eldest down: Elizabeth and Tim McKee, Richard and Pamela Ristau, Kenny and Katie Sonniksen, Josh and Jacklyn Sonniksen, and Marti and Chris Ingraham.

My talented and quite exceptional grandchildren: Jessie Evans, Mikayla Veith (Brayden), Matt McKee, Dylan Sonniksen, Ellie Sonniksen, William Ristau, Thomas Ristau, and great-grandson Roger Veith.

My dearest mother and sister: Joyce Renebome and Cheri Renebome Saunders.

The extended family I treasure: Sarah and Sean Akinyosoyes, Ricci and Mike Bailey, Sarah Bocher, Robin and Wayne Craig, Darlynn and John Haas, Marguerite and Cliff Happy, Fritz Lichty, Leslie and Kearney Martins, Uncle Al Martins, Anna and Dane Mumford, Jenny and Brian Riley, Becky and John Ristau, Jane Ristau, Peggy and Steve Ristau, Darlene and John Roseth, Shelby and Justin Rowland, Toni and Karl Sullivan, Crystal and Cliff Weeks.

My most treasured friends who offered encouragement when I needed it most: Chuck Bardin, Judie Brimmer, Roy Carlisle, Wayne and Kathy Choate, Andy and Caryn Collier, Diane Correia, Barb and Kevin Ernst, Lois Jane George, Leisha Medeiros Kelley, Melony Powys, Maria Salomone, Barbara Silva, Brad and Rosemary Turpi.

There are many people who came into my life and made it better. Time and distance are generally irrelevant. I hold you in my heart.

My sweet friends from around the globe include: Dick and Jane Abascal, Shelby Anderson, Geno and Jacqueline Andrews, Major Pat Antosh, Clive Arlington, Bill and Patti Barnhart, John and Sharon Barrett, Pat Baxter, Rodney Beason, Bill and Jean Benner, Betty Bilson, Ann Boessen, David Boring, Kathy Borner, Shelly and Johnny Bowden, Alexis Breeze, Karen Buck, Tom and Diana Buckton, Sharyl Burgeson, Brenda Burgett, David Carrido, Bob Carrizzo, Gail Casselman, Wink Chase, Kathy and Wayne Choate, Joe and Judy Coniglio, Tom Cox, Bob and Ruth Darula, Jack and Penny Dauler, Marsha Davis, SFC Ben Delaney, Lucy DiBenedetto, Jae Emery Eade, Diane Fitzpatrick, Patsy Fortenberry, Fred and Patty Gallegos, Patty and Jim Gittens, Bill and Carol Goodwin, Julie and Simon Goss, Mike and Gay Goss, JoEllen Grau, Gloria Grys, Dr. Gary and Libby Hall, Carol Jo Hargreaves, Scott and Carol Harris, Sharon Harsh, Mark and Toshi Hart, George and Helga Havener, Richard Hockett, Twylia Holm, Bob and Sue Jacobson, Bill and Mary Jackson, Frances and Joe Kamarad, Chuck and Marilyn Kilmer, Lou Kirkpatrick, Lyle and Donna Kleuver, Ann Kozy, David and Debbie Kroes, Pattie Laird, Dennis and Libby Lanagan, Rudy and Marsha Lara, Don LeBlanc, Ann and Don Lewis, Willie Lewis, Terry and Kate Lindberg, Anne Steele Loikits, Mike and Lorraine Long, Lisa and Jeff Malchow, Phil and Nella Mastagni, Mack and Tracy McDonald, Cathy Mead, Steve and Blanca Miller, Don and Gloria Monaco,

Mike and Grace Moran, Jody Morgan, Saralee Moorad, Marilyn Niles, SFC Jim Ober, Catherine Scattini O'Brien, Chuck and Kristi O'Brien, Sun Im Ohn, Richard and Mary Anne Olson, Jeff and Gail Pace, Ed and Jill Padilla, Aubrey and Diane Parish, SSGT Steve Payer, Shellee Husman Perkins, Diane Posey, SFC Gary Potter, Dr. Stu and Sheri Quisling, Duncan Reno, Fred and Mary Rieder, Major Dan Roach, Doug Roberts, John and June Rogers, Elvera Rollins, Phyllis Rose, Marianne Russo, Jeanne Sieling, Dolores Silva, Mark and Tammy Schmidt, Lois Schultz, Paul and Lois Smith, Lonna Albright Solnoske, Dr. Ted and Nancy Stahl, Lisa Stilwell, Dennis and Nicki Tobin, Gary and Kaye Tolbert, LaTrelle Uhl, Marilyn VanDoren, Valerie and Tag VanWinkle, Robert Wallace, Dr. Ron Weakley, Mike and Nina Wedlake, Gary Wein, Deb and Don Wendling, Melinda Whitten, Michelle and Dennis Wilborn, Max and Gloria Wix, Dr. Bob Wolfensperger, Quentin Wood, and Shelly Zeff.

I am also grateful for the help of the Marines Memorial Club in San Francisco, the VFW Post 1924 in Fallbrook, the American Legion, current and former Monterey County law enforcement officers, and Julia Reynolds (no relation to fictional character Chuck Reynolds), author of *Blood in the Fields: Ten Years Inside California's Nuestra Familia Gang* (published and available through Audible Publishing on Amazon).

I'd also like to thank those many authors, songwriters, newscasters, and others who post on the internet. Your research was invaluable to me, as I looked up names and places when my characters took off in directions I'd never intended.

Last, my special thanks and hugs to Florida friends Sarah Cusick, Liia Konovalova, Alice, and Erin from Cuveé 30A; Kat, Tom, and Tyler from Amici's at Inlet Beach; Jeff and Stephanie at The Old Florida Fish House; and fellow veteran Frank, and Chelsea from Kwiker Liquor in Panama City Beach, for your wonderful smiles and a glass of wine when my angels and I needed them most.

I do believe there are Warrior Guardian Angels among us, and that God and these Angels watch over all of us. We just need to seek, and we will find.